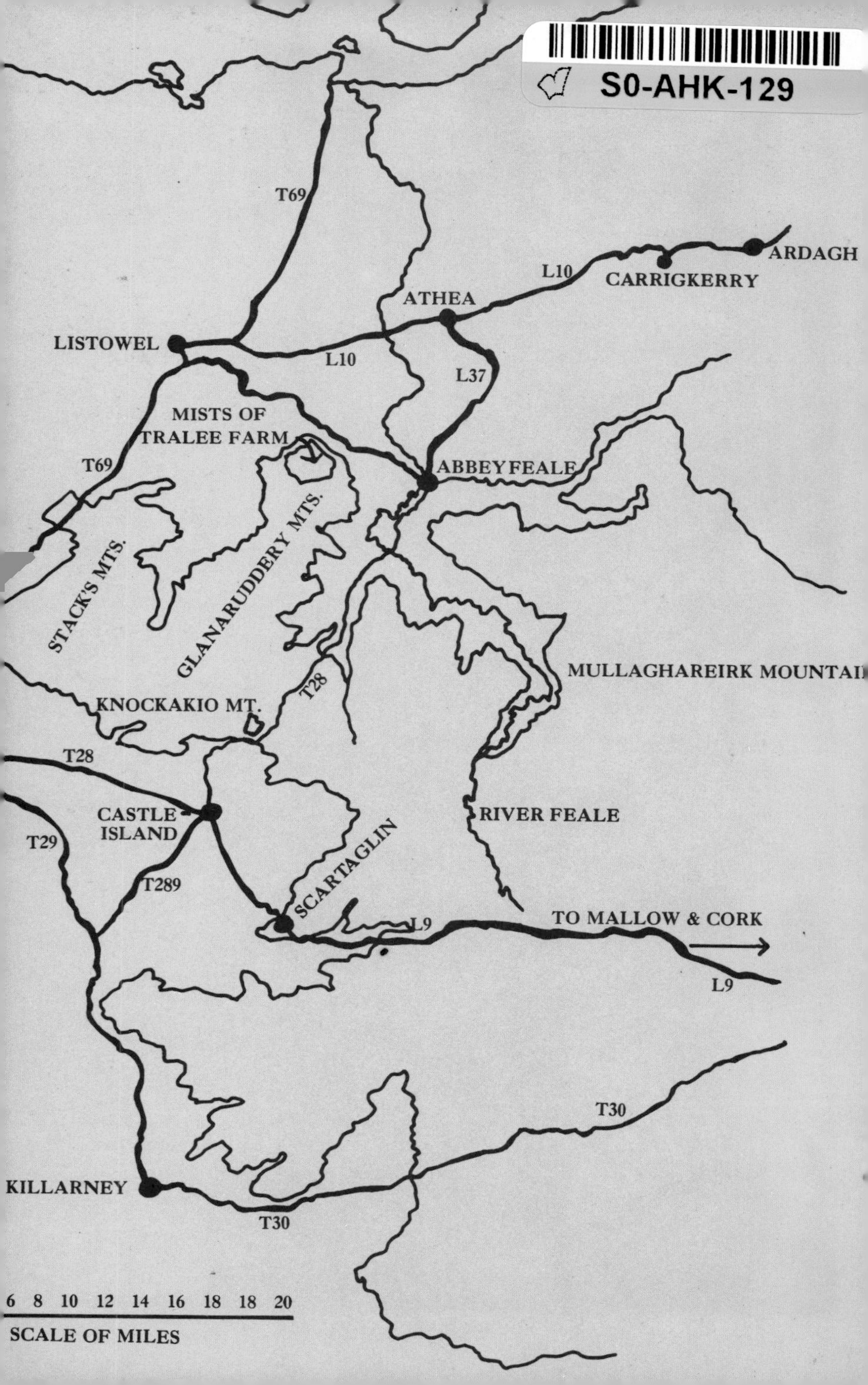
T69
L10
ARDAGH
CARRIGKERRY
ATHEA
LISTOWEL
L10
L37
MISTS OF
TRALEE FARM
T69
ABBEYFEALE
STACK'S MTS.
GLANARUDDERY MTS.
MULLAGHAREIRK MOUNTAI
T28
KNOCKAKIO MT.
T28
CASTLE
ISLAND
RIVER FEALE
T29
T289
SCARTAGLIN
L9
TO MALLOW & CORK
L9
T30
KILLARNEY
T30
6 8 10 12 14 16 18 18 20
SCALE OF MILES

THE SHOOTING OF THE GREEN

Books by Joe Poyer

THE SHOOTING OF THE GREEN
THE CHINESE AGENDA
THE BALKAN ASSIGNMENT
NORTH CAPE
OPERATION MALACCA

THE SHOOTING OF THE GREEN

Joe Poyer

DOUBLEDAY & COMPANY, INC.
Garden City, New York
1973

All of the characters in this book are fictitious, and any resemblance to actual persons, living or dead, is purely coincidental.

ISBN: 0-385-04498-4
Library of Congress Catalog Card Number 73-9173

Printed in the United States of America
First Edition

For Sandra Pilmore

THE SHOOTING OF THE GREEN

1

Cole Brogan dropped his cigarette into the dry grass and ground it carefully beneath his boot. He shoved his hands into the pockets of his jacket and shivered slightly in the icy wind sweeping down from the Elburz Mountains to the north as he leaned back against the jeep's hood to watch a military helicopter move in for its final pass. The helicopter paused above the far end of the field, then dropped abruptly and came in low, less than thirty feet above the wildly waving plants. A spray of colorless liquid burst from a tank slung beneath the fuselage and the copter roared diagonally across the field.

"We are ready, Mr. Brogan."

Brogan turned to the Iranian Army Colonel who was staring after the helicopter as it flew across the field to land beyond a collection of trucks parked along a rough dirt track. His thin face was grim but there was an expression of satisfaction in his eyes that Brogan wished he could share.

The Colonel turned to an enlisted man perched on the jeep's rear seat and motioned for the radio handset. He nodded to Brogan as if expecting an answer. After a moment's hesitation during which Brogan regarded him with a sardonic expression, he spoke impatiently into the microphone. The breeze chose that moment to freshen and it carried the distant sound of shouted orders across the field. A moment later, a jeep scurried away from the collection of trucks and went bumping along the rutted track, a red pennant waving from its radio antenna.

The field was roughly rectangular in shape, about twenty acres in extent and full of the same bulbous, dark-green plant that lay beside Brogan on the jeep's hood. Idly, he picked it up and turned it over in his hands. He studied it for a moment, paying particular attention to the deep-red, almost black, rudimentary petals that circled the pod. They looked like diseased leaves and gave the plant a rather mysterious and evil-seeming character. He shook the pod and heard a hard rattling sound.

"Now it ends," the Colonel said softly at his shoulder.

Without looking up, Brogan snorted skeptically, but managed to refrain from voicing his thoughts aloud.

"Yeah . . . maybe."

This was not an isolated mutation, he knew. At least if it was, it was the first one he had ever heard of that ordered itself into neat rows. He knew little enough about botany, but he did know that no new strain of any living thing, plant or animal, occurred in only one location and in neatly cultivated fields at that. During the early spring months he had investigated at least four other reports in different parts of Asia Minor and the Far East, but this was the first confirmed sighting to date.

The jeep was now almost out of sight on the western side of the field where the track dipped down into a shallow ravine. In the distance, khaki-clad army troopers moved forward with blazing torches and halted a few feet from the edge of the field as the jeep passed. At the sound of a pistol fired into the air, each man threw his torch as far out into the field as he could and leapt back. In seconds, the northern and eastern borders had become twin infernos of roiling clouds of smoke and tortured images of flame as the kerosene-soaked vegetation literally exploded. As the heat grew more intense, it lifted the smoke to reveal individual fires blending into one awesome front that began to advance rapidly across the field ahead of the wind. Now and then, pseudopods of flame leapt into the smoke as if to drag it back to shroud the destruction. By the time the jeep had completed its circuit and pulled to a stop nearby, all twenty acres were in flames.

Brogan watched the inferno, awestruck at the immensity of its power and devastation, then shook his head and turned as a young lieutenant stepped out of the jeep and walked over to join them. The Lieutenant spoke briefly in Persian to the Colonel, who nodded with satisfaction.

"He says," the Colonel translated for Brogan, "that the field is well alight and will burn completely. Afterwards, flame-throwers will be used to reburn any patches that survive, to make sure that no seeds escape to take root."

"You think that will do it, huh?" Brogan tried once more to keep the skepticism from his voice, but this time did not succeed.

The Colonel's smile disappeared. "Yes, I most assuredly do," he replied coldly.

"And to be quite sure, we will revisit this area several times before winter and reburn the field if necessary."

Brogan studied his face a moment, still unconvinced, then shrugged. Perhaps the Colonel was right, but he doubted it. There was *never* an easy way to stop this sort of thing. The seeds were here now, but they would show up elsewhere, naturally or by human design. And with that appreciation a sudden, almost indescribable weariness surged through him. All those years, and for what? he thought bitterly. There was never an end to it.

The field burned off quickly as the flames fed on the three thousand gallons of kerosene and the sickly sweet odor of hot opium began to pervade the air.

Brogan's weariness had become a living thing. All he wanted was to return to Tehran and his hotel room to sleep. Twenty-four hours ago he had been in London at the end of a hard day. Now he was standing in the middle of the District of Gilan, Iran, watching an illegal poppy field being burned. He turned toward the second helicopter squatting nearby, then hesitated. The two peasant farmers who owned the field were sitting on the ground, heavily manacled and guarded by two soldiers with bayonet-mounted rifles. Brogan picked up the flower again. The two Kurdish farmers were dressed in a collection of rags and dirt worse than anything he had ever before seen. Both stared sullenly at the ground.

"Where in hell do you suppose they found the seed for this?" He gestured with the flower. "It has to be a man-made variety. I doubt if it occurred naturally."

The Colonel shrugged. "They say that a man came to their village during the winter and offered a thousand rials to anyone who would harvest a crop for him. These two were the only ones to accept. They claim that they had no idea they were growing opium poppies."

Brogan snorted. "I'm no farmer and I can recognize poppy seeds when I see them. But what puzzles me is where they got this particular strain. According to that agricultural expert we talked to a while ago, these are mature poppies, similar to one of the Soviet oil-producing strains, Przewalski-222, yet they haven't any petals. That would mean one hell of a job to hand pollinate each flower."

The Colonel took out a leather case and offered it to him. Brogan shook his head and the Colonel opened it and selected a thin cigar. He wet the end and dug into his pocket for a match.

"That is probably the reason for their escaping your satellite detection system . . . I suppose."

He cupped a hand around the end of his cigar and struck the match, then inhaled deeply to set it alight.

"I suppose it was pure chance that one of our patrols ran across this field. From a distance, it looks . . . or did look . . . like animal feed. At least to the untrained eye."

"Damn it all," Brogan muttered. "If this is something new and it's very widespread, it's back to square one. How will you go about finding other patches?"

The Colonel shrugged. "The way we did before the satellite system was put up: by patrolling."

"Hell, it could take you a year just to check out this one province."

"That's very true"—the Colonel shrugged again—"but there is no other way. If the plants do not have petals, how will your satellites see them?"

Brogan swore savagely and threw the poppy down and ground it into the grass with his boot heel. The Lieutenant hastily bent down and retrieved the mangled remains.

"He does not want to take a chance on accidentally allowing any seeds to enter the soil." The Colonel laughed. "But I am afraid I did not understand your comment about square one."

Brogan shook his head impatiently. "It's just an expression . . . means to start all over again."

One of the farmers had glanced up as he threw down the

flower, and now he went back to staring at the ground. In that one glance, Brogan had felt pure hatred radiating from the man.

"What's going to happen to them?"

The Colonel shrugged. "They have been tried and convicted of growing opium poppies without a license, and for that the penalty is death. They will be shot tomorrow morning."

A sudden sick feeling overwhelmed Brogan, and for a moment he was unable to answer.

"Shot . . . My God, just for growing poppies? What kind of a trial . . . ?" he finally choked out.

"To raise opium poppies in this country without a government license is a capital offense," the Colonel replied. "Their trial was held this morning. They admitted to owning the field and cultivating the crop. They were found guilty and they will be shot. That is the penalty. Permission was granted immediately from the Supreme Court to burn this field, and your helicopter pilot brought written confirmation of the verdict and sentence from Tehran. In these matters our justice moves very swiftly."

"For Christ's sake, Colonel . . ."

"Mr. Brogan," the Colonel broke in, "this is neither Great Britain nor America. Iran is a major growing area. Would you have us return to the conditions that prevailed in the late nineteen-fifties and early sixties? We are, in spite of everything else, a nation of law with an international responsibility to prevent the unrestricted cultivation of opium poppies. Perhaps that is a conceit, but if so, it is one that we take quite seriously. In addition, we have our own internal problems with opium, problems which, as you know very well, are as difficult as those in America.

"We will never again allow our territory to become a source of illegal heroin. Nor are we like some other and neighboring countries that allow traffic in illicit heroin, *sub rosa* to be sure, but allow it nevertheless until a larger, richer nation offers to finance a restriction program that amounts to little more than a bribe. At least we are proud to say that we have recognized our responsibility and have never asked anyone to shoulder it for us.

"But these people"—the Colonel waved toward the helicopter—"do not understand that. To them, opium poppies are merely a cash crop. It is not that they do not understand the effects of what they are doing. It is merely that they are greedy. They are paid by the government not to grow the poppy . . . strictly from Iranian funds. Therefore, there is no hardship imposed on them. Pay no attention to their clothes. These two men are very well off by our standards. Their ragged clothes were but a poor attempt to appeal to the court's pity.

"You see, very few of these hill people have sufficient education to understand appeals to morality and reason; a problem not limited to Iran, of course. But they do understand the firing squad, and for ten years it has been an effective deterrent. These two thought they could escape detection because the poppies do not have petals and therefore could not be detected by air search or by your satellite monitoring system. They gambled and lost and now they will pay the penalty. And the rest of the farmers in their village will carry the word to all in this valley that the government is still seeking out and punishing those who break the law by growing opium poppies without permission. None of them will do so again for a long time."

The flames had all but died away and the freshening wind was beginning to whirl the nauseous smoke toward them. The Colonel left him to walk over to the helicopter's cockpit and speak to the pilot while the Lieutenant remained by the jeep, regarding Brogan with a quizzical expression.

Brogan took a deep breath and swallowed it to help steady his stomach. The Colonel's offhand manner concerning the fate of the two peasants had shocked him as few things ever had before. He rubbed his sleeve across his wet forehead and massaged his face.

The Colonel returned and spoke first to the Lieutenant, then to Brogan. "I have ordered the pilot to return you to Tehran when you are ready. The supply of seeds and plants for your investigators will be sent after you to London in a few days, under armed guard."

The Colonel hesitated, then grasped his arm in a friendly manner. "I understand your feelings, I think. You see, I was involved in the major campaigns of the late nineteen-fifties to stamp out the illegal cultivation of opium poppies and have conducted more than my share of executions, all so that one weak, ignorant man will not supply another weak, ignorant man with the means of killing himself in a manner of which society disapproves. I do not know which must be changed—the conditions that drive men to opium for solace, or the society that both creates the conditions and then denies to those who succumb this means of coping. I thought when the satellite system was put into effect that an end had been reached and the question was no longer valid. Now we have this to contend with.

"I have no other choice," he finished heavily, "the law is the law."

Brogan stood silent a moment. "Yeah, and that's the way . . ."

The Colonel raised a hand to stop him. "Please. Spare me. I know that to merely follow orders is no excuse. But that is an oversimplified evaluation. I have thought all of this through many times, most thoroughly, believe me."

Brogan nodded once more and glanced toward the distant mountains. "I guess you have to do what you think is right."

The Colonel nodded. "Yes I do, and so must you."

The two men walked to the helicopter and Brogan climbed in. The Colonel stepped onto the first rung of the ladder and reached inside to shake his hand, and minutes later the helicopter was airborne and behind them, the dense black column of smoke was already being whipped to tatters in the wind.

2

"Mr. Brogan . . . Mr. Cole Brogan, please come to the British European Airways information desk." The message was repeated once more, most charmingly in French, and smiling to himself, Brogan turned left on leaving Customs and walked across the almost empty concourse to the desk. A pert, dark-haired girl looked up as he approached and smiled.

"Mr. Brogan?"

He nodded, took the blue message form she handed to him and turned away to find a seat on one of the benches along the floor-to-ceiling glass windows. He put his suitcase down and frowned at the message, then slit the envelope open with his finger and unfolded the form.

> *Shipment located in Baltic. Receiver waiting for you Naval Command, Copenhagen. See Cpt. Olafsson.*

Brogan muttered an oath, crumpled the paper and stuffed it into his jacket pocket, wondering what the hell Vandervoort was on to this time. He got up and walked back to the BEA desk. He had just finished the long ten-hour flight from Tehran, and now this.

"Miss," he said in resignation, "which way to the SAS desk?"

It was a forty-five-minute direct flight from Paris to Copenhagen and the Trident touched down at Kastrup Airport at four P.M. Brogan managed to be first off the plane and, on the strength of his diplomatic passport, rushed through Customs. At the Avis desk he found that his secretary, Sandra, had been one step ahead of Vandervoort and had reserved a car for him. Blessing her efficiency, he begged a city map and by five P.M. was presenting his credentials to the uniformed guard at the Harbor District Naval Headquarters gate.

"That is the trawler there, Herr Brogan, the one moored beside the frigate."

Brogan stared out at the magnificent view of Langelinie Harbor and the bluish streak of Sweden across the Öresund. The harbor was filled with craft of every description, from lumber carriers to military ships. Closer in, a fleet of sailboats exercised, tacking in successions of twos and threes, white sails flashing like aspen leaves in the afternoon sunlight.

The trawler Olafsson had pointed out was so typical of North Atlantic fishing boats as to be almost nondescript. She was sixty feet long, higher in the bow than aft, and carried a single large mast surrounded by four angled booms for hoisting nets on the forward deck. A large, covered hold occupied the entire middeck, and the wheelhouse was mounted solidly over the stern. She was so weatherbeaten that little paint was left on her hull and upper works. What remained was stained or streaked to a dull, salt-encrusted gray. She had obviously spent several long months on the North Atlantic fishing grounds, but even so, her condition indicated years rather than months of neglect.

"What is her usual station?"

"The Greenland waters east to Grand Banks. In late summer she will go with the fleet north into the Labrador Sea after cod. One of our patrol ships, the frigate that you see, stopped her. The master must have been very sure of himself, as no great pains had been taken to hide the drug. It was found in the after trim tank."

"Do you do that with every fishing boat coming in—stop and search them?"

Olafsson turned and strode impatiently to his desk and sat down. He was a big, rangy man with the red, weatherbeaten face of a lifelong sailor and an air of impatience that said plainly that an office command was not to his liking.

"Of course not! She had reported engine trouble south of Cape Farewell and was returning. We had been watching for her since her first wirelessed distress signal. The Julianhabb station reported that she had departed eight days ago, and we had been expecting her to come directly across the North Atlantic. The Faroes Command had been alerted to watch for her and, when she was not spotted and not answering wireless calls, initiated an air search. Two days ago, the Dutch Navy reported a trawler of her type moving into the North Sea, close into their coast. Naturally, we were surprised and began to wonder why she would take such a roundabout way home with engine trouble. When she was in the Skagerrak, we stopped her. Smuggling has all but disappeared now that we are all in the Common Market together, but we still check whenever the situation warrants."

Brogan nodded and turned away from the window. "I see. So you found a load of heroin aboard and reported it to the Danish police, who notified INCC. How much?"

"I beg your pardon . . ." Olafsson said, confused by Brogan's abrupt question.

"How much heroin did you find?"

"Fifteen kilos," the Captain answered and Brogan whistled.

"My God. That's worth a hundred thousand pounds before it's cut and distributed. Maybe half a million after, and several million on the streets." He shook his head and half turned away from the window. "Fifteen kilos," he repeated softly. "That's the biggest load taken in two years."

The Captain remained silent and Brogan studied him for a moment. He gave the impression of waiting with barely controlled patience until Brogan was ready to leave, as if he were humoring a recalcitrant child. Brogan decided to ignore his attitude for a while yet.

"What does her Master have to say for himself?"

The Captain sighed. "Nothing. What would you expect? He will not talk and neither will any of his crew."

Brogan nodded. "That figures. Can I talk to them?"

Olafsson stood up briskly. "Certainly. My aide will escort you. But I must warn you that his solicitor has begun proceedings to have him released on bail."

"Released on . . ." Brogan exclaimed. "Good God, he was caught red-handed. . . ."

"The bail will be set very high." Olafsson frowned. "Of course, there is nothing but circumstantial evidence to associate him with the drug. And of course he claims to know nothing whatever of the heroin."

"Of course," Brogan repeated wearily.

"It will be only a matter of a few hours at most now until he is released. And I think we will never see him again in Denmark. They tell me that ten years ago the crime syndicates were more ruthless. Then they would have killed him so that he would not talk."

"No, that's not correct," Brogan said absently. "If that was the case, nothing would have been lost by talking and we would have cracked the syndicates wide open in a matter of years. No, they protect their own. This man's usefulness may be ended to them, but he will be taken care of, and he knows it."

Olafsson muttered in Danish and shrugged his shoulders. "I am a sailor. I do not know about these crime syndicates. But I do know this man for a smuggler, before the Common Market. Unfortunately, we were never able to convict him, and so he has no record. The most that we can hope for is to delay his release as long as possible."

Brogan stared down at the trawler again. Two armed sailors sauntered out of the deckhouse and sat down on the hatch cover to smoke. There was nothing else for them to do. Right under the guns of the frigate there would certainly be no attempt made to take the boat out, and no reason to try.

"So then what happens?"

The Captain laughed. "The police will probably follow him, since there is little else that can legally be done."

Brogan nodded once more and walked over to a large chart of the North Atlantic that covered most of one wall.

"Where exactly were they when the engine trouble was reported?"

The Captain came to stand beside him and pointed to a spot two hundred miles south and east of Greenland. "In this area here."

Brogan studied the map for a moment. "How long would

it take to run back to Denmark with a bad engine, and which direction would she be likely to take?"

Olafsson traced a route that led east of Greenland, south of Iceland to the Faroes, then southeasterly into the North Sea to the Skagerrak, the entrance to the Baltic. In all, a straight line some seventeen hundred miles long.

"Besides being the most direct, is there any other reason for her to have taken that route?"

"Of course, of course," Olafsson snapped. "She would be nearest help if she ran into serious trouble. It would take her about seven days at most."

"And it took her how long from the time she first reported trouble until you stopped her?"

"Nine days."

Brogan nodded thoughtfully. "Any reason for her to have followed a more southerly course—say, coming down into the Atlantic south of Britain? Storms maybe?"

Olafsson shook his head impatiently. "This season has been remarkably free of storms in the North Atlantic. Her fuel supplies would have been low, and going down into the Atlantic would have put her that much farther from help in case of drastic trouble."

Brogan nodded. "Then, if the Dutch reported her off their coast and you picked her up coming north, she *must* have run down into the Atlantic, which meant that she would have had to refuel?"

Olafsson snorted. "Of course. We have already thought of that. All possible ports in the North Atlantic have been checked. She did not refuel in any of them."

"At sea perhaps?"

"Possibly. But if so, then anywhere between the Barrier and the Bahamas."

"That she could reach in two additional days," Brogan amended. He continued to study the chart for several more minutes while the Captain wandered about his office, waiting for him to be gone.

Brogan shook his head. "Somewhere along the line he picked up that load of heroin. It's a damned cinch he didn't bring it with him from Greenland. It had to have been somewhere between Greenland and the Skagerrak, somewhere off the coast of the British Isles, France, Belgium or the Netherlands."

"Why not the Faroes? It is possible that he could have slipped in undetected. Or he could have picked the drug up from another ship at sea."

"Why not," Brogan agreed. It was obvious that the Captain was growing very impatient, but Brogan decided to stretch it just a bit further.

"If he came down south of Great Britain to the Channel, how much longer would that take?"

"At least two days, but . . ."

"Thank you, Captain," Brogan interrupted, satisfied that he had learned all he could here. "If we turn up anything, I'll let you know immediately."

Olafsson took a deep, frustrated breath, nodded curtly and pressed a button on his telephone. Almost immediately, the door opened and Olafsson snapped an order to the young officer, who then beckoned to Brogan. The Captain was already sitting behind the desk reading a file as the door closed. He did not bother to look up.

"Friendly son of a gun, isn't he?" Brogan said cheerfully, but the young officer just shrugged and shook his head, indicating that he did not speak English.

During the next hour, Brogan was able to learn nothing more than he already knew. The master of the fishing boat and his crew were completely noncommunicative, and although a naval officer was with him in the interrogation room to translate, they would tell him absolutely nothing.

Finally Brogan admitted defeat without learning anything more than the master's name, Lars Hansen. He shook his head in disgust and stood up. Immediately a guard came in and escorted the prisoners from the room. The translator perched himself on the table and offered Brogan a cigarette.

"They have been like that ever since they were brought in," he said cheerfully. "So don't feel bad. At their arraignment none of them would say a word. By the way, Hansen does speak English."

"But they are going to be turned loose . . . ?"

"Yes, I am afraid so." The officer frowned. "The evidence is circumstantial and I understand bail has been arranged. They will be out in less than an hour."

Brogan shook his head. "Great."

As he started to leave, the translator stopped him. "There is a man from the Copenhagen police in the lobby. Perhaps you might like to talk with him?"

Brogan shrugged. "It can't hurt."

The translator led him into the lobby and pointed out a middle-aged, well-dressed man sitting beside the information desk. Brogan thanked him and eased himself down into the chair next to the policeman. He extracted his card case, opened it to his I.D. card and held it up. The officer glanced at it, then back down at his magazine.

"So . . . ?"

"We are probably both waiting for the same man to appear."

"So . . . ?"

"Perhaps we can work together?"

"I have had no instructions concerning you."

"Probably not," Brogan admitted cheerfully. "But, I'll bet I can get you some."

The officer closed his magazine and stared at him. "In that case, do so, Mr. Brogan. Until then you are interfering."

Brogan grinned. "You know who I am?"

"Of course. Now please see what you can do about those orders." The policeman opened his magazine again. Brogan shrugged and left.

3

The sun, setting in a burst of red and gold, had gilded the drab buildings of the dock area, and the air of the long spring evening was soft and scented with the fresh breeze blowing in from the Baltic. Brogan glanced at his watch and was surprised to find that it was after eight o'clock. He let the door swing shut behind him and took a deep breath to rid his lungs of the disinfectant atmosphere of the brig, then walked slowly across to the parking lot and unlocked his car.

He settled himself behind the wheel, rolled down the window, and took out a cigarette. For a long time he sat, shoulders hunched, cigarette dangling from his lips and hands clasped on the steering wheel while he thought about what he had learned—and, more importantly, what he had not learned. Finally, he dug out his lighter and lit the cigarette.

A matter of hours before Hansen was released, Olafsson had said. But he had a feeling it was not going to take that long at all. On his way out, he had been elbowed aside by an officious little individual bustling down the corridor. From the size of the briefcase he carried, Brogan was willing to bet that he was a solicitor, Hansen's solicitor.

The last traces of the setting sun had disappeared into a soft, gray twilight when his guess was vindicated and Hansen came marching out of the brig accompanied by the little man. The two were a decided contrast. The solicitor was dressed in an expensive suit of green tweed that did little to hide an outsized paunch. As they passed his car less than fifty feet away, he got a good glimpse of the lawyer's florid face. The man was smoking a large cigar, and from the way he was huffing and puffing as he hurried along, Brogan was certain that he was well on his way to developing emphysema. Hansen was tall, angular and dressed in an ill-fitting jacket and slacks. A battered cap perched on a too large head. The total impression Hansen presented was that of being just a little too large. Hands, head, feet, arms, all just enough out of proportion that he appeared as a gangling scarecrow come to life. The effect was further heightened by strands of dirty, blondish hair straggling from beneath the cap. The comparison between Hansen's seedy appearance and his uncared-for fishing boat came immediately to mind.

The two men climbed into a green, late-model Mercedes 450 SL, and as they nosed out of the parking lot Brogan started his own car and followed. At the gate he handed over the temporary pass and drove out into the street. It was nearing eight-thirty but there was still sufficient light to follow the Mercedes.

As they left the area surrounding the docks, the Mercedes turned north onto the *Kalkbraenderihannsg.* Brogan maintained a discreet distance, knowing that with his headlights on in the gathering dusk, there was little chance that either occupant of the Mercedes could recognize him through the windshield.

After a mile or two, the Mercedes swung west onto *Strandvaengt* and continued on until they reached the intersection with the *Osterbrogade*. The Mercedes signaled for a left turn and they drove toward the center of Copenhagen. A few minutes later a Volvo slipped neatly between Brogan and the Mercedes, and at almost the same instant a second Volvo dropped in behind him. For several blocks they continued on in this fashion until it dawned on Brogan that the newcomers were police.

He quickly pulled to the side of the street and let the police car behind go past, then followed. He recognized the man on the passenger side as the policeman who had cold-shouldered him at the naval brig. Smiling to himself, he followed the three-car procession, knowing that the police were much better equipped than he to trail a car through the rapidly darkening streets of an unfamiliar city.

They continued the slow-motion chase for several more blocks, the police making no attempt to hide the fact that they were following the Mercedes, and Brogan taking no pains to disguise the fact that he was following the police.

It was not long before the driver of the Mercedes decided that things had gone far enough. The traffic light ahead began to flash and the Mercedes slowed. The brake lights in both police cars came on and all four coasted to a stop. Just as the light switched to red, the Mercedes swerved and accelerated suddenly, catching both police cars and a driver coming through the intersection from the left by surprise. Brogan stepped on the gas, then realizing instantly that the police cars were making no effort to follow, had to stomp on the brake to keep from rear-ending the police car ahead. He saw the officer at the wheel glance up into his rear-view mirror in surprise, then scowl. Brogan waved.

The light changed to green and the two police cars drove quickly through the light, but straight ahead rather than turning to the right as had the Mercedes. Brogan hesitated, then followed on through after the police. It became obvious, after only a few moments, that other cars were involved in the surveillance. The two cars ahead turned onto the *Oster Farimagsg* and, remaining at the speed limit, drove purposefully toward the center of the city. Twenty minutes later, they turned into the block in which the Hotel Europa reared above the surrounding buildings and stopped on the opposite side of the street.

Brogan signaled for a turn and slid into the unloading bay in front of the main lobby and stopped. He got out slowly, glancing around, undecided for a moment as to what to do next. The Mercedes was nowhere in sight, and both police cars were stopped on the opposite side of the street, apparently as puzzled as he was. He started to duck back inside the car when he caught sight of the Mercedes turning out onto the *Vesterbrogade* from the other end of the drive, but now with only one occupant, the driver.

The Mercedes sped away and Brogan waved, frantically pointing after it. One of the policemen jerked his head around, spotted the Mercedes, and made a U-turn in the center of the street and raced after it. Brogan grabbed his carryall from the seat, tossed the keys to the doorman and hurried through the double-glass doors into the lobby. He spotted Hansen at the registration desk and slowed immediately. Brogan waited as unobtrusively as possible by the doors until Hansen was safely inside an elevator. As soon as the doors closed, Brogan walked over to the registration desk and asked for the manager. He set the carryall down on the counter and dug out a cigarette, lit it and inhaled deeply, holding the smoke in his lungs for a moment to calm his agitated nerves.

"Yes, you wish to see me?"

Startled, Brogan choked on the smoke and coughed. "Yeah . . . yes, I do." He got himself under control and handed his I.D. case to the manager. The man studied it for a moment, then swept a hand to indicate a door behind the counter.

"Perhaps, my office . . ." he suggested.

Brogan nodded and preceded him inside. He was offered a chair, an ashtray and his I.D. case.

"My name is Chris Eriksen. What may I do for you?"

"A man registered here not more than five minutes ago. I believe his name is Lars Hansen . . . that is, if he is using his right name. I am very much interested in finding out in which room he is staying."

"I see," Eriksen said slowly. "This man you are following, he is a fugitive?"

Brogan tapped a knuckle on the desk for a moment, appearing to study it intently. "Look," he said finally, "I'll level with you. Hansen is not a fugitive from Danish justice. In fact, your courts have released him on bail. I would just like to keep him in sight so that he stays 'on bail.'"

"But you are not Danish. American perhaps?"

"Yes, I'm an American citizen. But I work for the International Narcotics Control Commission. I'm an investigator, that's all, not a cop."

"And you suspect this man of having something to do with narcotics . . . ?"

Brogan maintained a stubborn silence.

"I see," Eriksen nodded. He picked up the phone and spoke briefly in Danish, replaced the receiver and leaned back in his chair and studied Brogan quite openly. Brogan stared back, wondering if he had called the police, and they remained that way until the door opened a few moments later and an attractive young woman came in with a handful of cards.

Eriksen took them, thanked the girl and she went out, leaving a thin wisp of perfume that smelled of orange blossoms. Brogan turned his attention back to the manager.

"I should not do this. I could lose my position if it should ever be found out, but narcotics . . ." He shook his head and handed the cards across the desk to Brogan.

Brogan sorted through them with one hand while, with the other, he held the file card stolen from the brig when he had read through Hansen's record folder. The card, with Hansen's signature, a receipt for personal effects, had been the only thing small enough to palm.

As he had expected, none of the cards were in the name of Hansen. He went through them once more until he had three possibilities spread out on the desk. Carefully, he compared each of the signatures in turn until he was sure that he had the right man.

"This is the one. He is calling himself Hans Kopel."

Eriksen took the card. "Room 846, a single on the street side."

"Where he can watch the police cars out in front watch him," Brogan said wryly.

"There are police outside?"

"Yes, across the street. I imagine there is one at each entrance by now, probably watching from off the grounds."

"Ah."

"There is one more thing you can do for me, if you would?" Eriksen spread his hands questioningly.

"I'd like a room as near to 846 as possible, preferably close enough so that I could watch his door, and I don't want to use my own name to register."

Eriksen frowned. "That may be difficult. The hotel is crowded right now. Let me see . . ." He picked up the phone, asked for a number and, after a moment, spoke quickly in Danish. Almost as soon as he had hung up, the door opened and the girl came in again, this time carrying a large chart. She handed the chart to Eriksen and stepped back, shaking her blond hair away from her face. She smiled at Brogan—a professional smile, he thought regretfully.

"Perhaps 878 would do. It is a double room, but unfortunately around the corridor. It is as close to 846 as I can put you without asking guests to move, which might create sufficient disturbance to be noticeable. However, it does provide a view of both elevators and the stairwell door. If you wish me to move some . . ."

"No, please, that will do nicely."

"In that case," Eriksen smiled, "the room is yours. Anna will see you to the desk and take care of your reservation." He gave the girl instructions in Danish and she held the door open for Brogan.

He stood up and shook hands with the manager. "Look, I really appreciate this very much . . ."

"There is no need. We are always very ready to help."

Brogan followed the girl out, was registered immediately and had his bag sent up to the room. He took the key and walked over to the cigarette counter, bought a pack of Camels and, as an afterthought, a Danish-English phrase book. On the way to the elevators, he saw the policeman he had spoken to in the brig enter the lobby. The man glared at him but said nothing and continued on to the registration desk. Grinning to himself, Brogan went across the lobby to the bank of phone booths near the bar.

* * *

Shortly after one A.M. Brogan got up from the chair which he had positioned in such a way that he could watch both elevators and stairwell through his partly opened door. He stretched his aching muscles as he walked across the room to the windows and parted the curtains. The police car was still parked on the *Vesterbrogade*. A bored plainclothesman leaned on the hood, watching the lobby doors. Hansen had apparently kept to his room all evening as, for all intents and purposes, there were only two ways off the floor: the elevator and the stairwell. And even if Hansen had managed to slip past him, he would not have gotten past the police, or else the car would not still be parked across the street.

The corridor had been empty for almost an hour now. Brogan slipped on his boots and jacket and stuffed the electrical cord from the desk lamp he had dismantled earlier into his pocket. He stepped out into the corridor, stopped for a moment to press his ear against the elevator doors, then walked quickly around the corner to Hansen's room. Glancing up and down the corridor, he tried the doorknob and found it locked, as he had expected.

The police might be bound by certain restrictions and procedures, but as he was not a policeman, he was not required to observe those niceties of police protocol—as long as he was not caught.

He took a deep breath and rapped sharply on the walnut door panel. After a moment, a man's voice mumbled in Danish, "*Vem är där?*"

Brogan had occupied his vigil with a study of the Danish phrase book and, smugly, he called back, "*Oppna, Polis!*"

He heard more muttering and a few unmistakable curses, and after a moment the door swung open a crack to reveal Hansen's bleary face peering out at him. His expression turned to shock as he recognized Brogan and he moved to shove the door closed. Brogan, expecting just that, hit the door hard with his shoulder, flinging it open and knocking Hansen back into the room. Brogan stepped inside quickly and pushed the door shut. Hansen had tripped on the rug and fallen half across the bed, knocking the lamp onto the pillow. He lunged to his feet and rushed at Brogan, swearing as only a fisherman can swear. Brogan moved to meet him, sidestepped and caught him solidly in the stomach with his fist and, as he doubled over, hit him hard with the edge of his hand on the back of the neck. Hansen dropped as if he had been hit with an ax.

Rubbing his hand, he checked to make sure the door had locked behind him. Satisfied, Brogan dragged the unconscious man to the desk and used his belt to secure him to the chair. With the lamp cord, he carefully bound his feet and hands securely, then pulled the chair around so that it faced the nightstand and angled the high-intensity reading light so that it shone full on Hansen's face. Then he poured himself a drink from the half-empty bottle of akvavit on the desk and settled down on the bed to wait for Hansen to regain consciousness.

* * *

A blinding glare caused Hansen to jerk his head to the side and squeeze his eyes tightly shut. A stinging blow knocked his head back and he felt a trickle of blood start from his nose.

"Good evening, Captain Hansen."

Hansen squinted, trying to make out the voice's source, but the glare of light blanked out everything. His face stung from the slap and a heavy throbbing filled the back of his head. He was completely disoriented; bits and pieces came and went, a face he recognized at the door, falling on the bed . . . but the light and pain in his head kept him from piecing it all together.

"Now, no more games, my friend," the voice said again, but only isolated words meant anything to him. "I want information and I want it fast."

Hansen struggled to understand. "I . . . I . . ."

A solid blow rocked him back in the chair and he started to scream for help, but a hard-knuckled hand slashed him across the mouth.

"You aren't listening to me . . . I want to know when you picked up the heroin . . ."

The rest of the words were lost in a wash of abject fear. "My God," he thought, "my God, my God . . ." He began to struggle against the bonds holding him securely in the chair, but blows, hard, stinging blows almost reduced him to unconsciousness again. The beating also alleviated the panic and he slumped in the chair, his mind fighting through the sticky maze of conflicting thoughts and impressions until it fastened onto the remembered voice on the telephone, the voice that outlined for him in the greatest detail what would happen to him and his family if he should ever reveal anything concerning the arrangements for the heroin pickup.

Apparently, the man behind the lamp realized this, as the blows had ceased. He could hear the springs on the bed moving, then the sound of something dropped on the floor. A moment later, the light was abruptly angled away from his face and he raised his head as something grasped the front of his pajama pants and ripped them away. A second wash of panic seized him and he tried to squeeze his thighs together, but each foot was securely bound to a chair leg.

Hansen opened his mouth to scream and a thick cloth was rammed in.

"Look, you bastard. Open your eyes and look!" His head was yanked up by the hair. "Look!"

An implacably cold face stared at him, no trace of pity at all in the narrowed eyes. Slowly an object was raised into view, and it was a moment before he realized that it was the desk lamp without shade or bulb. The empty socket glared at him for a moment, then his head was yanked down and the lamp brought between his thighs. Frozen into immobility, he watched the socket end brought closer and closer.

"Two hundred and twenty volts at fifty cycles . . . You'll die from heart seizure, but it will take hours." The thumb pressed the switch and Hansen threw himself wildly about in the chair, screaming soundlessly into the gag until the world exploded into a staccato drum roll of pain that seared every nerve ending in his body.

Brogan felt sick. He swallowed hard and slumped down on the bed. The half-naked figure of the man tied to the chair groaned through the gag and rocked back and forth in the chair, legs fluttering weakly against the bonds.

"Once more," Brogan said thickly. "Where did you pick up the heroin?"

Hansen raised his head and stared dully at him as if he did not understand, then as Brogan lifted the lamp, his eyes grew wide with panic and he shook his head violently.

"Will you tell me?"

Hansen nodded quickly and Brogan removed the gag.

"All right. Where?"

The first words were a babble of incoherencies, and Brogan slapped him hard.

"Slow . . . and in English . . ."

"I . . . I . . . do not speak English . . . well . . ."

"Well enough. Get on with it." Brogan brought the lamp closer and Hansen shuddered back in the chair.

"In Bantry Bay . . . an oil tanker."

"Bantry Bay? Why there?"

Hansen shook his head quickly. "I do not know. My . . . my . . . instructions were to follow chart co-ordinates."

"You mean they didn't tell you . . . ," Brogan said dangerously. He snapped the light switch and thrust the lamp closer.

"No . . . no," Hansen almost screamed. "They told me nothing else. Only to be there."

Brogan leaned closer. "Where?" he demanded.

"I . . . I . . . do not know . . . I have forgotten . . . —" Brogan thrust the gag into his mouth and touched the outside of the lamp socket to his skin. Hansen's eyes rolled up and he sagged into the chair.

"Where, damn you . . . !" Brogan roared at him.

Hansen bobbed his head and Brogan pulled the gag away. "Where!"

"Fifty-one north by 10.22 west, off Dursey Head. Please, no more. I know nothing more, please." He lapsed into a broken stream of Danish, and Brogan straightened up.

"What was the name of the ship?"

Hansen sobbed once and made a pathetic attempt to gather himself together. "I do not . . . remember all," he choked. "Something . . . *MARU*. A Japanese ship . . ."

Brogan threw the lamp down on the bed, certain now that Hansen was nothing more than a delivery boy. The fact that the rest of the crew was still in the naval brig told him that Hansen was the only one among the crew that knew anything about the operation.

Hansen's eyes followed him, abject terror spilling over. The room stank of scorched flesh and fear. Suddenly Brogan retched. He managed to keep from vomiting and stumbled around the chair out of Hansen's sight until the spasm passed. Then he stepped forward quickly and hit Hansen solidly behind the ear.

Brogan unstrapped him and untied his hands and feet, then dragged him into the bathroom and draped him around and over the bathtub. With the amount of liquor already in him, he would easily sleep until morning. To heighten the illusion, he poured the rest of the akvavit over him and placed the bottle half under the bed. Then he put the chair back in place, reassembled the lamp, and straightened up the room. With any luck, he would be found by the maid, who would assume that, drunk, Hansen had staggered into the bathroom, fallen, and knocked himself out.

Brogan turned off the room lights, opened the door a crack and checked the hall, then went quickly back to his own room, where he called the desk for reservations on a nine-thirty flight to London, left a call for seven, and undressed. At that moment the sickness could no longer be denied and he vomited.

* * *

It was still dark when the insistent ringing of the telephone awakened him. With a groan, he rolled over and fumbled the receiver to his ear to hear a cheerful voice announce that it was seven o'clock. He muttered something semiobscene and hung up, then threw back the covers and rolled out of bed.

Brogan opened the curtains a crack and winced at the glare of the early-morning sun rising over the distant Öresund. The red brick and weathered wood of Copenhagen's buildings, huddled over narrow thoroughfares, lent a peculiarly northern and medieval aspect to the city, but Brogan was in no mood to appreciate the attributes of one of Europe's most beautiful cities. His head ached atrociously from too many cigarettes and not enough sleep and he was hungry. He found a bottle of aspirin in his travel kit and downed four with a glass of water, then he turned on the shower.

The hot shower, the steam and the aspirin had a mitigating effect so that, by the time he finished, the headache had subsided to a dull throb. He dressed quickly, collected his belongings and went down to the desk and paid his bill. Brogan was particularly anxious to be away from the hotel and, in fact, out of the country, if possible, before someone discovered Hansen.

An elevator took him down to the garage for his car. As he walked down the corridor to the attendant's cage, he heard voices coming from around the corner. Slowing out of a sudden cautionary urge, he heard a voice spelling the false name he had given to the desk clerk—carefully and with a distinct Danish pronunciation to the letters.

He stopped suddenly and took a quick look behind. There was no one in sight, so he knelt down and carefully peered around the lower edge of the corner. Two men were talking to an attendant beside a glassed cage in which a third man was rifling through the parking tickets. All were wearing business suits, and the attendant was being very deferential. That was all Brogan needed to see. He went back to the still open elevator car, keeping one eye on the corridor.

In the lobby once more, he walked casually across to the cigarette stand, bought a paper, looked around carefully, then went out into the street through a side door. Several cabs were waiting and he signaled to the first in line. The hell with the car, he thought, as the cab dove into the early-morning rush-hour traffic. He would send a cable from London to the Avis people, telling them where to find it. Those three buckos had the faint aroma of cops; and if he was mistaken, then they were friends of Hansen. Either way, the three of them could wait in the garage until they rotted—or at least until someone from the agency came to pick up the rented Saab.

The cab reached the airport a few minutes before eight, leaving him ninety minutes to wait for the London flight. He stepped into the coffee shop and took a booth near the back, where he could watch anyone passing, and considered his position. It appeared that someone just might be looking for him, police or syndicate, and it did not matter which. He doubted that he had been followed to the airport, but if he was wanted badly enough, the London flights would all be under surveillance. The waitress came and he ordered coffee and rolls, then went back to his brooding.

Fifteen minutes later, his breakfast half eaten, he stepped into a phone booth inside the coffee shop, puzzled out the number in the Copenhagen directory and called Sabena Airlines. A few minutes later, he walked into the men's room and locked himself into a cubicle to wait for the next commuter flight to Antwerp.

4

Brogan pushed his way through the crowd of tourists just off the latest charter flight from the United States, slipped through the "Nothing to Declare" gate at Customs and stepped onto the escalator. The crowd was all on the second level, and the main floor of Gatwick Air Terminal was practically deserted. He stopped at the newsstand to pick up the morning edition of the *Times*, then crossed the concourse to the railway ticket window and bought a first-class seat to London.

He went down the escalator to the platform and found a seat in the bright morning sunshine. The Brighton train was loading passengers on the opposite track and he watched the solid British tourist, complete with children and boxed pets, lunch hamper in hand, boarding without the hustle and shoving characteristic of Continental trains.

Brogan lit a cigarette and sat back, paper ignored, and breathed the clean English air, happy to be home again after four days of continent hopping. A born-and-bred Californian, Brogan had traded the sunshine, smog, and pleasant but vacant existence of Los Angeles some five years before, for the fog, soft rain and clean air, not to mention the sense of relaxation, that permeated the third most industrialized nation in the world, and never once considered himself the loser in the bargain.

The bustle of the airport and railroad station hummed around him as he closed his eyes and slumped back on the bench. He had slept badly the night before, angry not at what he had done to Hansen but at the fact that he had felt it at all necessary. He had seen too much of that in Vietnam, and ten years had done nothing to inure him to the repulsive concept of inflicting physical pain to gain a desired end. The cause had been less than worthy then, and if he took the Iranian Colonel's line of reasoning, this was no better. And where did that place him—no better than the Colonel, whom he had practically accused of a Nazi-like devotion to following orders?

The Victoria train slid into the station with a screech of brakes, and Brogan opened his eyes and stood up wearily. He wandered down the line, carryall in hand, until he found a first-class car that suited his purpose and climbed aboard. The train was half full when it pulled out, and his car was empty but for two excited elderly ladies, chattering over the sights along the way. He lowered the window and sat back, savoring the warm spring air as the train whistled past crossings and roared through tunnels on its way into London.

Presently, the two ladies got up and changed seats, closer to him.

"Pardon me," one of them said in a hesitant voice. "You are the first *real* Englishman with whom we have spoken. May we bother you for a moment?"

Brogan grinned and said, in his best Oxford accent, "Of course, madame. No bother at all."

The two ladies smiled happily at one another and the other shyly introduced them. "My name is Barbara Benson and this is my friend, Sara Walker. We teach school in Lansing, Michigan . . . that's in the Midwest, you know, the state shaped like a mitten."

She put a hand to her mouth. "Oh, I don't suppose you call them mittens over here. A mitten is a glove without . . ."

Brogan laughed. "Yes, Miss Benson, we call them mittens over here too, and I do know where Michigan is located."

Brogan hadn't the heart to tell the two ladies that he was as American as they. He continued the charade, exaggerating his phony Oxford accent, which all Americans seemed to feel was so British. It made for a pleasant trip into London, and he pointed out the row houses along the tracks and they exclaimed over the sudden contrasts between country and town life along the line as being so . . . so British. Brogan wisely refrained from mentioning that this was as typical of the

United States as of Great Britain or France or Germany, or Australia for that matter.

As the train rounded the last obscuring bend and the city itself came into view across a collage of elevated railroad platforms, buildings, and the river, Misses Benson and Walker fell into raptures, raptures that faded somewhat as the train shot through the reality of the industrial section of Brixton. Brogan distracted them by pointing out Chelsea across the river. He wrote down the names of two excellent restaurants and entertained them with a capsule version of London's two-thousand-year history until the train pulled into the dusty, superannuated structure of Victoria Station. His last sight of them came as they happily followed a West Indian porter down the platform to the taxi stand. Brogan shook his head and, recalling his own excitement as he had stepped off the train in London for the first time, chuckled to himself and followed.

He came out under the portico of the ancient, coal-blackened structure and decided that the day was far too nice to ride. He walked to the corner, crossed and started up Lower Belgrave Street. The afternoon sun shone brightly, producing a day that was exceptionally warm for May. The girls were all dressed in their lightest summer clothes and, in spite of the fact that it was Thursday, Brogan felt a holiday mood in the air which he knew existed only in his own mind. In fact, the air was the result of the produce market behind Victoria Station, and it was anything but holidayish. Nevertheless, he walked slowly north, enjoying himself thoroughly until the air turned chill as the sun disappeared behind a sudden bank of clouds. The girls who had been sauntering along so gaily a moment before were now hurrying, anxious to be out of the chill breeze that had sprung up.

Brogan flagged a cab going in his direction and settled into the back seat. "Corner of Park and Red Place." The driver made a right and went straight up Grosvenor Place onto Park Lane until they crossed Oxford and turned into Park Street.

The cab drew around the corner and stopped in front of a red brick, ground-floor flat. Brogan handed over the fare and got out. The doorstep was neatly cleaned and still glistening with water, and he unlocked the door and went inside.

The flat held, not an empty odor, as he had expected, but one comfortably sweet, and he knew that Sandra had been there earlier that morning. He found her note on the telephone, which she had disconnected from the wall plug. The note told him that he was not expected until tomorrow morning. The dirty dishes had all been washed and put away and his laundry sent out, returned and neatly hung in the closet. Brogan wandered through the rooms for a while, not really feeling drowsy although he was dead tired. His head began to ache abominably once more and his "returning home euphoria" died abruptly. He undressed, got into pajamas and turned the bed down. The windows were all shut, closing out the sounds of the city, and the air was stuffy. He opened a bedroom window that looked out onto a tiny garden which he had surrounded with a thick screen of Italian cypress, ivy and a huge yew hedge to close out the traffic noises. The sun was still struggling with the clouds, but fighting a losing battle. Moments later, a splattering of huge raindrops fell, an exploratory vanguard of a downpour.

He lit the electric log in the fireplace, adjusted the heat and got into bed. The heavy curtains, selected solely for their ability to screen bright sunlight, closed down the room, and the fire provided an air of coziness. Feeling somewhat self-conscious at this regression to the comfort of childhood, Brogan settled down and promptly fell asleep.

He awoke at six the next morning, more rested and relaxed than he had been in months. But during his shower and shave a feeling of depression began to intrude again until, by the time he had finished a meager breakfast, he had slumped into a sour mood. He left the flat before seven and drove to New Scotland Yard, showed a pass to a sleepy guard at the front entrance, a new man whom he did not recognize, and went up to the deserted offices of the International Narcotics and Control Commission on the ninth floor.

Always immensely dissatisfied at returning to office routine after the freedom of a field trip, today was no exception. He stared moodily around his office, noting the piles of paper stacked neatly in and beside his "in box," the "out box" reproachfully covered with a light coat of dust. He wandered around the main office for a moment, undecided as to whether he should stay or run, and after a struggle, decided to stay. It was just after seven-thirty, a good hour and a half before the regular staff came in, and if he got started he could make a sizable dent in the stack of useless paper on his desk.

As usual, the lackadaisical receptionist had forgotten to fill the coffee pot, and Brogan wandered down to the office of the Metropolitan Police Commissioner and filled his cup with the strong, half-chicory brew that policemen all over the world seem to favor and returned to his own office, counting himself fortunate that he had not had to say hello to anyone. He settled himself into his chair and took the first folder off the top and got to work.

By the time Sandra came in at nine o'clock, he had finished the two stacks by the simple expedient of throwing everything not marked URGENT or SECRET into the wastebasket, on the snobbish theory that if it was important it would be so marked; if not, then he was too highly paid to waste his time on the same kind of information available to file clerks and the like.

Sandra came in, started to say good morning, then paused. Brogan was poring over a quarter-inch map of some unidentifiable area, totally engrossed. Sighing, she hurried off to the library to sign out the map before another fight ensued.

Brogan did not emerge from his office until eleven o'clock and several long-distance phone calls had been completed. Even so, he was still not ready to talk to anyone. Sandra noticed this at once and pointed to the coffee pitcher on her desk.

"Have a cup. Mr. Vandervoort wants to see you as soon as you are available. That was an hour ago," she added warningly.

Brogan nodded and started for the door, hesitated halfway and returned. He bent down and kissed the top of her coppery colored hair.

"Thanks for cleaning up the place," he mumbled and went out, leaving Sandra glaring daggers after him.

Vandervoort's office was on the tenth floor and Brogan clumped up the stairs and pushed through the glass doors.

Vandervoort's secretary, a severe, prim old bat of the wire-stays-and-pursed-lips school, motioned to the door and watched him critically over the tops of her once-again-stylish but authentic granny glasses.

Brogan curled a lip at her and walked in without knocking. Vandervoort looked up, closed the folder he had been reading, leaned back in his chair and regarded Brogan with a jaundiced eye as he sank down onto the couch and put his feet up on the desk.

"Our wandering hero returns, does he? It is about time . . . spending the taxpayers' money on your world travels . . ."

Brogan shifted to a more comfortable position. "That's your fault and I'll tell them so at the next budget hearings. If you wouldn't send me off to Tehran, Copenhagen and other exotic places of intrigue and adventure with your cryptic messages left at airports around the world, like a good little counterspy, I could have been wasting my time around here, where you could keep an eye on me to see that I did it properly."

"Take your feet off my desk," Vandervoort snorted. "What did you find out?"

Brogan stood up and wandered over to the window with its magnificent view of the Thames, now barely visible through the falling rain.

"You may recall that I asked what you found out," Vandervoort prompted again.

Brogan shook his head without turning away from the window. "The rumors are true. Someone, somewhere is opening up a new heroin network."

Vandervoort laughed and Brogan swung around angrily. "For God's sake, what in hell does it take to make you admit that you were wrong? What do you need to convince you?"

"Do not mix your curses that way," Vandervoort replied in a mild voice. He picked up his pipe and toyed with it for a moment. "What does it take?" he asked finally. "To begin with, some hard proof, very hard proof . . . something more than your usual half-baked flights of fancy."

Brogan came back and sat down on the couch. "All right. This time you are going to have to give in. The Iranians are sending us samples of that damned poppy. When it gets here, I am going to bring one in and stuff it up your . . ."

"Now, now." Vandervoort held up a hand with a faint smile on his face. "Please remember that I am your superior and still approve your raises. You must be polite to me."

"Hell, if you are going to demand respect on the basis of the raises you get me, you're lucky I don't throw you through that window." He took a deep breath. "All right. When the samples get here, you'll see that there is no doubt that these blasted flowers do not have petals. Don't ask me why or how. I'm not enough of a botanist to answer that. All I know is that they don't, and I saw a twenty-acre field jammed full of them. And there is no chance, no chance in any way, shape, or form, that those flowers are confined to just that one field out there in the middle of Iran."

"And what leads you to that belief?"

"Look, those seeds were planted at least three months ago. Three days ago a major haul of reputedly high-grade, uncut heroin was intercepted off Denmark. For the first time in two years, a major shipment of heroin has been taken. For two years now, the satellite system has worked successfully, so successfully that it's all but closed down the heroin distribution system worldwide by cutting into the supply right at the source, the poppies themselves. You know as well as I do that since the U.S. completed the system, there has been no way to hide even a small field capable of producing a marginally economical batch. Now once more, and pay attention this time because it just may go over your damned head again, a major haul is made within a few days of the time we get our first hard look at a new opium poppy, one that grows without petals." Brogan got up and stalked across the room again to the windows.

Vandervoort chuckled. "Please, I ask a little more respect for your superior. Remember, your review comes up in another few weeks."

"Hell," Brogan snorted. "What few weeks. It was due three months ago."

"Did it ever occur to you that there might be a cause-and-effect relationship?"

Brogan gestured impatiently. "Of course. So what? It's too damned hard to sustain any amount of civility towards you for any length of time."

Vandervoort lit his foul-smelling pipe and resettled his bulk comfortably in the chair. "Surely you don't feel there is any direct connection between that insignificant little field in the middle of Asia Minor and this Danish shipment of heroin? Isn't it possible that someone has managed to grow sufficient of the old poppies to produce enough opium to manufacture . . . ?"

"Hell, no! How could they possibly? Every major and minor growing area is monitored at least weekly. The high-risk areas are surveyed every three days. There is no way for anyone to grow that many poppies without being spotted, and you know that as well as I do. I'm not saying that occasionally someone won't slip a small field past the satellites, enough to produce a few grams of opium, maybe even a kilo, but not the hundred and fifty kilos needed to make fifteen kilos of heroin. My God, they would have to cultivate fifty-two acres of the best-producing poppies to get that much. And fifty-odd acres of red and orange poppies would stand out like a sore thumb anywhere on the planet, no matter how much they broke the plots up. The odds against succeeding are astronomical."

"So, then"—Vandervoort stared at Brogan through the smoke —"where are these mysterious poppies being grown?"

Brogan rubbed the back of his neck. "I sure as hell wish I knew. This shipment was picked up as they tried to smuggle it into Denmark. And if the Danish Navy wasn't so damned efficient, they would have made it." He walked back to perch on Vandervoort's desk. "That Danish fishing boat was coming in from Iceland, two days later than it should have, according to the Danes. From what I was able to find out, the boat did not call at any North Atlantic port within range of their estimated fuel between the southern tip of Greenland and the Öresund. In fact, they were first spotted coming up through the Channel, past the Dutch Coast. Now, why would they be going the long way around . . . unless they stopped to pick up the heroin along the way?"

"I assume you have ruled out any possibility that the heroin was being brought in from North America via Greenland?"

Brogan nodded. "Yeah, I have. The market is still a hell of a lot bigger in the U.S. or Canada than it is in Europe. Except for a few really hard-core addicts in trouble with the law, there is no reason for them to buy from a black market since, with the exception of the Eastern bloc countries, heroin is now a prescription drug throughout Europe, even in West Germany."

Vandervoort nodded. "All right, so you have a point in your favor. Where does it lead you?"

"To something I found out from the master of that fishing boat. He came down the West Coast of Ireland and picked up the shipment from a Japanese tanker off Dursey Head on the South Coast. I've got a call into the U. N. Ships Registry to find out what ports she's called at since she left Japan."

"Is it possible that one of the Asian or African sources has opened up again? What about the Russians? There are some rumblings that the Caucasian fields are in operation once again?"

Brogan shook his head. "No, I don't think so. I talked with my contact in Chinese intelligence. The petal-less poppies are new to them, but they have been watching the Russians very closely since the Caucasian rumors started. Granted that the Russians have the resources to hide the fields, but what would they gain? They would have a difficult time producing and importing enough heroin into North America to absorb sufficient economic resources in the United States to make it worth their while. In any event, the Chinese don't feel that this stuff is coming from Russia or from anywhere in Asia or Africa. Our hard intelligence confirms theirs, down to the last detail."

Vandervoort was silent for a long while. Finally, he laid down his pipe. "All right. I still do not think that you are correct about these so-called petal-less poppies. But it is clear that something is going on that needs looking into. So look into it . . . but do not depend on me for support."

Brogan muttered sarcastically under his breath and walked to the door. "By the way," Vandervoort called out to him. He held up a sheet of flimsy paper. "This came through yesterday afternoon from Copenhagen. It is a Danish police warrant for your arrest. They wish to charge you with breaking and entering and assault and battery on a certain Lars Hansen, Master of the vessel *Friedland.*"

Brogan placed a hand on his chest. "Me . . . ?" he asked in mock innocence.

Vandervoort's expression was pained. "One of these days your cowboy tactics will land you in jail. And when they do, do not expect me to come rushing to your aid."

"Perish the thought." Brogan grinned for the first time that morning. "That's the last thing in the world I would expect from you."

"Sarcasm is not necessary," Vandervoort replied with dignity. "With all of the trouble you have caused us . . ."

"Trouble? That's trouble? A dumb arrest warrant? I was more worried about the three goons waiting for me in the hotel parking garage. Now I know who they were . . . cops. Nuts!"

"As I started to say," Vandervoort continued, "with all of the trouble you have caused, I hope that you have learned something worthwhile."

Brogan opened the door. "Yeah, enough to start me thinking anyway."

"Constructively, I hope."

Brogan closed the door harder than was necessary.

5

Feeling completely at loose ends, Brogan wandered down to the canteen and sat morosely through two cups of coffee. Back in his office later, he stared through the window until unconsciously he had memorized every rooftop and building within view. In the meantime, as the paucity of hard information replayed itself over and over again in his mind, his frustration began to mount. He snarled at Sandra, refused to talk to Vandervoort again, and brooded until the problem of the petal-less poppy was beginning to take on the dimensions of an obsession, driven perhaps by the knowledge of what he had done to Hansen. Only by turning up something concrete could he ever begin to justify that to himself.

He made two more phone calls, one to the *Sûreté* in Paris, the other to the Bureau of Narcotics and Dangerous Drugs in Washington. When they wouldn't or couldn't tell him anything, he even went so far as to walk reluctantly down a floor and discuss his problem with the Yard. There he met the guarded attitude traditional with the Metropolitan Police Force when dealing with illegal drugs. Afraid that a problem might develop where none had existed before, they preferred to pretend that heroin did not exist.

"We have our hands full dealing with marijuana, hash, and coke," they told him. "Why not talk to the Home Office?" Brogan swore vociferously, pointed out that the transfer could just as easily have taken place in British rather than Irish waters, and went back upstairs to stare out the window again. Narcotics investigation was slow, frustrating work, but never, never before had he been quite this frustrated. He could sense that something was building up, but he couldn't quite identify it, and this only added to his frustration. Go talk to the Home Office indeed.

By midafternoon he was reduced to sorting over and over the information that he had managed to gather, arranging and rearranging the scraps of data into various categories. In the end, he always returned to the same two classifications: hard information and speculation.

Into the hard-information category went the facts: fifteen kilos of heroin intercepted after a period of two years when the hauls were few and far between and limited to, at most, a kilogram; and the appearance of the petal-less poppy as confirmed in Iran. And Sandra had placed a cable on his desk after lunch reporting an unconfirmed sighting in Thailand.

The speculation column was even sparser. First, did the heroin confiscated by the Danish Navy come from the petal-less poppy? If so, then how to tie together the poppies in Iran and the interception off the North European coast, some four thousand miles away. He was not sure that he ever would be able to—unless the new poppy was being grown in sufficient quantity in Asia Minor to begin exporting opium or even pure heroin to Europe. If so, the questions then became, Where and how was it being shipped? And was the pickup off the Irish Coast headed for North America or Europe? Each question only produced more questions, and when he tried to list them on a sheet of paper he quickly discovered that he needed a computer to keep track of all the new branches opened up.

He stared at the world map that Sandra had dug up for him until he was convinced that photonic pressure was fading the inks. Theoretically, the International Narcotics Control Commission operated under United Nations auspices. In turn, its activities were primarily surveillance and investigation; and, accordingly, a worldwide monitoring system of listening and watching posts had been developed that supplemented the American satellite monitoring system. These posts took the form of contracts with and through Interpol, the independent International Police Organization, the intelligence agencies of various nations concerned with narcotics as an internal or international problem, selected representatives from every pharmaceutical company in the world manufacturing any drug classed as a narcotic, free-lance contacts, and certain semi- or completely underworld contacts, including one Mafia Capo in

Brooklyn that any Don would have sold his only daughter to know about. In any event, this surveillance system was supposed to watch the movement of all narcotic drugs, legal or illegal, after the satellites had located the source.

But even during the best of times, when the action was at its peak in the early seventies, the unwieldy system had been so riddled with holes as to be next to useless. Now, after two years of routine legal movements, the holes were probably big enough to drive a circus train through—one loaded with flowering poppies.

With a deep sigh and nothing better to do, he took out a red pencil and began eliminating the countries in Europe least likely to be involved. Since it appeared that transportation was by seagoing vessels, he marked out all those nations that did not border directly, or have easy access to, the Atlantic, Baltic or Mediterranean seas. In short order, he had penciled out Hungary, Austria, Romania, Czechoslovakia, Bulgaria, Lichtenstein, Luxembourg, Switzerland and Andorra, and he gave it up as a lost cause. The combined area remaining was still greater than half the United States.

The fifteen kilos captured by the Danes were reportedly ninety-two per cent pure and could easily be cut five or six times to two to three per cent concentration per dose, allowing a retail price on the streets in North America close to $32.5 million at the current price. He shook his head over the ability of a rather harmless (physiologically speaking) drug, through mass hysteria based almost totally on misunderstanding, to command such prices. Brogan had long ago disabused himself of the idea that heroin itself was a deadly killer. As the Iranian Colonel had suggested, heroin was only one other way that a morally or spiritually weak person found to cope with a world he had never made, in much the same way others used legal barbiturates, amphetamines or alcohol. After nearly one hundred years of existence, so little work had been done on the drug that even its primary toxic effects remained unknown. The best that could be offered to explain a death by overdose was respiratory failure, and the *exact* role of heroin in the process was unknown. He personally knew of three cases where people, participants in Britain's registration program, had used heroin constantly for thirty or more years with no overt systemic effects beyond mild cases of constipation. But of course that was in Great Britain, where a somewhat saner view of the problem was taken; although, unfortunately, the same thing could not be said for other hard drugs such as hashish and cocaine, for which there was a flourishing black market. Hash and coke were illegal drugs in Britain.

North America, by far the major market for illegal heroin, contrasted sharply with those countries in Europe where heroin was legally available by physician's prescription. Great Britain was a prime example. At the height of the North American epidemic, the mid-1960s to the mid-1970s, there had never been more than three thousand addicts in all of Great Britain, while the United States estimated over half a million: four thousand per cent higher, based on population. Yet, the U. S. Government persisted in its efforts to prohibit heroin use by legal ban, thus creating a black market in which users were forced to pay a terribly inflated cost—in terms of crime, human damage, and social disruption—to support a habit bred by poverty and criminal activity that fed on itself in a vicious cycle.

The satellite monitoring system was an expensive way to solve the heroin problem by cutting off the supply at its source. Although successful enough in slicing drastically into the supply, thus forcing the price for what little remained so high that it was all but priced out of reach, it had not been a complete solution. The addict population in the United States had been reduced from a high of 650,000 in 1976 to the pre-1960 level of about 50,000. But the underlying conditions still existed; the criminal syndicates had only rechanneled their resources, and a "customer base" was still in active existence, holding on until the "market" was again reopened.

And now a poppy without a petal, which could not be identified by satellite, was threatening to put the crime syndicates back into full-scale operation in the face of blind opposition from politicians who had repeatedly failed to provide legislation that would legalize heroin use under government medical supervision, thus wiping out of existence in one blow the crime syndicates dealing in heroin.

Brogan shook his head in disgust over the predicament. His

was an impossible job. It was no more feasible to end drug addiction by punitive measures than it had been to stop the use of alcohol by prohibition. Crime, social injustice and another cycle of poverty always followed any such ill-considered prohibition.

* * *

The afternoon was damp and rainy, matching his temperament perfectly. Sandra opened the door to his office, tossed his raincoat at him and hooked a thumb toward the elevator.

"Go out for a walk . . . and don't come back unless you are in a better mood."

Meekly, he got up and left, ignoring the hostile stares of the other secretaries as he shambled across to the elevators. Outside the building, he crossed the square and stopped on the corner of Broadway and Victoria, undecided as to whether he should head down toward the river or up into the city. Finally, he walked up Broadway and over into St. James's Park, which was practically deserted; even the pigeons had taken shelter. The rain began to pelt down again and he stepped under the shelter of an oak and waited for it to ease.

Brogan walked up the Mall, his chin sunk deep into his collar. A policeman standing under the arches watched him curiously as he crossed over to Trafalgar Square, where only a few very hardy tourists were about. The traffic was heavier than usual at this time of the afternoon because of the rain, and he dodged across the road, ignoring an angry taxi driver. He brooded up Charing Cross, barely aware of where he was heading until a sudden downpour drove him into Foyles, where he stared at the books on display until the manager came down to ask him if he intended to make a purchase. Brogan mumbled an apology and beat a hasty retreat. The manager came out under the awning and watched him down the street until he stopped a cab and rode it back to his flat.

Sandra brought his car that evening, let herself in with her key and found Brogan asleep beside the fire. She went into the kitchen, swearing under her breath at the mess, and put coffee on to perk. Then she went back to the living room, considered his damnably relaxed mien after sulking around the office all day, and kicked him in the knee.

"Ouch . . . damnation!" Brogan yelped, struggled upright in the chair and grabbed for his knee. He saw her standing beside him. "What the devil did you do that for?"

Sandra sat down on the couch without a word while Brogan hobbled about the room, trying to ease the pain. "What time is it?" he mumbled and, without waiting for an answer, went into the bathroom and doused his face with cold water.

He came back into the living room toweling his face and hands dry. "I asked why you did that?"

"Did what?"

"Kicked me in the knee?"

Sandra shook her head disdainfully. "Because you deserved it, that's why."

"Oh, hell . . . . and how did I deserve it?"

Sandra curled her legs under her and leaned back. "You have been acting like a perfect beast all day. You hadn't a civil word for anyone, me included."

Brogan started to protest, but she shook her head. "No, sir, don't you interrupt me. You remained cooped up in your office or down in the canteen growling at anyone who so much as dared to look at you cross-eyed, and you have Mr. Vandervoort upset with you again. People are beginning to wonder if it isn't about time that you were relieved or sent on to some other kind of work."

Brogan snorted. "Vandervoort never gets upset about anything, especially me. Anyway, you're right about another job. There are any number of less frustrating positions that I might qualify for: astronaut, lion tamer, mercenary, hired assassin, and so on. Any one of them would be easier on the nerves, not to mention what little brain I've got left."

"Oh, stop feeling sorry for yourself," she snapped. "I know you're worried about these poppies; you always get like this when you have a new problem. But this is starting out to be the worst siege yet."

Brogan stared at the electric fire for a moment before he answered. "Sandra, do you know what I saw in Iran?"

When she shook her head, he leaned back on the couch and lit a cigarette.

"Two men, farmers, owned that field of poppies, the new ones without the petals. They were both going to be shot the next morning. They were going to be shot just because they grew a special type of flower to make some money. They knew it was against the law, but they probably didn't have the haziest idea what the end product of their actions would be in terms of human misery. And you know something? That misery doesn't come about through what they did, but because some supposedly highly civilized and intelligent men in a couple of governments haven't got the guts to do their jobs and sell the public on the only way to stop this mess."

Sandra came over and knelt down on the carpet beside him and began to massage his shoulders. "I didn't know about that." She was silent for a moment. "But, Cole, there was nothing you could do about it, was there? Why are you worrying yourself sick?"

Brogan smiled half-heartedly.

"The eminent practicality of women. Sandra, I wish it was that simple, I really do. But if someone doesn't worry, those damned flowers are going to spread all over the world again, and this time the heroin epidemic is going to make the one a few years ago seem like a bad cold. So far, no one but me believes this. Vandervoort is a damned fool and can't see past his fat Dutch nose."

He was silent for a moment, staring into the red glow.

"You can almost trace the progression of heroin through the pipeline by the bodies it leaves behind. Somewhere along the line, if you count addicts who die from overdoses, dirty needles, gangland killings, whatever, one person dies for just about every kilo of heroin produced. Eventually, every illegal addict, unless he is lucky enough to go off and stay off, will die of that overdose, dirty needle, gangland killing, malnutrition or a policeman's bullet."

Brogan looked at his cigarette with distaste, then stubbed it out. "Same with these damned things. They cause lung cancer, contribute to emphysema and God knows what all; but people, myself included, have to have them because it makes life a little more bearable. Isn't it the same, to some extent, with hard drugs? Isn't the principle the same?" he almost pleaded. "A person, a Black kid in the New York ghetto, starts on heroin because of peer group pressure. But he only stays on if the drug fills some basic gap, some need in his make-up." He was quiet for a moment, staring at the curl of smoke from the ashtray.

"What was it Tennyson wrote . . . *Trouble on trouble, pain on pain, Long labor unto aged breath, Sore task to hearts worn out by many wars And eyes grown dim on gazing on the pilot stars.*"

Sandra got up and went over to the window to stare out into the wet night. She pulled the curtains shut and after a moment came slowly back across the room and stopped before Brogan.

"Cole, I . . ." She curled down into his lap and he put his arms around her and held her tightly, nuzzling his chin down into her soft hair.

6

On Monday Brogan was seated at his desk plowing through routine file reports when the buzzer on his phone woke him from a dull drowse. He glanced at it absently, and Sandra opened the door a moment later.

"Your Washington friend is on the phone."

Brogan raised an eyebrow. "Charlie?"

She nodded. "I'll get my pad and be right in."

Brogan attached the lead from the dictating machine to the phone, checked to see that a fresh cassette was in place, and as Sandra came back in, picked up the phone and punched the speaker button.

"Hello?"

The male voice of an international telephone operator was obscured by static, then cleared immediately.

". . . Brogan, please, Mr. Charles Conrad calling from Washington, D.C."

"Yes, this is Brogan, go ahead."

"Thank you. Go ahead, Mr. Conrad."

"Hello, Cole?"

"Hi, Charlie. How's the weather in Washington?" He glanced over to see that the tape was turning properly.

"Hotter than a pistol and muggy. The air conditioning is down again in the office, and it must be ninety or better in here. Look, something has come up about that problem we discussed on Friday."

Brogan sat forward in his chair, and reacting to the look on his face, Sandra opened her steno pad. "Let's hear it. I've got the tape going."

"Well, shut it off, then. This is confidential."

Brogan stopped the cassette and detached the phone jack. "It's off. Go ahead."

"Okay, here it is. Are there any oil refineries in western Ireland?"

"What the hell kind of a question is that?"

"Are there?" Conrad repeated the question insistently.

Brogan scratched his head. "Not that I know of. That's mostly an agricultural area, as I remember. There might be one or two around Bantry Bay, but nothing in the west . . . why?"

"I've just gotten a report across my desk from upstairs. It says there is a concentration of acetic anhydride somewhere in the center of County Kerry."

Brogan rummaged across his desk. "Hell! Sandra, see if you can find that map of Ireland, please . . . just a minute, Charlie."

Sandra cleared a pile of papers off the corner, dug out the map.

"Okay, I've got the map now. Where exactly was that location?"

"I don't know for sure. This was a test run and they found the concentration by accident. They haven't been able to pinpoint it any further yet. The overlay that I have shows it to be somewhere between the mouth of the Shannon and Tralee Bay. What puzzles me is that I can't see any reason for acetic anhydride in that area."

Brogan was silent for a moment. "Neither can I," he said finally. "We'll run a check to see if there are any oil refineries around there, but I doubt it very much."

"Do that, but we already have and there aren't; nor any metals-processing plants either, and there are no licenses issued in that area either. For one thing, the source seems to be inland quite a ways, at least thirty miles, and there doesn't seem to be any good road net to the sea in that area either."

"Okay," Brogan said thoughtfully. "I've got it. There might be something further north along the Shannon Estuary, perhaps up by the airport. We'll check it out."

"Good. Look, can you come to Washington? I really think that in view of what we discussed last week, this now bears looking into in some detail. You said the fishing boat picked up the shipment off Dursey Head, and that's down on the South Coast."

Brogan considered for a moment. The unexpected prospect of activity, no matter how remote the connection might be, was like a tonic, eliminating all traces of fatigue and frustration.

"Yeah, I think you're right. Look, I'll get a plane out of here as fast as I can. Sandra will call you later today with the flight number and I'll see you tomorrow."

"Good deal! Tomorrow, then."

Brogan pushed the disconnect button and stared thoughtfully at Sandra. "Charlie thinks he's on to something, something in western Ireland that may give us a clue to where that fifteen kilos of heroin came from."

"What is acetic anhyd . . . hy . . . or however you pronounce it?" she asked.

"Acetic anhydride," Brogan pronounced carefully. "It has two uses; oil refining and acetylizing morphine to make heroin. If there is enough there to detect, then someone is using a hell of a lot . . . but why Ireland?" he finished thoughtfully.

Brogan swiveled around in the chair to stare out the floor-to-ceiling window. "Sounds like a long shot . . . but let's double-check," he finished suddenly. "Get on to the Irish Consul and see if there are any oil refineries on the West Coast between Shannon Airport and Tralee Bay, as far inland as, say . . ."—he peered at the map—". . . Limerick. But, before you do that, get me a reservation on an afternoon flight to Washington. Have the tickets held at the airport and I'll pick them up there. Oh, and see if there is any money left in the travel fund. If there is, I'll take what's there."

"Don't you think Mr. Vandervoort . . ."

"The hell with Vandervoort. He'll just get in the way. Get me the tickets without going through the travel department and tell him tomorrow, after I'm gone."

"But wait just a minute. What would an oil refinery have to do with heroin? What am I looking for? . . ."

Brogan grinned at her. "I'll tell you when I get back if it makes any sense. Right now I'm not sure it does to me. It involves the Space Watch system somehow, and that's all I can tell you now."

"Cole, I know the Space Watch system is very highly classified, but I do have a 'Secret Clearance' . . ."

"Not from the United States you don't, Sandi, and that's the only reason why Vandervoort puts up with me. Take that away, and he might just see that I never got another job in Great Britain. One of these days the U.S. will start releasing some information, but until then I can't tell you anything."

Sandra heaved an exasperated sigh, but she knew better than to argue. Brogan shoved some papers into his briefcase as she came around the desk to the phone.

"There isn't anything left in the travel fund. In fact, Accounting wants your expenses from the last two trips before they will give you another advance . . ."

Brogan snorted. "Tell them that whatever they gave me as an advance, I spent. I'll use my own funds this time, and I promise," he said, raising a hand to forestall an outburst, "that I'll do my accounts the minute I get back."

He kissed her quickly and headed for the door. "I'm going home to pack. Let me know what airline and if it's any other airport but Heathrow. I'll see you in a day or so."

* * *

The light-gray Ford government car turned into the entrance to the parking garage and stopped. A security guard stepped to the driver's side and nodded to Charles Conrad as he rolled down the window and handed over his identification card. With the window open, the cool, soggy air of the air-conditioned interior was immediately replaced with the hot, soggy air of the exterior.

The guard examined the card carefully, leaned over to peer at Brogan, then glanced questioningly at Conrad.

"He's already been cleared. Name's Brogan, Cole Brogan."

The guard took another long look at Brogan, then nodded and ambled around the car to the guardhouse, where he took down a clipboard from inside the door and leafed through the pages. When he found what he was looking for, he sauntered back to Brogan's side of the car and motioned for him to roll the window down. Brogan did so, reluctantly.

"See some I.D., bud?"

"Leave your manners home?" Brogan muttered as he dug out his wallet and extracted his driver's license and identification card.

The guard ignored the question while he studied the I.D. Finally, he handed it back and motioned Conrad through. The car moved forward and both men quickly rolled up the windows again.

"You know, that bastard goes through this routine every time I come through . . . every day now for seven years. You'd think he owns the place. They won't let him on duty during rush hour or he'd have everyone backed up for hours."

Conrad shook his head as he wheeled the car into his reserved parking space. "Damned civil service. They make so much money nowadays for so little work that they think they own the government."

"It may be six years since I've been back here, but I haven't forgotten."

Shimmering heat haze hung over the courtyard and building, and Brogan was soaked with sweat by the time they had covered the hundred-yard distance between the garage and building.

"My God, how can you stand this?" Brogan panted as they entered the building to be engulfed by the chill air cascading from the air-conditioning system.

"I can't, but I also cannot afford not to like it. Put your jacket on or you'll catch cold."

The guard, seated behind a large walnut desk that served to block the entrance lobby from the main part of the Justice building, greeted Conrad by name. While they waited for clearance, Conrad led Brogan to a line of comfortable steel-and-vinyl chairs along one wall—rather good copies of the Barcelona, Brogan thought. Conrad shook out a cigarette and offered the pack to Brogan.

"No, thanks. I don't care for filters."

Conrad nodded and while they waited, making small talk about their years together in the Agency, Conrad had a chance to study Brogan. In spite of his approaching midthirties, Brogan was still lean and fit as a twenty-year-old. Gray was beginning to show in the dark hair, especially at his temples, and the deep tan was gone, probably washed out by the pale sunshine and rain of England. Schooled to pay close attention to minute details, Conrad was surprised to find evidence of stiffness in Brogan's face and movements. The hook in his nose seemed to have increased, and the faint hollows under his eyes had both deepened and darkened. He had already noted, as Brogan had walked beside him, that the spring had gone from his step, leaving a tense, hands-balanced gait. Was the pressure that bad on him, Conrad wondered. The pale face clearly showed enlarged pores and a sheen of excess sebum; and that, coupled with a line of muscle visible below the ear where the jaw joined the skull, made him wonder just what kind of strain he was under.

Brogan glanced at him, a quick flash of impatience visible in the way his shaggy eyebrows came together.

"Easy, Cole, Security takes . . ."

"Mr. Conrad . . ." The guard at the desk motioned to them.

The processing of Brogan's papers and I.D. had taken ten minutes, a fact that Brogan mentioned as they started down the hall. Charlie grinned. "It takes exactly thirty-two seconds to run your I.D. through the computers. The rest of the time is wasted by some clerk in Security digesting what's in the printout and transmitting it to the guard. If there had been the slightest indication that something was wrong with your credentials, you would have noticed about five more guards in the hall, all very polite while they asked you to step into a special office and explain yourself."

Brogan snorted. "What a waste of time and money. We have one receptionist who looks after the security of INCC offices in London."

"Yeah, but you're in the same building as the Metropolitan Police," Conrad pointed out.

"So what? They have a receptionist too. Three of them, in fact. One is in her midforties, and the other two in their twenties. They also have one guard in the lobby . . . one, and he is unarmed. Those cannons your crew carry could demolish a house."

Trading insults, Conrad led Brogan down a second hall to a bank of elevators, reflecting that at least his sense of humor hadn't totally disappeared. He used a key to open the sliding door of the one at the end. Inserting a different key into the control panel, Conrad selected the floor he wanted, and the elevator started down at a speed that surprised Brogan. Conrad watched with amusement while Brogan timed the ride and glanced around for the inspection certificate.

"You won't find it," Conrad chuckled. "They never put one in, because this is federal territory and we have our own elevator-inspection service. Posted licenses with declared speeds aren't necessary . . . inside the cars."

Brogan snorted. "Do you do classified work here, by any chance?" A moment later, the car stopped and the door slid open into a hallway where another guard watched them from behind another walnut desk. They went through the I.D. check procedure all over again, but much more efficiently this time. Then Conrad led Brogan down the hall and into an office with a brass doorplate that carried the initials "SWII" done in block lettering.

"Means Space Watch II, our name for the monitoring system. Very cleverly disguised, wouldn't you say?"

Inside they found a middle-aged secretary seated behind a desk overflowing with paper. Her typewriter maintained an amazingly fast pace as she glanced up, recognized Conrad, gave Brogan a semicurious stare and nodded to the inner office. Conrad knocked on the door, then opened it and ushered Brogan inside, where two men were seated on either side of a conference table.

"Brought our friend from across the water, I see," the older of the two chuckled. He was a big man, more resembling a lumberjack than a scientist. He had the ruins of a large black cigar stuck in his mouth, which he shifted from side to side as he talked. He was wearing a cotton shirt, well-worn jeans and half boots. The second man was quite a bit smaller and more conventionally attired in a business suit—without jacket, which hung over the back of a chair—and striped red-and-white shirt, with a solid red tie to match.

"Cole, this is Dr. Thaddeus Browning," Conrad said, indicating the larger of the two. "He's head of SWII. This is his assistant director, Dr. Peter Mayer. Gentlemen, this is Cole Brogan, special investigator for the International Narcotics Control Commission. He's one of the most important recipients of all those reports we crank out of here."

"Ha! Listen to him, will you," Browning roared. "*We*, he says. *We* crank out of here. Damned secret agent! Never has done a lick of work in his life." He glared at Conrad and shook Brogan's hand vigorously.

"It's good to meet someone on the receiving end, and it's nice to know that we are doing something useful."

"Unfortunately, it had to be by accident," Mayer added, laughing. "But there, it . . ."

"Sit down, sit down," Browning interrupted. "I think that what we have now will interest you." It was plain that he did not appreciate having his work treated lightly, by his assistant or anyone else. Browning shuffled through the pile of photographs at his elbow until he found the ones he wanted, swept the others aside and triumphantly tossed them across to Brogan.

"The first two photographs were taken yesterday, at four P.M. local time," he said. "The last two were taken at eight A.M. local time today and have just come in from the computer room."

Brogan stared at all four positives in puzzlement. They bore some faint relationship to aerial photographs taken from a very high altitude. It appeared that the color scheme had been inverted, but just how he couldn't have said. What should have been blacks were transposed to reds, and the whites in turn were in shades of green.

He said, puzzled, "I'm afraid these don't mean very much to me."

Browning snapped a suspicious look at him, then turned to Conrad. "I thought you told me that . . ."

"Hold on," Conrad said, raising a hand. "Let's not get into that. Brogan is from INCC, he's a field operative. All he wants to do is find out about that acetic anhydride source you've spotted. Nothing more. He's in no position to recommend more funding, but"—and Conrad stared hard at Browning—"he is in a position to throw a king-sized monkey wrench into the works if you don't help him out."

Brogan stared from one to the other, completely bewildered. Mayer caught his expression and laughed.

"Don't mind those two. There are some conflicting jurisdictions at work here. Now let's just concentrate on that acetic anhydride source." He reached across the table for the two sets of photos while Conrad and Browning fought a silent battle with angry looks.

"The point is, just what in hell is any amount of acetic anhydride doing in the west of Ireland? We have had our staff take a hard look at the area and there are no refineries of any kind within seventy miles of there. Now, as Mr. Conrad may have explained to you, the source was discovered quite by accident. I am sure that you are quite familiar with the Space Watch II system, even if you may not know all of its intricacies. So please bear with me a moment while I explain just one of them to you. As you might imagine, any system of cameras and sensors that is concentrated into one small unit the size of a space station with the sole function of monitoring what goes on six hundred miles below, has got to be a very complicated system, especially when its cameras are required to resolve objects six feet or more in diameter.

"Also, you might not be aware that the nature of that function is divided into three parts. The first is hard intelligence . . ." He skipped hastily on at a cold glance from Conrad. "The second is nuclear-test monitoring. And finally, the third, and as far as you are concerned, the most important aspect of the job, monitoring potential growing areas, searching for illegal opium poppies, which it spots by the color of the petals. This is the easiest of the three tasks, as the sensors are required only to watch for large patches of specific colors, all of which are programed into the computer."

Brogan was not as well informed concerning the technical aspects of the Space Watch II system as Mayer was giving him credit for. He was aware of some of the drawbacks, but other than those, he knew little more about the system beyond that it consisted of four unmanned satellites controlled from the single, twenty-four-man space station in a 2,000-mile polar orbit. The system produced coded reports on opium poppy sources, reports which he read religiously and saw to it that they were acted upon within INCC's ground-based surveillance system. But Mayer droned on relentlessly with a recitation of, to him, anyway, largely meaningless technical details.

"The four satellites are in 570-mile, near-polar orbits, and circle the globe each 103 minutes, or fourteen times a day. They can scan a strip 115 miles wide, running north/south at an angle of 80° retrograde to provide a slight overlap on each orbit as they proceed westward, thus achieving complete global coverage every eighteen days, or every 4.5 days per the entire system. We can cover any one spot, then, in less than twenty-four hours. The system uses a Multispectral Scanner Subsystem, which we call MSS, to transmit data to the Manned Orbiting Station, images in four spectral bands: green, red, and two near-infrared. In addition, the system employs two microwave radiometers and an infrared spectrometer and three 2.58 centimeter Return-Beam-Vidicon Television cameras built by RCA Astro Electronics Division. The data is relayed to the MOS, processed and telemetered to ground stations in California, Australia and Spain. Interpretation is done here at NASA's Data Processing Facility in Greenbelt, Maryland."

Browning began to fidget impatiently. Noting this, Mayer stopped and picked up a third set of photos and handed them to Brogan. "Because the poppy watch is the easiest," he said earnestly, "it is on this watch that routine maintenance is performed. The cameras and sensors can run unattended while the technical staff sets up for the next set of runs."

Brogan glanced at the photographs. They were similar to the other two, with the exception of a bright white spot in the left center of one of the photos. He picked up the magnifying glass that was lying on the table and examined the area surrounding the white spot, turning the photo around, vainly trying to recognize something concrete in the abstract pattern of colors.

"Here, try this." Browning handed Brogan an eight-by-ten-inch piece of glossy paper, a reference map of Ireland. He glanced from it to the photograph and, after a moment, recognized the Shannon Estuary. A few minutes more of study and the photo began to move into focus. He found that he could even discern the details of the coastline near the lefthand margin.

"Ireland?" he asked, looking up.

Browning nodded abruptly, his manner that of a man barely able to conceal his impatience on finding that he was dealing with an idiot child, and snapped, "Yes.

"The white spot in the second photo, taken this morning, is the acetic anhydride source. Of course it may not look like much to you," implying that Brogan was at fault, "but the on-board computer is coupled to the camera sensors. All data is fed through this computer, which is programed to isolate certain features in the data it procures. Certain subroutines then take over and call for closer visual observation, perhaps from the ground. Others may require more detailed sensor inspection in a variety of ways, most of them beyond even your classification. That is what happened in this case. Routinely, the computer ordered a spectrograph made of the source and interpreted it as acetic anhydride. Ordinarily, the technician monitoring the instruments would have noted this and immediately set up detailed plans for a source inspection on the next orbit. However, as Dr. Mayer told you, this was a maintenance run and the units were operating unattended. In addition, this was an intelligence-gathering test run in which the sensors were programed to search for specific chemical effluents through a variety of instruments. Acetic anhydride just happened to be one of them.

"So it was not until yesterday, twelve hours after the source was first noted, that the data was reviewed by Conrad, here. He called it to our attention and we immediately ordered another run."

"Okay, I think he has the picture now," Conrad broke in impatiently. "What are the results, dammit?"

Browning stared at Conrad with distaste, and Brogan

groaned inwardly. Wonderful, he thought. I had to walk into the middle of an intramural squabble.

"The results," Browning replied coldly, "are this. Subsequent runs verified the source and pinned its location to within six hundred yards. It appears to be a farm of some kind, three miles south of the village of Abbeyfeale in County Kerry, Ireland."

He stirred one of the photos with his finger. "This shot taken at nine o'clock this morning is the clearest. Last night's photos, as you saw, were obscured by cloud cover, and the results tended to be equivocal." He tapped an area near the center of the photograph. "Use the glass."

Obediently, Brogan picked up the magnifying glass and studied the area indicated. Now that he knew what to look for, he was able to make out buildings as flat, whitish, rectangular shapes connected by faint tracks that were probably roads. The farm was surrounded by fields for a great distance, and each field was evenly divided into neat parallel rows that met and boxed each other according to some pattern that he could not discern. He glanced up at Browning, but his question had already been anticipated.

"Those rows that you see are vineyards . . . for growing grapes."

For a moment, the revelation left him blank. He shook his head.

"What?"

"Vineyards," Browning repeated patiently. "The farm is a vineyard, for growing grapes, presumably for making wine."

"In Ireland?"

Browning shrugged. "That is the answer our research staff gave us. As I understand . . . and I do not know much about wine or grapes . . . there is no real Irish wine industry."

Brogan shook his head. "Not that I know of . . . unless you count drinking it." The others chuckled politely—all but Browning, who scowled at his levity.

"Are you sure that's what they are?" he asked finally.

In answer, Mayer selected another set of photographs from the pile on the table and spread them out in front of Brogan.

Through the glass, he could see the same fine parallel lines running through the fields.

"Okay, so what are these?"

"The first two," Mayer replied, "show the Napa Valley in California." He paused, reached over and checked the photos. "Yes. Now, that first one is the Napa-Sonoma winery, and the second is one of the Gallo vineyards. Both show the same distinctive pattern. The third is the Bordeaux area of France. Again, notice the tracings indicating a vineyard. We have others taken over Germany, Italy, Switzerland, what have you. All show the same marks, and the co-ordinates leave no doubt that what we are seeing are vineyards."

Brogan shook his head. "All right, so you have established that these are vineyards. Now, what the hell does it mean?" He stared morosely across the table at Conrad.

"Don't look at me, old buddy. It doesn't mean anything to me either."

An uncomfortable silence fell over the four men for a moment before Browning cleared his throat. "I am sorry, Brogan, but for the moment that is all we can do for you. As you are well aware, the sighting of the acetic anhydride source was pure luck. Ireland's atmospheric conditions are not the best, but of course we will continue to observe the area on a daily basis. Any more information will be forwarded to you through Conrad's office. I hope," he added sarcastically, "that Conrad did not mislead you into thinking that we would have detailed photographs of the area and a dossier on every individual within twenty miles."

Conrad started to retort but Brogan stood up abruptly. "Charlie, let's go get a cup of coffee and let these two gentlemen get back to work. Dr. Browning, Dr. Mayer, thank you very much for your able assistance. I don't need to tell you just how invaluable it has been. Charlie did not mislead me. He and I have been friends for years. He felt that I might be able to pick up something from a discussion that might not appear in a written report. A serendipitous approach, you might say."

Browning nodded, thawing a bit. "We do, I am afraid, allow our internal problems to get the best of us sometimes. But perhaps we have helped some pieces fall into place. I would like to think so anyway."

"It could very well be," Brogan replied. "I'll make some phone calls in the meantime and see what I can dig up, and I'm sure Charlie will keep you informed."

* * *

Conrad took Brogan up to a small cafeteria on the floor above, found a table and excused himself briefly to make a phone call. When he returned, he had a full lunch tray for Brogan and a cup of coffee for himself.

"Compliments of the Bureau of Narcotics and Dangerous Drugs," he grinned. "Probably the only thing for free you'll ever get out of them. This cafeteria is for security-level staff only, so you can talk pretty freely," he added.

Brogan nodded. "What the devil was all that down there about appropriations and so on? I thought you two were going to clobber each other."

Conrad frowned. "That doddering old fool. He guards those damned photographs like they were his harem. I don't know why they keep him around. He's more trouble than anyone else in the building. I merely hinted that you were INCC's appropriations boy. He's scared stiff that his little empire is going to fall one day."

Brogan nodded. "So you dragged me into the middle of an internecine fight."

"Yeah, I guess I did," Conrad grinned. "But I knew that if he thought you had some say in his precious appropriation, he would go to any length to get the data you need." Conrad paused and glanced around the room. "Damned fool," he snorted. "No matter what happens, we are not about to let the Space Watch project fold. It'll be continued, with or without INCC and the U.N."

Brogan shook his head. "Politics!" He grinned at Conrad. "All right. I've got the location of the source, but that's all. Where do we go from here?"

"Well, old buddy, I'll see that Browning runs a concentrated study on that area for roads, frequency of vehicular traffic, and make a thorough search of the grounds and the surrounding area. Beyond that, I'd say it's pretty much up to you."

Brogan nodded and bit into his sandwich. "My God," he exclaimed through a mouthful of bread and meat, "this is terrible."

Conrad laughed. "You don't see me eating any, do you?"

"Thanks," Brogan said, pushing the tray back. He picked up the fork and tentatively tried the pie. "What kind is it?" he asked suspiciously.

Conrad shrugged. "The sign said apple."

Brogan ate silently for several minutes, his mind churning with the confirmation of the suspicions Charlie had expressed over the phone.

"Damn, Charlie. I just don't get it. There are only three real uses for acetic anhydride: oil refining, metals processing, and synthesizing morphine into heroin. Assuming the first two are out, since there is no evidence to suggest that kind of heavy industry in western Ireland, why in hell would anybody make heroin in Ireland, of all places? The logistics are all wrong. You would have to ship raw opium or morphine, none of which is produced in any quantity in Europe, from North Africa or Asia. The Middle East fields are almost nonexistent, and the Indochina sources are nearly all dried up." He shook his head in puzzlement.

Conrad grinned. "Sure as hell is a knotty problem. About the best I can do for you is keep after Browning to make sure he keeps the surveillance on hard."

"Good luck," Brogan muttered, and Conrad chuckled.

"CIA does still have some clout over here. Being liaison officer with BNDD isn't quite as bad as you might think."

While Brogan finished his coffee, Conrad watched the brunette waitress behind the cash register.

"How's Sandra?" he asked abruptly. "Why haven't you married that girl yet?"

Taken by surprise, Brogan had to shift mental gears. He hemmed and hawed a moment, feeling his neck and ears begin to flush.

"For one thing, I doubt if she would have me . . ."

"Crap," Conrad chortled. "She would . . . in a minute. It's

written all over her, and I'll tell you this, you couldn't do any better."

Brogan shook his head, at a loss for words.

"When she called yesterday afternoon with the information on your flight, we had a long talk, courtesy of INCC . . . and don't you make any fuss over the phone bill. I'm the one who kept her talking. She didn't say so in so many words, but she is in pretty deep with you, and I got the feeling that something had better happen on your part pretty soon."

"Well, I'll be damned . . ." Brogan muttered.

"In your case, it's already a foregone conclusion." Conrad sat back, staring in amusement at Brogan's expression, now compounded of equal parts surprise and worry. Brogan toyed with his coffee cup for a while, then suddenly he shook his head and looked up at Conrad.

"Have you got a phone I can use? I want to make some calls."

"To Sandra?" Conrad asked slyly.

Brogan shook his head. "No, you jerk, business." Conrad shrugged. "All right, dummy. But it's your funeral . . . eventually."

7

Darkness had settled across the estuary by the time the big jetliner turned onto its final approach to Shannon International Airport. The scattered lights of villages along the river had thinned as the channel narrowed, leaving only the industrial park glowing in darkness. Bumping slightly in the wet air, the aircraft shouldered its way through the light rain, lined up with the end of the runway and settled gracefully onto the concrete. The stewardess brought him a hot towel and he placed it, still steaming, on his face and sighed deeply, then rubbed his neck and hands and finished the last of his scotch. There was always something so final about ending a long flight, but tonight Brogan was too tired to think about it as he put away the map of Ireland that he had been studying and sat staring through the rain-streaked window at the sign over the terminal loading bay that read SAOR—AERFORT NA SIANNA in bright neon Gaelic letters.

He managed to catch the last shuttle flight to Dublin. The Fokker commuter was cramped and stuffy after the spacious interior of the Pan Am 747, but Brogan was too weary to care. The rain continued with them to Dublin, and the aircraft bumped along just below the heavy cloud cover most of the way. The empty Irish countryside gaped up at him; only a scattering of lights here and there to mar the darkness, as profound below as above. It was after midnight when, half asleep, he reached Dublin. With the combined time changes between London, Washington, and Dublin, it was now thirty-two hours since he had been to bed and his internal clock was hopelessly out of whack. He found a cab, one of the few remaining at the almost empty terminal, and rode to his hotel.

* * *

At eight o'clock that morning, Brogan was seated near the window of the Intercontinental Hotel's grill, drinking his third cup of coffee and watching the city come alive through the rain-streaked plate-glass windows. Five hours of sleep had barely made a dent in his exhaustion and it was with great difficulty that he had dragged himself out of bed for the early phone call to Sandra that had confirmed his appointment with the Assistant Commissioner for Customs, his official contact for narcotics problems in the Irish Republic. She had also some information for him concerning the mysterious Japanese tanker that served to confirm his suspicions. He only hoped they would be enough to convince the Irish authorities.

The rain had eased somewhat since he had awakened at seven, but the puddles on the sidewalk still showed gentle spatters. The waitress came by with the coffee pot and he allowed her to fill his cup again.

Sharply at eight-fifteen, the door of the grill opened and a raincoated man wearing a gray fedora with a raincover and sporting a thick salt-and-pepper mustache stepped into the grill. He paused to shake his umbrella outside, then carefully folded it away until it was no more than a tube, four inches or so long, which he stuck into his pocket. He said something to the hostess and she pointed to Brogan. The man hesitated, then came toward his table. The description matched and Brogan stood up.

"Mr. Cole Brogan . . . ?"

Brogan nodded and they shook hands. "Commissioner Brian Strain, I take it? Please sit down."

Strain did so and Brogan motioned for the waitress to bring menus.

"Sorry I had to get you out in this rain, Commissioner, but this meeting is rather necessary, if unofficial for now."

"I am sure." Strain nodded as if he really were not convinced. "May I see your identification?"

Brogan grinned. "Sure. If you let me see yours."

Strain smiled a trifle and they both withdrew their wallets and extracted identification cards. Brogan added his passport and handed both to Strain, taking his driver's license and I.D. card in return.

"You are Irish?" he asked.

"Third or fourth generation, at least."

"Did you perhaps attend Notre Dame University?"

Brogan chuckled. "I'm afraid not. I spent my four years at USC . . . University of Southern California," he added, noticing Strain's blank look. "You might call it a rival school—football . . ."

"I see." He nodded absently and studied Brogan's identification card and passport. Finally, he handed them both back with a nod to indicate that he was satisfied.

"I am sorry that I have to be so careful. But occasionally we encounter a newspaper reporter representing himself as other than he is. It has caused us a great deal of embarrassment in the past."

Strain noted the surprise on Brogan's face. "I assure you that it does happen. Not more than a year ago, a man made an appointment with me, passing himself off as an investigating member of Interpol's narcotics squad, an agency with which I assume you are familiar?"

Brogan nodded. "Yes, we often work quite closely with them."

"Well, in any event, this gentleman was shown into my office one day and asked numerous questions about the drug problem in Ireland. I and members of my staff answered him as fully as we could. After he had left, I remembered a piece of information which I thought might be useful to him and asked my secretary to send it on. A letter came back several days later stating that a search had been made of their organization and they could find no one employed there by that name. Two weeks later, the story appeared in one of the Dublin papers."

The waitress stopped beside their table, pad and pencil poised.

Strain glanced up at the girl, reached for the menu, then changed his mind. "A cup of coffee, orange juice, providing it's freshly squeezed, and some toast."

Brogan ordered porridge, two eggs and Canadian bacon, toast, a glass of milk and orange juice.

When she moved away, Strain sipped at his cooling coffee

and continued. "The Dublin newspapers, as you might know, see themselves as the guardians of Irish morals and honesty, particularly where the government is concerned. In your country during the last century I believe they called that 'yellow journalism.'"

"Well, not quite," Brogan grinned, "but I think I understand."

"We do have a drug problem of course, but it is limited to the other hard drugs, barbiturates and amphetamines . . . and it is not widespread. We do not generally make this information public, as we have learned by Great Britain's hard experience. They did not have a serious drug problem until 1967. By that I mean, it was nowhere near epidemic proportions. In that year, as you may recall, the Home Office asked the Metropolitan Police to conduct a drug-abuse program in schools throughout the country. Scotland Yard did, and within a year the use of drugs had doubled in both numbers and severity. In 1967, there were 1,729 known heroin addicts in Great Britain. By the end of 1968, the number had risen to 2,782. Of course the heroin problem is now back to pre-1965 levels, but other drug use, hashish and cocaine, is up drastically. I am not suggesting that the increase was due wholly to this program; however, we are certain that it contributed substantially."

Brogan watched narrowly over the rim of his coffee cup as Strain sat back with a satisfied air, certain that he had made his point. Wonderful, he thought to himself—a civil servant in fact as well as title. What the devil was there about governments that caused them to turn out these *Punch* caricatures in such great numbers? They were always right, no matter how wrong they were. Obsessed with secrecy, they were resentful of any outsider who might attempt to meddle in their affairs. He would do well to keep that in mind.

The waitress interrupted his internal assessment at that point by bringing the first breakfast dishes: toast and juice for Strain, and porridge and milk gently warmed in a china-blue pitcher for Brogan. During breakfast they continued to skirmish with one another, testing and probing the other's credentials in small talk relating to the politics of international drug control. By the time they were through, both were satisfied.

Strain studied him quite openly as they finished their coffee. "All right, Mr. Brogan," he said. "We can talk more comfortably in my office and not have to worry about being overheard."

Brogan nodded and motioned for the waitress. "Fine. The check is on me of course, since I had to drag you all the way down here."

Strain nodded without a word and Brogan handed the girl two one-pound notes and they left the grill. Outside, the rain still had pretensions, but in the west the sky was beginning to show a bit of blue. Strain hailed a cab and they rode in silence to the Customs House.

"All right, now, Mr. Brogan. Shall we get down to business? What exactly do you want from us?" It was not a question on his part, but a statement. Commissioner Strain was safely ensconced once more behind his massive desk in his own office and completely certain of his ground.

"I take it, from the tone of your voice, that you have doubts about my reasons for being here at all?" Two could play "ambiguity," the game of government subalterns. Brogan knew that he had to maintain, if not the upper hand, then at least an even-handed relationship with Strain, or he would find himself ramrodded right out of the country. Strain was obviously a game-player and would look for the forms, and he proceeded to prove Brogan right by sitting back in his chair and loading his pipe, taking a great deal of care in tamping the tobacco down into the bowl with his thumb. He struck a match and moved it gently back and forth across the tobacco until the flame at each puff was several inches long, exhaled a great cloud of aromatic blue smoke, and only then turned his attention back to Brogan. He found him staring out the window.

"Yes, you might say that I do question your reasons for being here," Strain said with a trace of annoyance at not finding Brogan squirming with impatience.

"I believe it was your secretary who phoned yesterday afternoon with your request . . . ?"

Brogan nodded.

"Well, she hinted at something mysterious and possibly far-reaching that you had apparently uncovered. Something to do with Ireland." He chuckled and waited for Brogan to deny it, to admit that perhaps she had overplayed the urgency to gain an appointment.

But he was doomed to disappointment. Instead, Brogan nodded solemnly and Strain removed the pipe from his mouth.

"Oh?"

"Sorry, but it is true."

"Perhaps you had better start . . ."

Brogan stood up and wandered toward the window.

"Uh, sorry," he apologized absent-mindedly. "I think better on my feet." He hunched his shoulders, then relaxed. "Okay, here it is from the beginning."

For the next few minutes, Brogan described the events of the past week involving his trips to Iran, Denmark and Washington, omitting only the exact manner in which he had extracted the information from the Danish fishing master and the part played by the Space Watch II system.

"And so," Brogan concluded, "we are certain that this location in western Ireland does not belong to any legitimate industry but in fact to a heroin-processing laboratory."

Strain sat quietly for several minutes, staring moodily past him at the rain. Finally, he cleared his throat and removed the pipe from his mouth, examined the bowl carefully and began to clean out the crumbs with a thin knife that he extracted from the tobacco humidor on his desk.

The office was quiet, he noticed, as he walked back to the chair and sat down. The heavy oak paneling shut out even the sound of the typewriters beyond the door. Strain's office was furnished in impeccable taste. What appeared to be Hepplewhite chairs stood at attention around a massive conference table. His desk was a delicate Regency style which contrasted handsomely with the table. The rug was a thick-piled, modern Kodel fiber in pale blue. Carefully placed lamps shared an air of warmth in spite of the gloom creeping in through the curtained windows.

"We should perhaps review the events that have led you to the conclusion that there is some type of heroin-processing laboratory on Irish soil," Strain said at last. He inserted the pipe into the holder and sat back, adjusting his jacket carefully. "First, there is the matter of this petal-less poppy which you claim to have seen . . ."

"I have seen them," Brogan interjected sharply. "Samples are on the way to London now and there is no doubt that they are fully mature poppies that grow without petals. The Iranian Agriculture Department's opinion is that they are mutations which have been carefully preserved."

Strain pursed his lips and nodded skeptically. "All right, then, assuming that the poppies are an established fact, they could definitely be a source of trouble to the entire international monitoring effort in coming years—providing, of course, that they can be grown successfully on a large scale. Be that as it may, I don't see how you can relate them to one shipment of heroin uncovered by Danish authorities. It would seem that all this merely tells you that the police are still sufficiently alert to stop such traffic." He studied Brogan intently for a moment.

"The question, of course, is, Where did the drug come from? What are your thoughts about that?"

Brogan shook his head. "I haven't the faintest idea, Commissioner."

"I see," Strain said finally.

Brogan hunched forward. "Look here, Commissioner, I am almost convinced that there is a heroin-processing laboratory in Ireland, as far-fetched as it sounds. Ireland is relatively uninhabited and underdeveloped; but in spite of that, the country certainly does not lack an educated population from which to organize and operate a heroin-processing syndicate. What's more, in a way Ireland is ideally located to supply both Europe and North America."

In his agitation, Brogan jumped out of the chair again and began pacing about the office.

"Let's just follow it through and see where it leads. First of all, concerted international pressure on the drug syndicates and the growing and distribution network have cut the flow of heroin to a trickle. The majority of the drug reaching the largest customer, the United States, is now coming from Southeast Asia through Hong Kong direct to the West Coast, or through the Panama Canal Zone and then into the country through southern ports, and has been for several years now. Even though the traffic has been reduced to less than twenty per cent of what it was in the early seventies, it is still sufficient to maintain the heroin problem as a problem in the States. Now with the price of heroin almost out of reach of the addict population, a new source, a dependable source, is worth not millions of dollars any more, but literally billions. That means the risks and investments have to be correspondingly higher.

"Let's suppose that someone has succeeded in culturing this new poppy strain . . . a strain that is undetectable by the drug syndicate's worst enemy, the Space Watch system. If we assume that the opium poppy is being grown in quantity somewhere in the world, somewhere close enough to transport it to Ireland economically, then, my God, we are right back where we started ten years ago. And if you couple modern agricultural techniques to its production you can double or triple yields. Now, assume that you are a syndicate boss. You get wind of a special opium poppy that can't be detected by the satellites . . . wouldn't you be interested? You're damned right you would be," Brogan answered his own question. "And you would spend whatever you had to, to find out if it was true. And then you would spend whatever you had to, to make sure that you had the corner on the new development. So you are going to be just as leery of your compatriots as you are of the U.N. or the police. You know damned well that as soon as heroin starts showing up in the streets in any quantity again, the drug bureaus and secret services of at least twenty nations are going to be after you. So you pick your location carefully, damned carefully. Since the poppies have no petals, you aren't worried about the Space Watch system, just the ground-based police and narcotics bureaus that go around poking their noses into anything that smacks of heroin. You find some out-of-the-way country, one whose officials can be persuaded to look the other way."

"Where?"

Brogan shrugged irritably. "I said I didn't know yet. Maybe somewhere along the Atlantic coast of Africa or South America. From there the raw opium or morphine could be shipped by sea to Ireland. It wouldn't even have to be landed. The West Coast is empty enough and wild enough to safely carry on a smuggling operation of this scale."

"But . . . Ireland?" Strain shook his head.

"There are a number of reasons why Ireland is an excellent choice for the processing laboratory," Brogan replied.

"And if I might ask, what are those?" The sarcasm in Strain's voice was hardly disguised.

Brogan crossed and uncrossed his legs, finding that he was too tired to be comfortable in any position. "Precedent, for one thing. When the heroin traffic was at its peak in the nineteen-fifties and sixties, the syndicate's raw-material sources, processing and distribution networks were spread over four to seven thousand miles. The poppies were grown inside a belt five hundred miles or so wide, stretching from Turkey to Turkestan. From there, raw opium gum was transported to the nearest seacoast, and smuggled aboard a ship, or sent overland through Bulgaria and Yugoslavia to processing plants along the Mediterranean coast of France, where it was reduced to morphine and synthesized to heroin. Those labs were all closed in the early seventies by French authorities. The Indochina route is similar, only longer and has to cross the Pacific to South or Central America.

"Today the old grounds in Asia Minor and Indochina are too well policed, both on the ground and from space, to grow poppies on that scale. The Iranians proved that again just last week, and I have an unconfirmed sighting in Thailand. And as I said, the old labs in France, Burma, Laos, and Hong Kong have been closed for years.

"Of course, these factors alone," Brogan continued, "would not be sufficient in themselves, as many other countries can offer conditions similar to Ireland. But Ireland is unique in that it further provides an ideal geographical location . . . one of those reasons that has attracted so many foreign industries in the past ten years. Europe and Great Britain are right next door, and North America merely a few houses down the block, so to speak. And like any businessman, the syndicate boss watches distribution costs."

"I see your point," Strain said slowly. "You are suggesting that Ireland's problem is not drug use, but drug manufacture." He sat quietly for a long moment, sucking on his pipe. "But you have no proof of your assertions?"

"No, not actual proof. But enough circumstantial evidence to convince me that at least one processing plant has been established."

"What evidence, may I ask?"

"The shipment of heroin found aboard the fishing boat by the Danish authorities, for one. You would have seen the details in the Interpol report. Well, there was one unexplained point—why the fishing boat took two extra days to cross the North Atlantic to Denmark. The reason, I found out, was because she came down the West Coast of Ireland to receive the heroin from a Japanese oil tanker just off Bantry Bay."

"That wasn't in the report," Strain said in surprise.

"That's true. You might say my methods did not involve the police."

Strain pushed back in his chair and stared at Brogan for several moments.

"Just how, may I ask, did you find out where the fishing trawler obtained the heroin?"

"I have sources of information that are not available to the police. I admit it was not easy, but I am convinced of the reliability of my source."

Strain made as if to say something further, then decided against it. He picked up his pipe, examined the bowl, then reached across the desk for the box of matches.

"Not only did the fishing boat pick up the heroin from that Japanese tanker," Brogan continued, "but she did so off Dursey Head. Yesterday we found out that the tanker had called in at Cork . . . when she had no need to. She was on her way to Iceland, and"—Brogan paused for effect—"as you may know, there isn't an oil terminal at Cork where she could have loaded or unloaded. She picked up a bonded cargo and left after less than three hours. The cargo must have contained the heroin."

Strain nodded and toyed with his letter opener for a moment.

"What other bits and pieces of evidence have you?" His voice carried all of the sarcasm that his words implied, and Brogan, perhaps on edge from lack of sleep, thought he detected a hint of relief as well.

"As I told you earlier, the source and nature of that data is classified by the U. S. Government. But I am sure that they will make all pertinent details available if it turns out that I'm right and the Irish Government decides to prosecute." Brogan went on in a cold voice. "The situation is serious enough, in my opinion, that a closer investigation, on the ground and in force, is warranted."

This last was pure bluff on Brogan's part, but there was little else he could do at this point. He had hoped to build a strong enough circumstantial case that Strain would be willing to mount an immediate investigation. Now he realized that by challenging him with suspicions that something was happening on his home ground that he did not know about, he had only succeeded in antagonizing the man. The hard information concerning the acetic anhydride source might be enough to convince him, he knew, but the obsessive predilection for security displayed by the U. S. Government precluded that approach at the moment.

"I wonder, then," Strain snorted. "I am certain that if a heroin-processing laboratory existed anywhere within the Republic that some rumor would have reached me by now. I do have my sources, you know, and we are not as backward in Ireland as it is fashionable to believe; in fact, we . . ."

"No doubt," Brogan interrupted wearily. "And in time I am sure you will hear. But do your people have available to them the same tools I have . . . a large computer network for data gathering and reduction, internal agents, plus the co-operation of just about every intelligence agency on earth in these matters."

Strain regarded him coldly without replying. "Assuming that

you are correct, just where might this processing laboratory be located?"

Brogan shrugged. "At this point, my telling you will probably be more of a hindrance than a help. The suspected location has been identified as a large vineyard south of Abbeyfeale."

"A vineyard?" Strain exclaimed. "A vineyard yet . . . in Ireland?" He sat back in his chair and laughed uproariously.

"Almost the same way I reacted," Brogan admitted. "But the manufacture of wine is a fairly complex process, as it turns out, and requires techniques that are often trade secrets in each winery. So tight security and secrecy would not be unexpected."

"I see," Strain said, grinning broadly. "But there is no native wine industry and never has been."

"That's true. I did some reading on the plane to confirm that. But there is a large farm that contains several very large vineyards. Not only that, but the existing collection of buildings suggest some type of processing plant . . . as you would expect from a farm with large vineyards engaged in wine making. The location of the farm, the Glannaruddery Mountains just east of Tralee Bay, is certainly remote enough to help maintain secrecy. My contacts in Washington have checked with a large French winery; no winegrower in his right mind would consider spending the half-million pounds and the four to five years that it takes to establish a vineyard in the cold, damp climate and boggy, peaty land of western Ireland."

"And that should lay to rest your own suspicions as well," Strain said disdainfully.

Brogan nodded. "Ordinarily, I would agree. Unless of course the operation is run entirely by or subsidized by an outside organization. The returns are more than adequate to justify the investment.

"Look here," Brogan said sharply, beginning to lose his patience. "Let's go over it all again. The cost of heroin on the illegal market is such that high expenditures can be risked. Ireland is one of the last places in the world where you would expect to find a heroin-processing plant, yet from a distribution standpoint the country is ideal. One shipment of heroin has already been intercepted, and we know it definitely originated off the Irish Coast and most probably from Cork. A vineyard has been identified in County Kerry, and vineyards for any reason are rare in Ireland. The area, when you examine it, is ideal. Highways T-36, -68, -29, and -28 surround the region, each leading to a sizable city, Limerick, Tralee, Killarney, Mallow or Cork, all with airports and all but two, Killarney and Mallow, with direct access to the sea. A convenient choice of shipping points, and Abbeyfeale, where the farm is located, is about as isolated a town as you can find in Ireland, but still large enough to supply immediate necessities. Damn it, the evidence *is* circumstantial, but it bears looking into and I can't do that without your permission and help."

He took out the crumpled cigarette pack and extracted the last cigarette. The sound of his lighter stirred the Commissioner and he looked up and across the desk at Brogan.

"I see," he said finally. "The case you have built is, as you say, circumstantial at best, but there is a certain logic."

"Then you'll start an investigation . . . ?"

Strain shook his head. "You are as familiar with legal processes as I am. Our laws are the same as yours. You simply have not given me enough information—evidence, rather—to ask for a search warrant with any expectation of success."

Brogan shook his head. "Damn it all, what about the source . . . ? That alone bears investigation."

"Not by my department. That would be a matter for the police and the Board of Trade to handle, and how can I ask them to investigate when I don't even know what you are talking about?"

"No police," Brogan held up a hand. "That's why I came to you. We get them involved and their heavy-handed approach will ruin it all. At the very least, you could put a watch on the place while we trace both ends of the pipeline . . . Couldn't you at least mount an undercover investigation? Surely, your regulations allow you that much latitude?"

Strain thought it over a moment. "All right," he agreed reluctantly. "That much I can do. I will have a very discreet investigation conducted around the district. I don't know what we can expect to find, but that much we can do."

Brogan repressed an angry retort. It was not exactly what he had hoped for, but it might be enough to get an investigation started. Perhaps if more information were uncovered, Strain could then be persuaded to ask for that search warrant.

The final few moments of their meeting were spent in general but rather strained pleasantries. A cab was called for Brogan, and the Commissioner walked to the door with him and shook hands.

"I will keep in touch with you and perhaps by the end of the week there will be something concrete to report."

Brogan nodded, mumbled his thanks and left. He found his way down to the main floor, shrugged into his coat and stepped out under the canopy to stand shivering against the stiff wind that had sprung up and was now blowing gusts of rain down the streets. The scattered patches of blue sky had completely disappeared beyond the lowering black cloud blowing in from the Irish Sea. A cab slid to a stop at the curb and Brogan dashed down and slipped inside.

"Hotel Intercontinental," he muttered and slumped back into the cushions, finding that, after the inconclusive morning, he felt as exhausted as the night before. Bleakly, he thought of everything that should be done, had to be done yet and wondered, not for the first or even the thousandth time, if any of it was worth the energy.

8

Sandra was to have met Brogan at the airport with the car, but by seven P.M. he had given up on her. Somewhat annoyed, he took a taxi into the city, wondering what had happened, and at the same time he found himself thinking about Conrad's lecture. He was not quite sure just how that was going to affect their relationship, and in fact was still not quite certain that he wanted it affected. In any event, he mused as the taxi wriggled through the city traffic in a light but persistent drizzle. He would have to wait until tomorrow to find out.

He paid for the cab and started to unlock the door, then changed his mind. He was hungry and, in spite of being tired, did not care to fix his own dinner. Accordingly, he wandered three blocks north to the Nun's Nose, his favorite pub, where he slouched at the bar, munching beef sandwiches and joking with the barmaid until nine-thirty. He took his time walking home, enjoying the drizzly spring night. It occurred to him as he unlocked the door that Sandra might have tried to phone him. "It would serve her right," he muttered to himself, "to worry a little." Next time she wouldn't leave him stranded at the airport . . . it was a three-and-a-half-pound cab ride in from Heathrow, after all.

Brogan turned on the lights and started to take off his coat, but the flat was chill and he changed his mind. He turned the thermostat up, then lit the fire in the bedroom and pulled back the covers to warm the bed. Sandra's blouse, the light-blue one he had given her on her last birthday, was bunched up next to the pillow.

Before he touched it, Brogan took a deep breath, then went out into the living room to make sure that the door was securely fastened. He checked the back door and made a quick survey of the windows. Only then did he re-enter the bedroom and pick up the torn blouse. There was a small streak of blood near the collar. A note was stuffed into the breast pocket and he unfolded it slowly.

Sandra Duncan is our guarantee of your co-operation. If you do not ring the number below by 10:00 p.m., you will find her body in the city morgue tomorrow. Below was printed a London phone number: 837-6457.

Brogan sat down on the bed and stared at the unsigned note. What the hell? he thought.

After a moment, he looked at his watch. It was twenty minutes to ten. He reached over and picked up the telephone, dialed and listened to the buzzing on the other end, half afraid that it would not be answered.

The receiver clicked as it was lifted from the cradle and immediately a man's voice asked:

"Mr. Brogan?"

His mouth and throat were suddenly dry.

"Yes . . ."

"Listen to me, then, Mr. Brogan. I believe by now that you have found your girl friend's blouse?"

Brogan remained silent, not trusting himself to speak.

"All right, have it your way. But I warn you, we are not playing. This girl has only one chance to live. You will leave your flat at exactly eleven o'clock P.M. and drive your own car to Russell Square. You will park it on the Square, at the corner of Bedford Way, and enter the park by the northeast entrance, directly opposite the Russell Hotel. Do you have all that?"

Brogan repeated the directions.

"Fine. Do it just that way. A man will be waiting for you near the center ring. He will be wearing a black raincoat. Introduce yourself and go with him."

"Why?" Brogan's voice was flat and harsh.

"We want very much to talk with you, it's as simple as that."

"I'd like to speak to Sandra first."

"Now, now, Mr. Brogan. Let's not be foolish."

"Who is *we*?"

"You will find that out when you get here. Leave your flat at eleven o'clock and be at the park at exactly eleven-twenty. Do not talk to anyone on the way or make any telephone calls. If you are not here on time, then at midnight the girl will die—most painfully, I can assure you."

"Listen, how the hell did you find out about Sandra or me . . ."

The line went dead and, thoughtfully, Brogan put the receiver onto the cradle and stretched out on the bed. For a long time he stared at the fire.

There was no doubt in his mind that they, whoever *they* were, they had Sandra, or she would have met him at the airport. If he hadn't been so preoccupied he would have realized earlier that something was wrong. He was also somehow certain that *they* were connected with his supposed narcotic syndicate in Ireland. Whether or not she was still alive was another question. He was ordered to come to Russell Square. Why there? Why had they not just waited for him at his flat; they had managed to get in to leave Sandra's blouse? Why set up a mysterious rendezvous in the park? Were they waiting to see if he would contact someone else? If so, one of their own people would be waiting to follow him . . . and, his phone was probably tapped to intercept any phone calls.

He sat up and lifted the receiver. Now there was no dial tone; they had gone one better and cut the phone lines. Now he knew for certain that the flat was being watched.

Thoughtfully, he stretched out again. Why did they want him to come to them—unless, and the thought suddenly became a dead certainty, Sandra was, or would be at the Square when he got there. They were going to stage a lover's quarrel and leave them both dead, a murder and a suicide in a public place.

Brogan swung his legs off the bed and sat up. Of course! That way anything he might have already reported about the Irish heroin operation could easily be discredited as a product of an unbalanced mind.

He thought furiously. They had told him to be there at eleven-twenty and it was now ten after ten. Moving deliberately now, Brogan went into the study and unlocked his desk, opened the center drawer and extracted his Colt .357 Magnum and shoulder holster from the small compartment he had built into the thick desk top. He slipped into the holster, settled it comfortably, then checked the revolver. It was loaded, the hammer resting on an empty cylinder. Satisfied, he slid it back into the holster and added a dozen more cartridges to his pocket.

He went into the bathroom and opened the cupboard. Sandra kept some clothes and toilet articles there and in the top cupboard. He found a blond wig she seldom wore. He took it out, studied it a moment, then with a pair of scissors he held the wig over the wastebasket and snipped away the curls, trimming it down into the semblance of a man's shaggy hair style. He tried it on twice before he was satisfied with the effect. The wig was badly butchered, but in the dark and under a hat it would pass.

He went back into the bedroom and changed his suit for a pair of old tan levis, a sweatshirt, nylon windbreaker and a battered Australian tennis hat. He pulled on a pair of hiking boots, laced them up and went out into the garage, where he took down his old pack frame and emptied the camping equipment out onto the floor. From the pile of newspapers his housekeeper kept beside the trash barrels, he wadded up several back editions of the *Times* and used them to pad out the bag. This done, he shrugged into the straps, readjusted them until they were loose enough so that, with a single motion, he could drop the pack off his left arm while reaching for the revolver with his right hand. Then he took the pack and shoved it into the back of his Datsun 240Z and returned to the flat.

During the next twenty minutes he dictated a report to Vandervoort covering the events of the past two days, ending with an account of Sandra's kidnaping and describing what he was about to do. He removed the cassette from the recorder, slipped it into a mailing carton, addressed it to the INCC offices and shoved it into his jacket pocket.

Then Brogan sat back in the chair and lit a cigarette. His hands were shaking so badly that he had to use three matches. He knew that his analysis of *their* plan represented a good deal of wishful thinking, and his strategy to beat them at their own game was, at best, more of what Vandervoort sneeringly referred to as his "cowboy" tactics. But he was also well aware that this represented Sandra's only chance. If he went to the police, Sandra would die quickly and her captors would disappear forever.

He finished the cigarette and got ready to go. Now came what was probably the most difficult part of his plan. He had to find the man watching his flat. In the darkened living room, he studied the street through the parted curtains. He doubted that he would be inside any of the buildings along Green Street, as they were all private flats or houses and he knew most of his neighbors. So it was a good bet that the lookout would have to be waiting somewhere outside.

Brogan let himself out the back door of the flat and clambered over the fence into the garden of the house directly behind. A padlock secured the gate leading out into North Row, forcing him to climb the wooden fence, gathering three sizable splinters in his hands as he did so. Just as his feet cleared the top of the fence, he heard a rush of air and the click of teeth. An instant later, a very large dog hurtled into the fence, barking loud enough to wake the dead. Brogan scuttled down the alleyway and across to the opposite side of the street, breathing hard and swearing under his breath. The dog continued to bark for a few moments, then gave it up as a lost cause.

Head low against the rain, Brogan hurried around into Red Place, keeping well to the side of the buildings both for protection from the rain and the cover provided by their shadow. The shaggy wig was soaked before he had gone fifty feet and, in spite of the hat brim, the water trickled down into the neck of his jacket.

The tiny church was visible as he came around the corner at the end of Green Street, and in front was a car, its parking lights glowing dimly in the rain. As Brogan drew nearer he could see that the wheels of the car, a Viva, were canted into the street as if prepared to drive away quickly. He glanced at his watch, 10:25; he was cutting it fine. He crossed the street and hesitated in front of the church, as if undecided which way to go from there. He glanced up and down the street and scratched his head, then hurried over to the car and rapped on the window. There was only one man inside, dimly visible in the meager street light. He glanced at Brogan and motioned him away angrily. Brogan rapped again.

"Hey, mate, can you . . ."

The man inside rolled the window down a few inches. "Get the hell away from . . ."

He stopped abruptly as he found himself staring up the barrel of Brogan's .357 Magnum.

"Open the door, mate," Brogan said emphatically. "Very carefully now." The man did so, never taking his eyes from the pistol.

Brogan stepped back and with his left hand held onto the door as it was pushed open.

"Get out."

Holding his hands well away from his body, the man started to edge out, glaring angrily at Brogan. When he was half out, Brogan grabbed his shoulder and held him in that awkward half-in, half-out position.

"Sorry, friend. I know I wasn't supposed to leave until eleven o'clock, but I got restless."

"What are you talk . . ."

"Shut up! Now, I want you to tell me exactly what is supposed to happen in Russell Square?"

His eyes widened slightly and Brogan knew he had the right man. "I don't know what you are . . ."

Brogan chopped the gun down hard on the man's hand where it rested on the top of the car door. He yelped in pain and struggled to get out but Brogan hit him again, harder.

"Stay there . . . now once more, what's going to happen in Russell Square?"

"I tell you, I don't know what you're talking . . ."

Brogan hit him hard on the side of the head twice and shoved him back inside the car. He knew he hadn't any more time to waste and this bird wasn't going to tell him a thing. He slipped the revolver back into the holster and wrestled the unconscious form across into the passenger seat, swearing like a trooper at the man's weight and bulk. He drove the car quickly down the street and stopped beside his flat. He checked to see that the man was still unconscious, then jumped out and unlocked his garage door and backed the Datsun out, leaving its engine idling. Then he drove the Viva inside and set the parking brake. Quickly, he located some wire and dragged the man out of the car, trussed his hands and feet securely and passed a short loop around and through the Viva's bumper to hold him.

Brogan paused and looked at his watch. Ten thirty-five. Time was running short, and quickly he found and ripped a strip of cloth from an old paint rag, fished the man's handkerchief out of his pocket, shoved it into his mouth and secured it in place with the cloth. Then he closed the door, satisfied that the man was safely out of the way for at least a few hours. Outside, he climbed into the Datsun and swung hurriedly into Park Street. He waited for the light at Oxford, then turned right. At this hour on a Tuesday night the traffic was light. He changed down at Oxford Circus, barely slackening speed; then, keeping to a fast forty, he was at Giles Circle in less than three minutes. Before turning, he double-parked long enough to drop the mailing carton in a post box. A few minutes later he shot across Gower, ignoring the sparse cross traffic, and rolled to a stop in the thick, unlit shadows of the British Museum. He shut off the engine and parking lights and rolled down the window.

The night was thick with the sound of the steady rain and the muted traffic noises of the city. Ahead he could just barely discern the west end of Russell Square, the high iron fence and the spreading oak trees delineating it from the block of flats and business offices. It was eleven-five. Brogan lit one last cigarette to try and relax the knot in his stomach. Incessantly his fingers insisted upon drumming on the steering wheel. When he forced them to stop, the toe of his right foot began to tap the floor. At last he couldn't stand the waiting any longer and threw away the half-smoked cigarette. He stepped out into the rain and closed the door quietly without locking it, then went around to the rear window, opened it and lifted out his back pack. He shrugged into the straps, zipped his jacket partly open so that he could reach the revolver, and went back down the block along the Museum and out onto Bloomsbury, where he walked quickly down and turned east onto Russell Street. He hurried along past the front of the Museum to the light and crossed to the other side of Southampton Row.

The digital clock in the Barclays window read 11:09. At the ABC store, he stepped into the doorway and studied the street, trying to make it seem as if he were merely sheltering from the rain. A police car cruised slowly past and the policeman inside eyed him carefully. There was no one else along the street in either direction, so Brogan pulled his collar tighter around his neck and continued on. At ten minutes after eleven, he crossed Southampton Row where it became Woburn Place and paused on the center island to let a cab go by, then sprinted across in rain that had become a downpour. It streamed down his face, seeped beneath his jacket and squelched inside his hiking boots as he paced steadily toward the entrance to the Square. The lamps, scattered among the trees, provided only the meagerest illumination, but just inside the open gateway, half hidden by bushes, Brogan spotted someone. Without a moment's hesitation, he hurried through the entrance to the Square. As he did so, the man stepped out of the bushes in front of him.

"Wait a minute . . ."

Brogan stopped. "What's the matter?"

The man stepped closer, peering into his face. "What do you want in here?"

"What the hell do you think I want? I want to get out of the rain." Brogan stepped back a bit. "Who the hell are you?" he asked suspiciously, "police?"

"Never mind. Just turn around and go find someplace else to sleep. That way you won't get hurt. You don't want to ask . . ."

He stopped abruptly as Brogan showed him his revolver. "Not a sound, not a word." He motioned the man back into the shadows. "Turn around!"

The man did so reluctantly, and holding his breath, Brogan hit him behind the ear. He shoved the unconscious form back into the bushes, wishing there was time enough to tie him securely, and shoved the man's pistol into his own pocket.

So far so good, he thought. The sodden wig and the pack had fooled one of them. He glanced at his watch, turning his wrist to catch the lamplight. It was 11:15, still a few minutes before the deadline.

Huge oak and elm trees filled the parklike interior, casting shadows deep enough to hide an army. Scattered about were street lamps standing above deserted park benches, but their combined light in the heavy rain was insufficient to show more than gross details. He tried to remember exactly how the park was laid out. It had been nearly two years since he had last stayed at the Russell Hotel across the street but, as he recalled, a walk circled the perimeter, sending branches off to the four exits, located at each corner. The entire park was surrounded by a high iron fence covered with ivy. Near the front, the walk widened into a cobbled court containing three fountains—all shut off for the night. Separated from the fountain stones by twenty or so feet was a low building containing restrooms and a concession stand.

Brogan studied the area around the concession stand as being the most likely location for an ambush. There was an old-fashioned lamp on a curved rod mounted on one end of the stand, and as he watched, a figure stopped directly beneath, reached up and unscrewed the bulb. The area was plunged into total darkness and Brogan took a deep breath. He could feel his pulse increase as the nervous warmth of adrenaline rushed through his body.

At twenty after eleven, two men walked through the Woburn entrance. They hesitated, glanced around, then continued down the path to the fountain stones, where they stopped, their backs to Brogan. One man waved toward the street.

A third man, clutching a girl, hurried into the Square to join them. The three talked for a moment, then one of them returned to the Woburn entrance, leaving the other two holding the girl between them. Brogan began to breathe again. At least Sandra was still alive. The two men at the fountain stone looked around nervously and Brogan considered his position. The one hidden in the shadows of the concession stand was going to be the major obstacle now.

Brogan watched carefully, nerves on edge, as he tried to decide what to do next. As he hesitated, a fifth man stepped from the shadows near the Montague exit, the one Brogan had chosen for their escape due to its proximity to the car. He swore viciously under his breath. He had been boxed neatly. God, what an organization they must have if they could mobilize six gunmen, counting the one he had disposed of near his flat.

There was no time now to even plan. Depending on the rain to cover any noise, he pushed through the bushes toward the concession stand, staying as near to the fence as he could. The dense alder and yew finally forced him onto the brickwork that ran around the base of the fence until he was directly in back of the concession stand.

He stepped down into an ankle-deep puddle and swore under his breath. The rain was still pelting down, its noise providing a blessed cover. The man was hunched under the overhang of the roof, leaning against the building. Beyond him, Brogan could see outlined in the light from the overhead lamps, the two men and Sandra. Sandra raised her head at that moment and appeared to say something.

Brogan jumped forward, revolver raised. Warned perhaps by the sound of a footstep, the man started to turn but the revolver butt hit him squarely on top of the head. Brogan grabbed for him but missed and the man collapsed into the mud, his pistol clattering onto the sidewalk. Desperately, Brogan broke out of the bushes and dropped to one knee, bringing his revolver up in both hands. The distance was less than twenty feet and, not daring to consider the consequences if he missed, he shot the man on Sandra's right. Sandra broke away at his scream and Brogan fired twice more at the man on her left as he dove for the ground.

"Sandra!" Brogan roared.

She stopped for an instant, then veered toward his voice and he was up and running. He swept Sandra around and pushed her toward the bushes as the guard at the Woburn exit came running into the park. A shot snarled past Brogan's ear from behind as he hurled himself into the cover of the bushes.

Sandra was sobbing from the exertion, but Brogan did not dare stop. He dragged her behind the concession stand and along the fence back the way he had come. The spiky branches of the yew hedge scratched at them as they stumbled along the top of the brick base. Through the iron palings, Brogan could see the front of the Russell Hotel, where someone had stopped under the main awning to watch the rain. A taxi went by and a pedestrian could be seen coming up the street from Southampton Row. But the damned fence was fifteen feet high and offered no handholds!

"Here!" he warned Sandra and led her through the bushes, stumbling over the man he had knocked unconscious less than five minutes before. He grabbed Sandra's hand tightly and pushed through the screen of bushes. As they came out to the entrance to the park, he heard a shout.

"Run," he panted and dragged her across the walk and into the street.

Brogan plunged across Woburn Place on a dead run, dodging a cab which swerved and honked in angry protest. Another shot was fired which ricocheted off the front of the hotel. The two of them raced across the sidewalk and up the steps to the hotel entrance. Brogan caught a glimpse of a man running across the street, and he pushed Sandra through the revolving doors, knocking the head porter off his feet as he rushed to see what was happening. He pulled Sandra after him along the hallway to the left, ignoring the startled faces behind the registration counter. As a violent argument erupted behind him involving the battered porter and two of their pursuers, he ducked to the right into the bar and through the doors leading back out onto Woburn Place.

"Stay with me," he panted and hurried around the corner into Colonnade. At the end of the block, next to a deserted newsstand, he spotted a gleaming Underground sign, a circle bisected with a line indicating a tube stop. They raced down the short street and whirled through the revolving doors into the Underground and crowded into the elevator as a sleepy Pakistani operator looked up, startled out of his light doze.

"Move it!" Brogan roared.

"Here naow, mon, you . . ."

Brogan thrust a pound note into his hand and yanked the gates shut.

"Goddamn it, get this thing moving!"

Wide-eyed, the operator did as he was told and the lift began to move. As the floor rose slowly above them, Brogan saw the revolving doors spin angrily, then the view was cut off by the ironwork of the elevator shaft.

He jittered back and forth during the seemingly endless ride down while the operator stared from him to the note in his hand and back again. Sandra had slumped against the wall of the car, breathing deeply, her eyes glassy. Brogan squeezed her hand and she stared blankly at him.

The lift stopped with a jerk and the operator jumped to open the doors. As he did so, Brogan wrenched the control lever outward, bending the marker against the dial so that it was jammed into place. He pushed the protesting and now angry operator to one side, grabbed Sandra's hand again and dragged her after him down the tiled hallway lined with advertising placards for movies, lingerie, and soaps. The hall suddenly opened out onto a platform and Brogan stumbled to a halt. The schedule board above the northbound track read 11:40, ten minutes away. The damaged control lever would not hold that long; he swung around and stared down the other track at the southbound schedule board which read 11:30, only three minutes.

"Are you all right, Sandra?" he demanded.

Still winded, the girl looked at him and nodded, then shook her head, plainly confused, but color was returning to her face and her eyes were no longer glassy.

"I'm okay . . . just out of breath . . ."

"All right, look; they're right after us . . . no time to go around to the other platform. We've got to go across the tracks and we only have a couple of minutes. Okay . . ."

Sandra started to protest, but he yanked her to her feet and to the edge of the platform. He jumped down onto the oily gravel between the tracks and reached up for her. There were only four feet between them and the high-voltage third rail. Brogan trotted down the track a short distance to a concrete service step.

"Go on now, step well over and climb up onto the platform," he commanded.

A roar of air down the tunnel announced the approaching train as Sandra stepped high and placed her foot on the outside rail, then leaned forward until her knee was on the platform. Brogan leaned dangerously over the electrified rail, placed his hands under her backside and pushed, sending her sprawling onto the floor of the platform.

He risked a quick glance over his shoulder to see the headlight of the train showing at the curve of the tunnel. A man and a woman who had just come down the steps stopped, transfixed by the sight as Brogan vaulted up onto the cement step and leaped for the platform. He teetered on the edge for a moment, then fell forward as the train slid by.

He picked himself up, helped Sandra to her feet and into the first compartment. The couple followed, the woman expostulating angrily at them. Brogan sank down in a seat next to Sandra, took a deep breath, then jumped up to kneel on the opposite seat to watch the platform. Two men with drawn pistols raced down the service stairs and onto the platform as the car doors whooshed shut and the train moved away. Brogan waved as the car slid into the tunnel and one of them started to raise his pistol, then thought better of it. Both turned and ran again for the stairs.

Brogan took an even deeper breath this time and sank down in the seat next to Sandra. The woman was still going on, her voice shrilling at them. Brogan ignored her and gathered an armful of rain-soaked, sobbing girl into his arms and kissed her gently.

"Well, I never," the woman all but screamed and lapsed into sputterings. Her husband shook his head, nudged her, and they got up and left the car.

Sandra was half sobbing as she kissed him, long and hungrily. Finally she laid her head against his chest and cried quietly while Brogan stroked her hair, matted into curls and tangles by the rain. As disturbing as he found her nearness and the wet scent of her hair, he forced himself to study the chart of the Piccadilly line over the opposite windows. The next stop was Holborn, and he knew that the men following would never be able to get there fast enough to board the train. From there on, the train could outdistance their cars on city streets at a three-to-one ratio, unless they cut directly across the city to Knightsbridge or beyond. He concluded that Leicester Square was as far as they dared go, at least on this line.

Sandra stopped sobbing after a few minutes and pushed away from him and rubbed at her face with her hands. Brogan reached into his parka and extracted a damp but serviceable handkerchief.

She dried her face, blew her nose and pushed back her hair, moving to catch her reflection in the window opposite. As she did so, she gasped and rummaged in her coat pocket for a comb.

Brogan smiled at this feminine gesture, knowing that she was all right now. He pulled the revolver from his pocket to reload it. Sandra glanced at the weapon apprehensively. "Just a precaution, Sandi," he grinned. But the grin disappeared as the first of the Holborn signs slipped past the window. In spite of his conviction that the train was traveling fast enough to outdistance any pursuit, he could feel his heart beginning to pound. As the train left the tunnel, Brogan pushed Sandra down in the seat. The train came to a stop near the end of the platform, and as the doors slid open, Brogan ducked around and, crouching beside the doorway, glanced up and down the platform.

Except for an elderly couple getting into one of the rear cars, the platform was deserted. The doors slid shut and the train picked up speed. Brogan staggered back to his seat as they swayed into the tunnel.

He plopped down beside Sandra, stretched his legs and groaned. "My God, am I tired!"

Sandra leaned over and kissed him. "Thanks," she murmured. "It goes against my liberated grain, but thank you anyway."

Brogan grinned, but wisely kept his mouth shut. For a little while they sat quietly in the empty car, satisfied with each other's nearness. The train stopped at Covent Garden, then at

Leicester Square, and Brogan got to his feet and they hurried out as the doors slid shut behind them.

"Are they . . . ?" Sandra began, but yanked along behind Brogan, she was soon out of breath again.

He hurried down the platform, found the exit and stopped near the foot of the escalator before he answered.

"No, at least not yet. But if we stay on the Piccadilly line their chances of catching us increase with every station from now on. And we only have until midnight . . . when they close this place down. So stick close behind me because we are going to move fast. Okay?"

Sandra nodded and Brogan started up the escalator, trotting up the moving steps past other, less hurried travelers. At the top he ran into an unexpected problem; a beefy woman dressed in a uniform demanded their tickets. Brogan explained that they were in such a hurry that they had forgotten to buy them, at which the woman raised her eyebrows.

"It's true," Brogan protested. "Look here, I'll pay for a full two tickets." He extracted two fifty-pence coins from his pocket and offered them to her. The woman stared at Sandra leaning wearily against the railing behind Brogan and clutching her coat tightly around her. She smiled at the ticket taker and moved forward to lean her head on Brogan's shoulder. The woman relented.

"All right. 'Tis a bit irregular, but just so's you don't do it again." She made change for Brogan and they pushed through the turnstile and hurried along the hall to the large map of the London Underground near the Charing Cross entrance.

Brogan studied it a moment, his hands thrust into his pockets. "You know, we could ride this thing all night, and the chances that they would find us are pretty damned remote. Still, we've got to get off sometime."

"Why not here?"

Brogan shook his head. "No. This is the most obvious place and the one they would cover first. I think we'll take the Northern Line to Warren Street, then back down on the Victoria to Victoria Station. We can get a cab there."

Sandra nodded wearily and Brogan steered her to the Northern Line ticket window.

For the next twenty minutes, they rode from one station to the next, dodging back and forth between lines in all-but-deserted stations. Brogan knew that the chances of being at the same station as any of the gunmen, who were certainly looking for them, were becoming more and more remote with every stop. Yet each time they hurried through the echoing halls of a station, he clutched the revolver tightly in his hand, anxiously watching for the odd man in a business suit hurrying down the stairs between the escalators to draw a gun.

As the train left the Goodge Street Station and slid into the tunnel, Brogan pulled Sandra closer to him and leaned back in the seat, staring blankly at the darkened glass across the aisle.

"How did it happen?"

"Mmmm . . . ?"

"How did they get to you?"

"Who . . . ?"

"Whoever they are . . . the men who kidnaped you?"

"Oh . . ." Sandra pushed herself upright and brushed a strand of hair away from her eyes. "They were waiting as I left the office. One man walked up behind me and said that he had a gun. He made me walk down to the corner where a car was waiting. We drove to your flat. They made me let them in and take off my blouse. Then they gave me an injection and that's all I remember until I woke up in a car just as we were stopping outside a park. . . ."

"Russell Square."

Sandra glanced at him. "I didn't know . . ."

Brogan shook his head. "How the hell did they find out . . . and who the hell are *they?*" he added.

Sandra laid her head back against his shoulder. "Oh Cole, I was so frightened. I didn't know what was happening."

Brogan shook his head and slipped an arm around her shoulders. "I don't understand it . . . did you recognize any of them?"

"No, I don't think I've ever seen any of them before. Cole, who were they, what did they want?"

Brogan was silent for a moment, almost preoccupied with

the noise of the train as possible explanations swirled in his mind, none of them making any sense at all.

"I just don't know," he said finally. "They were after me. For exactly what, I really don't know at this point."

The train slowed for Warren Station and as the platform came into view, Brogan searched it carefully. They left the train and he glanced at his watch.

"We've got about ten minutes before they close the Underground. Let's see if we can make the last train to Victoria."

Hand in hand they ran through the echoing halls to the Victoria line platform, catching the last train by inches.

They found seats near the end of the car and Brogan sank down, letting the weariness loose for the first time. His legs ached abominably and so did his head. Who . . . what . . . when kept echoing and re-echoing through his thoughts. The BNDD in Washington and the Customs Service in Ireland—Conrad, Vandervoort, Sandra and Strain—no one else knew what he was up to. Yet *they* had managed to find out, find out his home address, the fact that he was out of town and would return by ten o'clock and about Sandra. Somewhere along the line there was a leak. One hell of a leak.

As they drew into the Victoria Station, Sandra reached up and removed his hat and the sodden wig. "My wig," she wailed, holding up the bedraggled hairpiece. "It looks like a drowned rat." Brogan grinned sheepishly.

"I guess I didn't need it, after all."

It was close to midnight, but still Victoria was a scene of hurrying people and shouting, arguing porters. Sandra and Brogan walked carefully toward the entrance, watching the crowds of people moving around them. It was raining as they came out under the canopy, but not nearly so hard as an hour before.

A cab pulled forward and Brogan waved it away and they walked down the street.

"Why did you do that?"

Brogan shook his head. "Just being careful. There's another cab stand around the corner."

They took the last one in line, over the driver's protest, but Brogan told him to shut up and start driving. He did so, reluctantly, waving an apology at the angry drivers ahead and the doorman who had come running out from under the awning, whistle bleating into the rain at this breach of etiquette.

"Where to, Chief . . . ?"

Brogan thought for a moment. "Try Harrods."

The driver half turned and growled. "Look, Chief, you got me in enough trouble already. Harrods is closed."

"Too bad. Go anyway."

The driver subsided, muttering to himself.

Brogan flopped back into the seat and delivered a long, heartfelt sigh. After the fumes of the Underground stations, the cold, wet air of the London night had never tasted sweeter.

"We've got to find someplace to go . . . and we can't go to your place or mine." He thought for a moment. "Do you have any friends in London where we could stay for the night? The Datsun is just a little too small for sleeping."

Sandra opened her eyes and roused only long enough to shake her head. "I've some friends, but not one-o'clock-in-the-morning-can-we-stay-here friends . . ."

Brogan nodded and sat back to think. The driver turned onto Kensington Road from Exhibition and a few moments later slowed across the street from Harrods.

"Okay, Chief. There it is."

"Is the meter running?"

"Of course it is. What do you think I do out here all night?"

"All right, go on up Knightsbridge to Park Lane, then cut over to Park Street. Go slow as you make the turn back onto Park Lane."

The driver muttered some more but did as he was told, turning into Park Street ten minutes later, and cruised slowly down the street as he had been instructed; but it was too dark and too far away to tell if his flat was entertaining visitors.

The light changed and the cab moved forward. "Okay now, friend?" the driver called back. "Where do we go from here?"

"Scotland Yard."

The driver turned around to stare at him, shrugged, and the cab moved forward. Fifteen minutes later, they stopped in front of the modern steel-and-glass building housing Scotland Yard.

The cab driver leaned over the seat and peered at them through the window. "Look, my friend, if this has been just for the fun of it, I'll be inside there yelling for a copper before you can . . ."

He shut up abruptly as Brogan handed him his last five-pound note. The meter read £3.80, but Brogan waved away the change and opened the door. He practically had to lift Sandra out of the cab and carry her into the building. He showed their passes to the skeptical guard and punched the elevator button.

"Where are we?" Sandra asked sleepily.

"The office. They won't be able to get at us here, even if they think to check. You can use the couch in my office."

"That's nice," she murmured and snuggled closer to him.

9

During that winter and spring Brogan had watched the heroin traffic plunge to its lowest ebb since the years immediately preceding World War II. The combined efforts of twenty nations, spearheaded by the United States and utilizing the Space Watch satellite system, had succeeded in reducing the world production of illegal opium from a high of three thousand metric tons in 1974 to something less than one hundred metric tons, of which it was estimated that less than thirty tons had been successfully diverted to heroin production. In North America heroin had become both a rare and expensive commodity for the first time since the turn of the century. Yet rumors of a breakthrough in the drug syndicate had been rife for months among the international underworld organizations specializing in narcotics, and in spite of signs of an impending crisis, most law-enforcement executive levels continued to bask in the warm glow of publicity following the United Nations pronouncement that the worldwide narcotics epidemic was at last coming to an end.

That particular summer would turn out to be one of the gentlest periods in recent memory. The Middle East's permanent crisis had at last been resolved. Eastern Africa was quiescent, and South America seemed to have come to terms with itself. An era of international co-operation was being trumpeted from every capital, editor's office, and pulpit. A new interest was extant among the generation coming to maturity; a new interest that was a modification of the ideals, hopes and tactics of the young of the sixties and early seventies. Drug use was in disrepute and abuse was plummeting. Unfortunately, very few people were in a position to, or would trouble to, appreciate the significance of the shadow cast by a new poppy that flourished without a display of brilliantly colored petals, and whose seed pod contained the foundation on which the international underworlds might rebuild their shattered structures.

Brogan was well aware of all this as he trudged into Russell Square next morning. That much had been more than evident from Vandervoort's reaction. So far, only Conrad and his irritating colleague Browning, fearful that funding for his satellite surveillance system might evaporate, had taken him seriously. Vandervoort had laughed and Strain had humored him; yet less than twelve hours later, there had been an attempt to kill him. Unfortunately, it had been too neat an operation. All he had to show for the night's activities was the kidnap note, which he had remembered to tuck into the package along with the tape.

The tape recording had arrived at INCC headquarters with the morning post, and Vandervoort had gone over it word by word before surreptitiously sending it down to the Yard's lab. Brogan did not need to be told that he was extremely skeptical.

Two detectives had gone directly to his flat from Scotland Yard as soon as he and Sandra had reached the office, but the bound and gagged driver had disappeared. The padlock on the garage door had been unlocked rather than broken, which told much about their resources. Brogan paused beneath an ancient beech and lit a cigarette, wincing at the acrid taste in his mouth. Uniformed policemen stood at each entrance, and several detectives were wandering about the area between the fountain stones and the concession stand. In spite of the flimsy evidence comprising only the note and his recording, the Yard was going about the investigation with its usual efficiency.

A small trace of blood spotted by a sharp-eyed policeman on a bush lining the walk into the park was the only other piece of evidence to back up his story so far—that and the hotel staff's account of a mad chase through the sedate lobby of the Russell in the middle of the night. But the Underground lift operator, when questioned, refused to provide any information. Apparently, he was scared witless. He had gone so far as to blame himself for bending the operating lever. Privately,

Brogan suspected that the bruise high up on his cheek had helped to convince him to keep his mouth shut. In any event, it probably would have done little good to question him extensively. There was little the terrified Pakistani could have told the police beyond the fact that a man and a woman had been chased down into the Underground.

Inspector Robert Layton, one of the few men on the Yard's force whom Brogan knew and respected, turned away from his examination of the concession stand as Brogan sauntered up.

"Found anything yet?"

Layton shook his head. "Not much, beyond this . . . up here." He stretched and tapped a splintered gash where a hole had been smashed into the wood. Brogan examined the bullet hole, then stepped back and turned around until he was facing the fountain stones.

"It probably came from one of the two men holding onto Sandra. I was kneeling just about there." He pointed to a spot in front of a chrysanthemum bush. "I shot the man on her left. The other ducked, and when Sandra ran toward me he fired at least once. I think he was on the ground, which might account for the high angle."

Layton nodded. "It's possible," he murmured.

"All right, damn it," Brogan growled. "I'm an inspector for the International Narcotics Control Commission, not some witless bystander."

Layton looked up sharply, then nodded. "I realize that, Cole. But the evidence is certainly limited, you must admit. All any of the hotel staff can recall is that you and Miss Duncan came running through their lobby, you waving a gun. Two men followed, that's true, but no one can describe them satisfactorily."

"Well, what about hospitals?" Brogan demanded. "Surely they would have taken the man I shot to a hospital?"

"We are checking every hospital in London . . . in southern England, in fact, which they could have reached by now. So far none have reported admitting a gunshot wound during the night. We are also checking all physicians in the area. But there are over three thousand in London alone." He shrugged. "I, personally, am willing to take your word for what happened. But there just is not enough evidence to support your story. I have no reason to doubt what you say . . ." he started to repeat, but Brogan cut in impatiently.

"But no reason especially to believe me either. All right, Bob," Brogan sighed. "There doesn't seem to be any more that I can do here, so I'll get out of your hair."

The inspector nodded and motioned two uniformed policemen over. "This is Sergeant Winslow and Constable Sykes. I have assigned them to you and Miss Duncan for now . . ."

Brogan nodded absently. "Thanks for that anyway. I'm going to get Sandra out of the city for a while until this thing is settled one way or the other."

Layton raised a hand. "Just a moment, Cole. There are certain charges pending. I must ask you not to leave the city . . ."

Brogan whirled on him, temper exploding.

"Look here, you two-bit civil servant. If I leave Sandra in this city, even with the two lunkheads you assign to protect her, they'll get her in a matter of hours. And this time they won't play around. You have no legal hold on me until you arrest me. And if you do, I'm going to put up bail and do as I damned well please anyway. So stay out of my way, Inspector, just stay the hell out of my way." And with that, he spun and stalked away.

The two uniformed policemen hesitated and looked to Layton for instructions. He contemplated Brogan's retreating back for a moment, then motioned them after him.

"Stay with him, you two, until he sends you packing." Then shaking his head, he walked over to a sergeant who was waiting for him with the crowd of newspaper reporters.

Brogan drove first to his flat, where he found the last of the police laboratory crew packing up their equipment. He took a quick shower, shaved and dressed while the two policemen waited outside. The sky was beginning to clear as they left once more and drove onto Fulham Road. Sandra shared a flat with two girl friends on Mulberry Walk in Chelsea, and he had offered to pick up some fresh clothing for her on his way back. He stopped the car in front of a three-story walk-up, part of the block of flats lining either side of the narrow street, and got out, followed by the policemen, both glad to escape from the confines of the cramped Datsun.

Sandra's flat was at the end of the second-floor hall, and her roommate was a nurse who worked at St. Stephen's Hospital. He recalled Sandra telling him that she was on nights this month, and so as not to disturb her, he used the key that Sandra had given him. The door was unlocked. Glancing at Winslow, he pushed it open. The nearly nude body of a young woman lay huddled in the middle of the floor. Brogan motioned to the door closing off the bedrooms and kitchenette and handed his revolver to Winslow. As they pushed past, he knelt down and turned the girl over gently and felt for the pulse at the base of her throat, then lifted her onto the couch and rearranged the torn nightgown.

The two policemen came back into the room.

"Alive?" Winslow asked and handed back the heavy revolver. "Here, take this one," Brogan said and gave him the pistol he had taken from the man in the park. "I forgot to hand it in last night. She's okay. Someone hit her pretty hard behind the ear . . ."

As he spoke, she murmured incoherently, choked and shot bolt upright. Brogan grasped her shoulders and eased the terrified girl back down on the couch.

"Take it easy, Linda, it's Cole. You're all right now."

For a moment she struggled against the pressure of his arms, then, recognizing Brogan, she sank down and burst into tears. Brogan pointed to the kitchen.

"The cabinet just inside the door, top shelf. There's some liquor. Bring her a small glass of brandy."

Winslow nodded and a moment later was back with a glass. Brogan helped her to sit up and coaxed the drink into her. A few moments later she blew her nose on his handkerchief, took a shuddering breath and wiped her eyes.

"All right now, Linda," Brogan said quietly. "I want you to tell us exactly what happened."

The other policeman, Sykes, hung up the phone and came across the room. "I've called the Yard and they are sending two men around immediately."

Linda glanced at him, still too dazed to comprehend. "Oh, Cole, I . . ."

"Take it slow, Linda. Just tell us what happened." She took another deep breath and rubbed a hand across her eyes. "I had just gotten to sleep when someone knocked on the door. They said they were policemen and I let them in. But they weren't. One of them ripped my nightgown and threw me down on the couch. The other yanked my hair and told me that if I didn't tell them where Sandra was that they would rape me and then kill me."

"I think I became hysterical, because one of them hit me several times," she rushed on. "I told him that I thought Sandra was at work, that I hadn't seen her because I worked nights. They hit me again and threw me to the floor. I think I fainted because they . . . then you were here . . ."

She put her hands to her face and began to cry. Brogan held her tightly for a moment, then lifted her chin.

"Come on now. It's all over now. You're okay and some policemen are here to watch out for you. Now, I want you to tell me anything else you can."

Linda nodded and wiped her eyes with his handkerchief again. "I . . . I can't. That's all I remember . . . Sandra . . . Cole, where is Sandra?"

"Sandra's safe. She's at the office and no one can get at her there." He eased her back down on the couch and smiled. "Look, I'm going to get a doctor in. You just relax. Let him check you over and don't worry. There will be a policeman inside your apartment from now on until this whole thing is over."

"The police surgeon is coming along as well, sir," Sykes interjected.

Linda raised a tear-stained face and brushed back the hair that was clinging to her wet cheeks. "What thing, Cole? Has this something to do with you . . . ?"

Brogan nodded. "Yes, I'm afraid it does. Look, I can't tell you anything about what's happening now, but when it's all over, you'll hear the full story."

She nodded, then glanced up with a stricken look. "Cole! Denise! What about Denise?"

"Oh, my God! You stay here until someone comes," he yelled at Sykes and bolted through the door, followed by Winslow. They ran down the stairs, across the walk and piled into the Datsun. Brogan leaned on the horn and yanked the car into the street before the doors had fully closed. Ignoring the honking horns and angry drivers, he floored the accelerator and took the corner into King's Road on two wheels.

Sandra's third roommate, Denise Crown, worked in a small boutique on Knightsbridge, near the Scotch House. Close to panic, Brogan barreled through the heavy traffic on King's Road and slewed through a traffic signal. They passed a police car coming from the other direction and Brogan caught a glimpse in the rear-view mirror as it made a U-turn and accelerated after them, siren whooping.

With staccato blasts on his horn, he cut dangerously through the traffic and narrowly missed a pedestrian who insisted on his right-of-way. Brogan slammed the car to a halt in front of the boutique and both of them rushed onto the curb as the police car skidded to a halt behind.

Brogan burst through the door just as a tall, well-dressed man yanked Denise by the arm toward the back of the shop. He caught a glimpse of another man hurrying out the back door as he yelled and pulled his revolver. The tall man tried to swing the girl around in front of him as a shield, but Denise stumbled, went down on one knee and was pushed away. A third man materialized in front of Brogan, pistol drawn, and the boutique echoed to the crashing report of Winslow's pistol.

The two policemen entered the store at that moment and hesitated in astonishment. Brogan, down on one knee and revolver cradled across his wrist, yelled, "Stop!" as the tall man tugged desperately at his jacket. The weapon came free and he pivoted, bringing it down in line with the girl's head, but Brogan's heavy revolver and Winslow's pistol fired together, smashing him back into a glass counter that shattered under his impact into slivers of flying glass.

For a moment, the mingled echoes of gunfire filled the store, then a devastating silence followed that was as fragile as a crystal wineglass.

Brogan stood up slowly and walked to where Denise was huddling on the floor, while behind him the two policemen exploded into a volley of profanity and a customer fainted dead away.

* * *

INCC Director Jacques Druie, in an unprecedented appearance, had journeyed down from the eleventh floor to Vandervoort's office to occupy the large, leather-covered morris chair, from where he stared out the window at the thunderous sky. Vandervoort sat morosely behind his desk tapping a pencil, and Brogan sprawled on the couch, weary beyond belief, yet angrier than he had been in years.

"Now, Cole," the director began once more soothingly, "all this does not necessarily bear out your claim that the attacks on you and the three girls are involved with this mysterious heroin laboratory which you think you have located in Ireland . . ."

Brogan forced himself up into a sitting position and regarded Vandervoort, pointedly ignoring the director.

"Damn it, Van! Do we have to go through this all over again? You both have expressed the opinion that I'm a damned fool and you have my resignation. So stop trying to convince me that this is all a figment of my imagination."

Vandervoort grimaced and moved his bulk into a more comfortable position and started to reply, but Brogan swore again. "Damn it! Don't you give me any of that *now-see-here-Cole* nonsense. I'm finished with trying to get through to you two. I've given you just about everything but a sample of heroin. What more do you want?"

"Just that you agree to wait until we can have the proper Irish authorities check your theory, then . . ."

Brogan interrupted him by standing up abruptly. "It's no good, Van. For one thing, it's beyond the theory stage. For another, if you turn the police loose on this thing, the syndicate will be long gone from there before they can get within ten miles of the place. For God's sake, can't you two see that they know we are getting close? They tried to shut me up by grabbing Sandra. When that didn't work, they tried to get to me through her friends. Unless we move now, right now! they'll disappear in a couple of days." He spread his hands, as if appealing to both of them.

The director shook his head. "I'm sorry, Brogan," he said in a cold voice, "but there is just no hard evidence to back up your story, nothing at all to link last night's and today's events here to your farm in Ireland. Those men may have had something to do with this affair, as you claim, or they may not. Until we can conduct a proper investigation . . ."

The door slammed, cutting off his words. After a moment, the director got up and went over to the window to stare out onto the rain-spattered Thames. Finally, he sighed and turned his back to the window.

"You read what he did to that man in Copenhagen in the police report?"

Vandervoort nodded unhappily. "I did. But you have to admit that he learned what was needed."

The director was silent for a moment. "I still do not like it. I do not like what he did. That is the way the Nazis acted . . . and the way we reacted. You remember that as well as I do."

Vandervoort nodded, thinking of a certain day in 1944 when he had been a much younger man. "I remember . . . and I remember the reasons why we did what we did."

"Suppose we take him out of the field after . . ."

"He'll leave," Vandervoort said calmly.

The rain was streaking the windows in long runnels. A flare of lightning sharpened the buildings across the river for an instant.

"Headstrong young man, isn't he?"

Vandervoort clasped his hands over his huge stomach and swiveled the chair toward him.

"Yes, he is . . . that is what makes him so good." He paused for a moment, an intensely unhappy expression on his face. "I only hope that this is the right way to go about this . . ."

"Yes," the director said, some of the complacency gone from his voice. "Yes, I hope so, too."

10

At three P.M. the alarm went off. For several moments Brogan lay still, trying to shut out the grating buzz, then he dragged himself out of bed and stumbled across the room to shut it off. He was halfway back to the bed before he remembered why he had set the alarm. "Aw, hell," he muttered and staggered into the bathroom and turned on the shower. Ten minutes later, feeling somewhat like death warmed over, he finished dressing, shrugged into a heavy knit sweater and went out into the living room. Winslow glanced up as he came into the room.

"You look terrible."

"I feel worse. Is Sandra still asleep?"

Winslow nodded to the open door of the other bedroom. "Just looked in on her. Still asleep. Everything else is quiet. The outside man reports traffic normal and no one lurking in the bushes."

Brogan dragged a chair over to the fire and poured himself a cup of coffee from the pot on the sideboard. "Go ahead and laugh if you feel like it," he muttered.

Winslow shook his head. "Not after this morning, no, sir. Not after this morning, I'm not laughing."

Brogan stared into the cup and tried to sort through the rambling thoughts that insisted on fading in and out. Aldershot was a sixty-minute drive; no, better add half an hour for traffic. What about Winslow . . . would they let him come along?

"I'm taking Sandra to some friends in Aldershot tonight. Will they let you go that far?"

Winslow lowered the newspaper. "My orders are to stick to you no matter what happens. Just let me call the missus and tell her I won't be home tonight."

Brogan nodded. "Good. But don't tell her where you're going, in case they have the phone bugged again."

While Winslow went to phone his wife, Brogan got up and wandered through the flat, double-checking doors and windows. Then he stepped outside for a moment to look at the street. The policeman on duty turned and nodded to him, then went back to watching the traffic trickling by on Park Street. Across the way, Brogan noticed curious neighbors at the windows, wondering what the commotion was all about.

It had begun to drizzle again and the streets were wet and glistening. He shivered and stepped back inside.

"All set," Winslow said as he came back into the room. "I called the station house and told them I would be going with you. I'll call in later and say where."

"Fine. You'll be a great help if you come." He poked about the newspaper for a few minutes and glanced at his watch. He forced himself to sit back in the chair and light a cigarette, but it was more than he could do to finish it. He crushed out the cigarette and went into the spare bedroom and sat down on the bed.

Sandra was asleep, half turned on her side, one hand under the pillow beneath her cheek. The soft blankets outlined her slender figure, knees drawn up and her face partially obscured by her hair. Only the dark lashes lying along one soft cheek and her short, slightly tilted nose were visible.

He touched her cheek, then slipped back the blanket a bit and caressed her bare shoulder. She shivered comfortably, then slowly turned and pulled the cover back up. From under the mass of chestnut hair she opened one eye carefully and looked up at Brogan. Before he could say anything, she had flung her arms around his neck and was holding him closely. For a long moment he held her tightly, one hand absently running through her hair.

"Time to get up, beautiful," he said finally.

Sandra shook her head.

"Yep. We have to leave here as soon as it gets dark . . ."

She shook her head again. "I don't want to leave," she mumbled.

Brogan smiled. "I don't want to either, but it's not safe. I want to get you hidden well away from London before I leave."

Sandra let go of him and flopped back down on the pillow. She drew the blanket under her chin and stared at him with mock hostility.

"Go where . . . ?" she demanded.

"I quit the Commission this afternoon. Told them to fly a kite, or words to that effect."

"Cole, you didn't!"

"The hell I didn't." Brogan studiously examined a broken fingernail, not quite daring to meet her eyes. "Even after all that's happened, Vandervoort refuses to believe that there is anything to this petal-less poppy business. He thinks it's all a figment of my imagination."

"But the director? Have . . . ?"

Brogan shook his head. "Look, Sandra, I've tried every way I know to convince them. They just won't see it. The director was there all right, and he all but ordered me to drop the investigation, said it wasn't doing our relations with the Irish any good. I don't know whether he meant the government's relations or the Commission's, but in any event they were very clear as to what they wanted. And that was simply for me to drop this case."

He shook his head and said softly, "And there's not a chance in hell of that ever happening."

Sandra was silent for a while. Her expression puzzled him; it was completely unreadable. He couldn't tell whether she was angry, glad or indifferent.

He had done a lot of thinking about Sandra during the long hours that he had spent that morning at Scotland Yard. He had inventoried all of the usual attributes that a man wants, or thinks he wants, in a woman when he is interested in nothing more than a good time: looks, a nice figure, a sense of humor, a basic compatibility, mutual attraction . . . sexual and otherwise. Sandra had all of these and then some. But as he was well aware, as interest on both sides deepens, the surface attributes became less important and other factors came to the fore. And it was these that Brogan had reviewed in some detail.

How deeply was she interested in him? He had Charlie's

word that she was in love with him, and there was no reason for Charlie to lie. Were they compatible? She had been his secretary for two years now, a position in some ways more demanding than that of a wife, as it required the woman to acknowledge male supremacy, to subordinate herself completely in order to perform the menial jobs such as typing, fetching coffee, arranging travel schedules, running errands, and in general acting as a personal servant. But beyond that, they had gone together quite regularly over the past two years, and neither of them had dated anyone else seriously in that time. Were they compatible sexually? They had been intimate for almost as long, and he knew that they could both answer yes to that question.

Brogan had gone through the standard self-questioning. Would they still love each other in ten years? Answer: How the hell was he to know what the situation would be like in ten years? Did he really love her? Did she really love him? Answer: What the devil did that mean? He had come to the conclusion that there was no one else he would rather spend his life with, and he had good reason to be certain that she felt the same way.

Brogan glanced down at her, so appealing, so vulnerable, and in the end, made the decision, as every other man before him has done, on the basis of the moment's emotion. He asked her to marry him.

Sandra closed her eyes and pulled the covers back up to cover her shoulder.

"I can't, not now, Cole."

Brogan sat up with a jerk. "Hunh . . . ?"

"I can't answer that question now, Cole."

"You mean no . . . ?"

She shook her head. "No, I don't. I mean that I can't give you an answer now. Cole," she rushed on, drawing her knees up and struggling into a sitting position, "I . . . this job, this job is doing something to you. It's changed you terribly in the past year or so. As things stand now, I couldn't marry you. I mean I would never know from minute to minute how you were going to react to anything. Your mood goes from one extreme to the other, and there doesn't seem to be any in-between any more. The pressure is getting to you and I think that you are standing right on the edge. When you're like that, no one could live with you for long . . . and Cole, if we are married, I want it to last, forever and not just for a year or so until we can't stand the sight of each other any longer."

Brogan got up and slowly closed the door. He stood leaning against the frame for a minute before he turned. "Look, Sandra, I . . ." He stopped and at the same time thought to himself, Charlie, you total bastard you . . .

He rubbed his forehead and shook his head. "Sandra . . ." he started again.

"Cole . . . Cole, please, come and sit down, please?" Sandra swung her legs away under the blanket and patted the bed. Still shaking his head, Brogan sat down. Sandra took his hand and held it tightly.

"Cole, I haven't said no, and I won't, ever. But I just cannot say yes now, the way things are with you. You've been pushing yourself so hard over these damnable poppies . . . you're just ruining yourself. . . ."

Brogan took a deep breath, then shook his head. "What do you want me to do? I've quit INCC . . ."

"Yes, yes you have, but you haven't really. Cole, do you see what I'm saying?" she pleaded. "Until you get away from narcotics work altogether . . ."

"Sandra, for God's sake, what else can I do? Go back into intelligence or the army? Hell, that would be even worse. But those are the only other jobs I can do. That's all I know."

Sandra shook her head. "Cole, it has to be more than that. I don't know what right now. We need time to think about it. Both of us."

Brogan stared down at the blanket. "Yeah, maybe we do," he mumbled. "Maybe you are right. I don't know. But not now, not until this thing is finished."

Sandra watched his face, fingers plucking at the blanket. Then she turned away from him so that he would not see her tears.

"Get dressed now," he said quietly. "We'll be leaving shortly."

* * *

The rain had stopped by the time Brogan had repacked the camping gear and backed the car out of the garage. He drove slowly east on Oxford, turned north around Oxford Circus into Regent, then quickly into Cavendish Place, where he dodged back and forth through the mews. During the next half hour, he worked his way westward, almost imperceptibly, until he was on the Wellington Road, going north. Winslow, hunched into the luggage space, where he shared the narrow compartment with the pack frame and hiking equipment that Brogan had rescued earlier that morning from the Square and Sandra's only suitcase, bore it all stoically. Once Sandra asked him if he was uncomfortable, and he replied that it reminded him somewhat of his years in the Royal Tank Corps.

By eight o'clock Brogan was satisfied that they were not being followed, and he found an entrance to the M-4 and dove into the stream of traffic flowing west out of London. A few minutes later he cut off onto the Great West Road connector to the M-3.

"Where are we going?" Sandra's tone expressed pure puzzlement.

"Just to see some friends of mine."

"Cole, stop it. I want to know where we are going."

Brogan relented. "All right, sweetie, we are heading for Aldershot . . ."

"Aldershot?"

"Yeah. Can you think of a safer place than the middle of England's largest army base?"

"But why there?"

"Because I have friends there who will help Winslow look after you."

"Oh. And where will you be all this time?" Sandra asked archly.

"That, my dearest, I am not going to tell you. You are going to stay with these friends of mine while I settle some business."

"Ah . . . well . . . Mr. Brogan," Winslow broke in, "you see, I will have to come with you, then. My orders are to stick with you and Miss Duncan . . ."

"Sorry, Sergeant, but you would only get in the way."

Brogan floored the accelerator and passed a lorry creeping up the long incline outside Camberly. He kept the pedal down and the speedometer shortly was nudging ninety. Winslow cleared his throat and Brogan dropped back down to seventy.

"Whether or not I would get in the way is a moot question. The fact is that my orders are to stay with you . . . like a leech, I believe, is how the inspector put it."

"Okay, have it your way, then." Brogan shrugged. "But do your orders allow you to go outside the country?"

"Outside the country?"

"Yeah, to Ireland."

"Cole," Sandra wailed. "You aren't going back there . . . ?"

"The hell I'm not. This is the time when they will be least expecting me. Vandervoort and Druie want proof . . . then they sure as hell are going to get it."

The road sign for A-325 came into sight and Brogan edged over into the lefthand lane and took the exit without slackening speed. The Datsun rocketed around the loop, and Brogan braked hard at the roundabout to slip between a lorry grinding past a bus, which he followed through the circle and swung off onto A-325.

Sandra maintained a hurt silence for the next few miles and Winslow was busy mulling over his instructions in the light of Brogan's plans. Brogan concentrated on his driving meanwhile, weaving quickly in and out of the forty-mile-an-hour traffic. When the city limits of Aldershot slipped past, Brogan slowed and drove more sedately into the center of town. He turned north again and followed the road through the hills to the main gate of the Royal Army base.

A sentry stepped from the box as they approached, and Brogan doused the headlights and stopped.

"Yes, sir?"

"I'm Inspector Brogan, International Narcotics Control Commission. This is my secretary, Sandra Duncan, and this is Sergeant Winslow, London Metropolitan Police. We would like to see Colonel Winston Saunders."

Brogan shoved his I.D. card through the window and Winslow handed his over as well. The military policeman glanced into the car and said respectfully, "One moment, sir."

He stepped into the sentry box and picked up the phone. Brogan lit a cigarette and lounged back in the seat. Sandra glared at him and he grinned.

"Cole, do you really know what you are doing?"

"Sandra," he asked in a tone of mock hurt, "when have I ever not known what I was doing?"

Sandra pursed her lips, then leaned over and whispered fiercely in his ear. "You are not going to Ireland without me, do you understand?"

He was spared having to answer for the moment as the guard handed the two I.D. cards back through the window. "All right, Inspector Brogan, you are cleared." He slipped a visitor card under the windshield wiper and stepped back to the window.

"The Colonel and Mrs. Saunders are at the Officers' Club. They will leave immediately for their flat and meet you there. If you will follow that Rover ahead of you, sir, he will lead the way. It can be very confusing for a visitor, especially in the dark."

Brogan thanked him and eased the car into gear as the Rover pulled onto the road from the parking area and started toward the distant line of lights. The Rover stopped five minutes later in front of a long, modern two-story row of apartments. The driver got out and came back as Brogan rolled down his window.

"Colonel Saunders lives in 123, sir. If you need a guide to find your way back, I'll be happy to wait."

"Thanks, but it might be a while."

"Well, in that case, if you would call the gate, I will come back when you are ready."

The soldier saluted and drove away. Brogan pulled into the parking space and stopped.

"Here we are, folks. Everybody out. Come on, Sandra."

"*No!*" Sandra hunched down in the seat. "I told you you were not going off to Ireland and leave me here, and that's that."

Brogan leaned into the car and said very quietly, very calmly, "Sandra, you told me that I have to get out of this business. All right, but not until I've finished what I've started.

Now, get the hell out of that car before I drag you out."

"Cole," Sandra started.

"Out, damn it. Now!"

Sandra flung herself out of the car and hurried up the walk. Winslow cleared his throat in embarrassment and began to unload the Datsun. Brogan grimly followed her up the walk.

11

"I do not care what you want to do! You will not do it in Ireland without my permission . . . Is that understood?"

Brogan stared up at Commissioner Strain from the deep leather chair as Strain turned away, forgetting to hand him the whiskey that he had poured. He started back around his desk, realized that he still held the glass in his hand and abruptly handed it to Brogan.

"All right, Commissioner, then why haven't your people gotten anywhere . . . ?"

"How the devil could they?" Strain roared. "They have only had one day!"

"For God's sake! What do you want?" Brogan cried in exasperation. "Do you want a lorry to leave that farm, drive down a public highway to some deserted bay, unload into a fishing dory, then watch it row out to a freighter waiting offshore while the crew lines the side and cheers you on?

"My God, Strain, grow up. These are the big leagues you're playing in now. These people are clever and they are deadly. I told you what they tried in London . . ."

Strain dropped wearily into his chair. "How do you know there was any connection . . . ?"

Brogan muttered under his breath, then snorted. "Commissioner, INCC can bring a sizable amount of pressure to bear, and you know it damned well." He let the threat hang between them.

Strain gave him a cold stare in return. "I take it this is in the nature of an official request from the International Narcotics Control Commission?"

Brogan smiled but did not answer.

"Brogan, you are an unprincipled, bloody bastard."

"Flattery will get you nowhere," Brogan grinned. "Now what do you say? Are you going to help or do I call London?"

Strain sat back and contemplated Brogan for a long moment. Then, as if reaching a conclusion, he sat forward to lean his arms on the desk.

"What do you want me to do?"

"That's more like it. Pull any of your people out of the area and stop any and all surveillance you might have operating now.

"Then I want a car with a radio, and not the police frequency either, and I want complete freedom of movement. You are not to contact me. I'll get in touch with you when I'm ready. But when I do call, I want you to come in fast, and that means you have to have a troop of cops or soldiers or whatever ready and waiting. From the time I call you until the farm is surrounded can't be any longer than one hour, do you understand?"

"Now, where am I going to get enough police or soldiers to surround that farm on one hour's notice?" Strain asked in a sarcastic voice. "This isn't Great Britain or the United States, you know. We don't have twenty thousand men under arms in the entire Army, and if there are two thousand policemen in all of Ireland, I would be very much surprised."

"That's *your* problem," Brogan snorted. "Get them together now and keep them ready, because if I call, it will be no later than the day after tomorrow."

Strain started to shake his head, but Brogan leaned forward and asked coldly, "Do you dare take a chance that I'm right? If I put in that call and your people don't show and this whole thing goes bust, just how much do you think this cushy job and plush office are going to be worth to you?"

Strain fidgeted in the chair and glared at Brogan. "All right," he said finally. "You'll know the arrangements in the morning."

Brogan stood up and started for the door. "Fair enough." Then as an afterthought, "Chin up, Commissioner, I'm going to make a hero out of you in spite of yourself."

Strain shook his head. "Damned if I know what you are up to," he said, half in perplexity, half in admiration. "But whatever it is . . ." His voice trailed off.

He stood up and came around the desk, his face relaxing into a smile. "Look, I'm going down to my boat at Greystones this evening. Why don't you come along with me. It would give you a chance to relax, and both of us time to discuss details."

It was with some difficulty that Brogan concealed his astonishment. The proper civil servant, unbending so far! It was almost more than he could believe.

"All right," he replied in amusement. "That sounds like it might be interesting."

"Very good," Strain smiled. "I'll give you directions from Dublin . . . You do have a car, don't you? . . . Good, then you'll have no trouble at all finding it. Here, let me draw you a map."

Strain stepped back to his desk and quickly sketched a rough map. "Just follow T-7 down the coast, through Dun Laoghaire and Bray, to Greystones. Keep on through the village and watch for the sign for the marina."

Brogan glanced at the map quickly. "Looks easy enough. What time?"

"Say about eightish. We'll have dinner on board." They shook hands and Strain opened the door and escorted him through the office, smiling and joking. As Brogan rode the elevator down, he found himself wondering at Strain's sudden change in attitude. It raised a particularly interesting question . . . Why? Had Strain decided, after all, that it was in his interests to co-operate? Had his people discovered something more than Strain had told him, after all?

At a few minutes before eight, Brogan wheeled the rented Austin through the silent fishing village of Greystones. A low stone wall separated the narrow roadway from the drop to a stony beach. Below he could see one or two fishing nets drying in the sea breeze, but from that distance could not tell if they were real or were only local color for the tourists.

The tarmac road edged gingerly down to the small bay, where a number of motor and sailing craft lined a double *H*-dock arrangement. A small side road ran down toward the beach and, as if to make the obvious even more so, a large green-and-white sign labeled "Marina" pointed toward the dock half a mile away. Brogan turned onto the narrow road, musing on the incongruity of the Spanish word in Ireland before he recalled that it really wasn't so. Legend had it that the Celts had come from the Iberian Peninsula nearly two thousand years ago.

Brogan stopped in the nearly empty car park and got out. The sea breeze was beginning to die away as the sun dropped nearer and nearer the horizon.

"Cole . . . over here!"

Brogan looked over the top of the car to see Brian Strain striding toward him. He stepped down off the dock and came across the walk, hand outstretched.

"You made it, I see. Good, good. Come along now. We'll be having dinner shortly. Leave your car here, no one will bother it. We can get your bags later."

With one hand on Brogan's shoulder he led him up onto the dock and along the line of polished yachts.

Brogan shook his head, grinning to himself. Strain caught the gesture.

"Something wrong . . . ?"

"No." Brogan laughed. "No, not really. It's just that I wasn't ready for this. Seeing you in the office the proper civil servant, you'd never suspect."

Strain laughed without any trace of self-consciousness. "One must sometimes play a role, you know." Gone were the severe dark suits of the civil servant. Instead, Strain was wearing a pair of cream-colored flared slacks, a red-and-white striped shirt open at the throat, and a burgundy sport jacket. He looked twenty years younger, and by comparison, Brogan felt like a slob in his tan levis and nylon windbreaker.

"Here we are," Strain said, indicating a forty-foot, gleaming teak and brass motor yacht. That in itself was surprise enough, but Brogan was stopped completely by the two girls waiting for them as they stepped down onto the deck.

Strain laughed, a deeply resonant baritone laugh, and took each of the girls by an arm.

"Now, Cole, I thought we should have some agreeable company. This is Glynda," he said, inclining his head first to the stunning blonde on his left, then to the equally stunning brunette on his right, "and this is Kathleen. Both are very old friends of mine, and I'm sure that we'll all have a good time."

Kathleen took Brogan's arm and pressed against him. "Hello," she murmured. "Brian tells me you're a Narc."

"Now, wait . . ." Brogan backed away in surprise.

"Oh, come on." Strain waved a hand airily. "There are no secrets here. Don't worry, they won't tell anyone else. Besides, it makes you seem a bit glamorous."

"The hell with that," Brogan said angrily. "Just what . . ."

"Oh," Glynda pouted mockingly. "You blew his cover, Brian. He's an undercover agent . . ."

Strain chuckled and handed Brogan a drink. "No, he's not. Now come along, Cole. We are all friends. Drink up."

"Yes, do. We are already several ahead of you, Cole. So hurry along," Kathleen all but cooed.

"How do you like our marina? This is all brand new." Strain waved a hand expansively. "It was finished just this past winter and every space is now reserved. Some thought is being given to expanding it, even though there is already room for seventy-five yachts. They've widened the harbor and dredged the channel to make it one of the best moorings on the Coast." He stepped down into the cockpit and opened a large plastic freeze chest. "We have everything ready. The girls have put together what looks like a delicious cold supper." He rattled the chest and Brogan heard the unmistakable clink of wine bottles.

Strain laughed. "I brought champagne. California, in honor of our guest. It seemed to me that we should have a celebration. I tried to get Irish wine, but you know how it is . . ." He laughed and the girls exchanged delighted grins.

"Why would you want Irish wine?" Glynda asked in a mocking voice.

Strain laughed again. "A private joke, dear, a private joke."

In spite of the fact that they seemed to be going out of their way to make him the butt of their not-too-subtle jokes, within ten minutes they were all settled comfortably around a table that Strain had arranged in the cockpit. Ice cold martinis seemed to pour endlessly from the thermos that Glynda kept near her. And for the first time in days, Brogan began to relax as he finished one martini after another. He had even managed to put out of his mind the thought of what Sandra would say if she were ever to find out. Kathleen's dress was clinging and brief in spite of the cooling evening, and she was running her bare toes up and down his leg. He lit a cigarette and leaned back and let the peace of the Irish evening flow through him. Across the bay, the roofs of the tiny fishing village gleamed in the sun as it neared the horizon inland. A large fishing boat with a party of anglers and tourists was making its way into the harbor, and the entire scene framed against the jut of Bray head was one of summer's peace and plenty. Not far from them, a sixty-foot ketch was putting out from its moorings, and the sound of laughter and music floated across the marina.

"There goes Petros Balkis again," Glynda said, disgust turning her voice brittle.

"Now, Glynda," Strain admonished with some amusement.

"I don't care," she muttered. "He's a conceited, pompous ass, and someday someone is going to push him over the side . . ."

"Glynda is mad because he wouldn't choose her for a part in the movie he is making at Ardmore," Kathleen leaned along his arm and whispered into his ear. "He's a Greek movie producer who likes to work in Ireland because of the talent here . . . and because it's cheaper," she giggled.

"Is Glynda an actress?"

"We both are," Kathleen replied comfortably. "Neither of us is really very good, but we certainly are good enough for the trash that Balkis produces."

Brogan flicked his cigarette into the water, got up and walked to the side. Kathleen followed him and together they leaned on the railing, staring down at the placid water.

"How much did Strain tell you about me?" Brogan asked.

Kathleen laughed and shrugged her shoulders, sending the light dress dancing.

"Not very much. Just that you work for an international something or other that polices narcotics. I never bother very much about that sort of thing. Why?"

Brogan shrugged. "Just wondered, that's all."

"Why?" she asked again. "Are you on a case, or whatever you call it? Do you do dangerous things and track down heroin smugglers around the world?" she finished, laughing.

Brogan grinned in return. "Hell, no. I wish I did. It would certainly make my life more interesting. I spend most of my time stuck away in a little office in London reading newspapers and tons and tons of reports."

"Nothing else? Don't you get to go here and there and chase people?"

"Hardly ever."

"Why are you in Ireland, then?"

Brogan hesitated, then smiled at her while thinking, with some admiration, that she was a skillful little bitch. She might be an actress, but it certainly wasn't in the movies that she used her talents.

"Sort of a combined vacation and business trip," he replied finally. "I've just come over to clear up some last-minute business with Commissioner Strain."

Kathleen turned so that her back was to the rail. The satin-finish material of her dress was dangerously close to slipping completely away, and Brogan, as he was supposed to, concentrated on the soft expanse of gently tanned flesh while at the same time cautioning himself. He stepped closer to her until he was pressing her tightly back against the rail and kissed her soundly.

She didn't struggle, but instead reached up and placed both hands around his neck and returned the kiss. She was an actress, all right, Brogan thought, somewhat disjointedly.

Kathleen relaxed the pressure of her arms and leaned back. With one hand she fiddled with the zipper on his jacket for a moment, then looked up at him. Her eyes, he noted, were almost violet in the evening light. Her brown hair cascaded luxuriously around her shoulders, and she shook her head to clear a strand from her eyes.

"Do you have to go right back?"

"Go right back when?"

"When your business is finished?"

Brogan shrugged. "No. I'll probably take a day or two and just relax for a while."

He noticed that Strain and Glynda had gone below, leaving them alone. The evening was still. A light breeze rippled the quiet waters of the mooring, and here and there lights were beginning to come on as the dusk increased. A low moon was just visible above the sea, to the east, round and swollen.

Brogan walked over to the table where he had left his glass and poured another drink from the thermos. He held Kathleen's empty glass up and she nodded. He brought both back to the railing and they sipped the icy, tart liquid without speaking for several minutes.

Finally, Kathleen broke the silence. "It's so peaceful here. I just love it."

"It's the air of affluence." Brogan grinned. "That always helps."

He watched her carefully to see what her reaction to this sally would be. Surprisingly enough, she giggled. "You're right. It does have the feel of money to it. And there isn't much of that in Ireland, I must say."

She leaned again on the railing and said in a quiet voice, "Ireland has always been such a poor country. We have so very few resources, including people. And we all seem to have such a violent, self-destructive streak in us. It drags us back each time we begin to make some progress. You can see it plainly in Joyce and Yeats. They are both so typically Irish and, like most Irishmen, so committed to ideals that in the practical world soon cease to matter. We can destroy ourselves for an ideal. The troubles in the North are a recent example. Irishmen killing Irishmen for the sake of minor variations in the same religion, no matter how much they prattled on about economics and civil rights in the process. Ireland is a country that has never progressed past the seventeenth century, and might never."

"My, what morbid thoughts," Brogan answered quietly.

Kathleen smiled. "Yes, aren't they."

What the hell, Brogan thought, wondering if this was a put on. Strain's little sex and drinking party with intellectual overtones yet.

Kathleen glanced up at Brogan again and he caught the

glint of mockery in her eyes before she turned away as Strain's head appeared at the top of the companionway.

"Steaks are on," he called. "You had better come now."

Dinner proceeded uncomfortably for Brogan. He had become the center of attention, carefully targeted by Strain, who threw out hints concerning Brogan's business in Ireland every time the conversation flagged.

No matter how hard or how pointedly Brogan changed the course of the conversation, Strain always brought it back and both girls gleefully dug away at him, professing entrancement with his work. Finally, Brogan gave up and began to feed them stories about international heroin smuggling, describing how it had been in the years before the worldwide concerted effort began to make itself felt, hinting at the fact that a great deal of smuggling still went on simply because it was impossible to plug all loopholes.

But this satisfied neither, and the questions became all the blunter and more insistent until Glynda demanded he tell them exactly why he was in Ireland. The conversation froze at that point, and the two girls looked at him expectantly while Strain sat back and folded his arms smugly.

He looked directly at Strain, "I can't tell you anything, can I, Commissioner? Because if I did, then the Commissioner would have to answer some questions of his own."

Strain smiled carefully across the table at Brogan. "You are right of course. Much of what we have talked about should be considered confidential, I suppose. What . . . ?"

Brogan had jerked his head at the companionway and stood up.

"I think we had better go outside and talk this over."

Strain studied him a moment, his eyes hooded while the two girls watched. Finally, he stood up. "If you wish . . ." and he gestured to Brogan to lead the way.

The sun had now set completely and, except for the few lights of the town and the almost deserted marina, the darkness was complete. The light from the companionway spilled out in a brief fan. Brogan led the way to the stern and steadied himself against the railing.

"All right, Commissioner," he said harshly. "Let's have it. What the hell is this all about?"

Strain was a half-seen shadow against the dark sky, his expression invisible in the darkness.

"Let's have what?"

"The reason for the boat, the soft lights, this sex party and the constant digging and prying. What the hell do you want to know?"

There was a low chuckle in the darkness. "My dear Cole, your American upbringing is overreaching your common sense. You see plots at every turning, it seems. You aren't becoming paranoid, are you?"

Brogan snorted. "Paranoid? Hell, no. It's just that everyone is against me."

He sensed rather than saw Strain's hesitation, then his laugh at the feeble joke.

"No, Cole, come along now. I am a bachelor, I have a very nice boat, some very nice and compliant friends, and I have taken a liking to you in spite of your suspicious nature. In my office this afternoon you looked a bit wound up, a bit tense, and since I was coming down tonight, I thought you could do with a bit of relaxation. Do not let the girls intimidate you. They are very intelligent and they like to ask questions."

Brogan snorted. "Come on, you don't expect me to believe that, do you? They may like to ask questions, but you are making damned certain they ask the right ones. You've been leading the conversation ever since we sat down to dinner."

There was silence for a moment. "I see. Somehow we have offended you. I did not think we . . ."

"Damn it, give me a straight answer! I don't like beating around the bush."

"So your superiors have informed me."

A long minute passed before Brogan replied. "When?"

Strain's laugh was quiet yet somehow menacing. "This morning, before you came to my office. Your Mr. Vandervoort telephoned to tell me that you had resigned from the International Narcotics Control Commission. He suspected that you might attempt to continue the investigation on your own and he wanted to inform me that INCC disavowed your further activities completely."

Brogan turned away to the bay where a light breeze ruffled the waters. The quiet of the night was all-encompassing, yet it did not affect him. Internally, he felt as if a howling gale were raging.

"Then, why didn't you throw me out of your office and be done with it?" he asked tightly.

"Why?" Strain took out a cigarette pack and offered one to Brogan, who accepted absently. A match flared. Strain held it cupped in his hands, and as Brogan lit his cigarette he could see by its light that Strain was watching him closely.

"I do not take my orders from the INCC, a point I made to you in our first discussion. Now, I won't say that you have convinced me that you are on to something, but it does seem rather shortsighted of INCC to cut you off so abruptly. But then, also, I received the impression from your *friend* Vandervoort that he did not consider you entirely reliable."

Brogan laughed bitterly. "That's very true. It has been a damned long time since the two of us have agreed on anything."

Brogan flicked the half-smoked cigarette into the water and straightened up.

"What do you intend to do now?" Strain asked.

Brogan shrugged. "I really don't know. You were the last hope I had. There was a possibility that your people had come up with something . . . but they haven't, and I guess that makes Vandervoort right and me wrong, all the way round. It looks like I was being truthful when I told Kathleen that I was on an extended vacation."

"Are you going to give it up, then?"

"What the hell else can I do? INCC wants no part of me . . . I can't do anything here without your permission . . . which, I suppose, I do not have . . ."

"That is correct, I am afraid."

"Well, that's it, then, Commissioner. Only"—Brogan paused, then finished bitterly—"don't say I didn't warn you."

Strain clapped him on the shoulder. "I won't, old man. And I wouldn't worry about the investigation. I have absolutely no intention of dropping it. But we will not be moving at your headlong pace, I am afraid."

"Yeah, I expect that you wouldn't," Brogan said grimly. "Just watch out that they don't slip through your fingers while you are methodically crawling through the bushes."

Strain chuckled. "Don't worry about that. Well, now that everything is settled, don't you think we have left the girls alone long enough? Put your problems behind you for tonight. Kathleen can be very diverting if handled properly . . ."

Brogan shook his head. "No, thanks, Commissioner. I'll go back to Dublin tonight. I want to get a flight back to London first thing in the morning."

Brogan pushed past Strain and climbed up onto the dock. As he walked away, Strain watched, but did not call him back.

12

It was not yet dawn as Brogan sat in the rented car, studying the one-inch-scale map with the aid of a flashlight. The eastern horizon was just beginning to show a flush of pink and the hundreds of frogs in the bog below were in full cry. Brogan had driven the one hundred and sixty miles from Greystones since midnight to reach a point just four miles north of the village of Castleisland on Highway T-28. In the half-light of the approaching dawn, he had pulled off the road to follow what was probably an old sheep track leading partway up the slope of Knockakin Mountain to a grove of trees where he could conceal the car.

Knockakin Mountain was eleven miles south-southeast of Abbeyfeale, according to the map, but that still did not provide him with a clear picture of exactly how the vineyard lay in relation to the town. And the more he tried to puzzle it out, shifting the photos and map this way and that, the more confused he became. The rudimentary road net shown on the map that surrounded Abbeyfeale compared well with the satellite photos. However, he could not quite locate the farm on the map as it was shown in the photographs. The best he could do was to approximate its location some two miles south and west of town. With a sigh, he decided that he had better start earlier than he had planned, in case he had to search. No rest for the wicked, he muttered, refolded the map and reached over the seat to stuff it into the map pocket of his back pack.

He had decided before leaving London that he stood a better chance of approaching the farm safely if he appeared to be just one of the numerous back packers and campers who infest Europe every summer. Entrance to the farm itself would be something else again, he thought grimly. He was certain that it would be heavily guarded, and the guards supplemented with personnel-detection devices.

The visit to Aldershot had done double duty. It had not only placed Sandra safely into the hands of a very good friend in the middle of a British military base, but it had given him the opportunity to borrow one of the latest military reconnaissance cameras and some anti-personnel-detection equipment. Unable to resist the urge to play with it once more, Brogan shifted the metal case to the passenger seat and unlocked the lid.

The camera resembled a Super-8 home movie camera, but a closer examination disclosed that it was definitely not for home movies; in fact, it was far more than a ciné camera. Rather, it held two magazines—one containing infrared film, and the other, the new 1600 ASA Ektachrome color film. An image intensifier built into the lens turret gave him the capability of recording the activities of a black cat at midnight in a coal bin, if necessary. In spite of all this, the camera weighed less than two pounds, fully loaded and with batteries.

Brogan checked the battery charge for the tenth time, replaced it in its case and opened the car door, dragging the pack after him. A sleeping bag was tied to the pack frame, the outside pockets were full of candy bars and rations, and a plastic bottle canteen was jammed into its holster. Before leaving London, Brogan had added a change of clothes, one hundred pounds in ones and fives contained in a small wallet sewn into the flap, and an extra box of ammunition for the revolver, both wrapped in lead foil to get them through the metal detectors at the airports. He had also added some battery jumper wire and other odds and ends that he felt might be useful. He fastened the flap down, lifted the pack, which weighed less than twenty pounds, and slipped his arms into the straps. After checking to make sure that the spare key to the car was in its magnetic case beneath the bonnet, he locked the doors and struck off into the hills.

By the time the sun was fully up, Brogan had covered the first mile. The going was much more difficult than he had anticipated, as the hills were steep and covered with knee-high bracken. A low mist began to settle in shortly after sunrise, which obscured everything beyond several yards, so that

Brogan found himself walking through a gray world in which the only color was the faded green of the vegetation immediately around him. Without his compass, he would have been hopelessly turned around in minutes.

The mist burned off by noon, and all around him the softly rounded mounds of the Glannaruddery Mountains pressed against the hazy blue sky. The area was completely deserted, not even sheep grazing, nor was there any sign that they had done so recently. Once he came across a dusty road empty of even the faintest tire trace. There had been a fence along either side, a stone fence, but it had long ago fallen into a half-buried pile of rubble.

As he paced along, the sun climbed higher and higher into the nearly cloudless sky. A mild breeze fluttered through the winding hills and the bracken began to give way to low, spring grass covered with wildflowers. Mountains were a misnomer to someone brought up in California, he thought. These were nothing but high hills, none more than two thousand feet high. But they were empty, completely empty of human life in any direction that he cared to look.

By late afternoon, Brogan reached a wooded crest less than a quarter of a mile south of where he suspected the farm to be. From the vantage point of the hilltop, he searched the valley below with his binoculars. In the middle distance he found something entirely unexpected: acres and acres of greenish nylon cheesecloth.

Brogan gave a low whistle and swept the glasses from side to side. There was no mistaking the fact that the fields were covered by the green nylon; huge swaths of cloth were mounted ten to twelve feet off the ground and covered entire sections of the field. On the far side, where one vineyard spilled over the side of a hill, Brogan caught the glint of sunlight on metal. He shrugged out of the pack and knelt down in the grass to minimize exposure and focused the binoculars on the hillside.

Two tractors appeared to be moving slowly across the rim of the hill, one towing a trailer on which was mounted a large drum—as he watched, a green ribbon fed off the drum and was manhandled into place along the tops of high posts set twenty feet or so apart.

"So that's how they're doing it," he muttered. "That's pretty damned clever." Like a softly rolling sea or a tinted snowscape, the cheesecloth stretched in either direction as far as he could see. Around the periphery of the vineyards he could discern a barbed wire fence that ran up and over the hills until lost in the light mist. What looked to be tiny white placards were mounted at intervals on the fencing, and he guessed that they were to warn potential trespassers away. Then he noticed a spot of red on each fence post and focused the binoculars more carefully. Insulators, four to a pole, were spaced vertically eighteen inches or so apart. The placards weren't to warn against trespassing, they were to warn that the fence was electrified, a precaution he had half expected.

An ancient beech tree crowned the top of the hill on which Brogan stood. He moved toward it, noting how the branches spread densely on all sides some sixty feet above the top of the hill. He dropped his pack beneath the tree and stood looking up into its branches. Heavy, gnarled limbs rose out of the ten-foot-thick trunk, newly fleshed with spring leaves. The tree was filled with birdsong and he could hear the mild buzzing of insects, so quiet was the late afternoon.

Brogan sat down and lit a cigarette. Here he was, he thought to himself, within a quarter of a mile of the damnable farm that was causing him so much grief. In the days since his trip to Washington, he had never once doubted that he was on the right track. It all fitted so well: the fishing boat carrying heroin from and not to Irish waters, the vineyard where one should not have been, the acetic anhydride source. But that had been only a part of the entire picture. All the time the question of where the heroin had come from had gone unanswered. Economically, in spite of his rationalizations to that damnable dilettante Strain, it made no sense to transport morphine base from Central or Southeast Asia, or from anywhere else for that matter, to Ireland. Now the question had been answered for him.

He had seen those cheesecloth tents before in the Connecticut River Valley, where a variety of Havana cigar-wrapper tobacco was grown. The cheesecloth tents raised the temperature and humidity to levels comparable to those in Cuba to allow the fine green wrapper leaf to grow a thousand miles further north. Obviously, the syndicate was following the same procedure. By using the cheesecloth tenting, the temperatures could be raised high enough to grow opium poppies. The tents would also provide any further camouflage from satellite detection necessary to the poppies and, as a bonus, provide rich, ripe grapes from which wine could be produced, thus cementing the vineyard's cover solidly into place.

Where before when he faced the farm, challenging it, as it were, to prove itself innocent, he had experienced serious misgivings. After all, he had put his reputation on the line, not to mention his job, and all he had were his convictions, convictions that would not be sufficient to sustain him if proven wrong. The vineyard could very well have been a vineyard. After all, if they could establish a vineyard in Ireland, might not the owners be on the verge of opening up a large market for Irish wines? Nonsense, he snorted and knew he was right. Somewhere beneath those shade tents Brogan had not the slightest doubt that he would find opium poppies.

The afternoon was warm and still, and the combination was proving too much for Brogan in spite of his elation. His head was nodding and it was with difficulty that he forced himself to his feet and glanced at his watch. It was 5:30, leaving him at least another four hours to sunset, and at least an hour or so after that before it would be dark enough to move. He needed sleep desperately, but even more, a place where he would be safely out of sight.

He looked up at the tree again. The lowest branch was just above his head; it would be an easy climb, he decided. He slung his pack onto the branch, shoving it back against the trunk, and pulled himself up, hooked a leg over the branch and swung his body up. Carefully, he stood and began to climb, dragging the pack behind. The leaves were dense around the outer fringes of the tree, but the interior was open enough so that he experienced no difficulty. A rush of wings announced a mass egress of squawking birds, and in moments he had most of the tree to himself.

At forty feet, he found a thick branch extending out from the main trunk in such a way that it formed a small platform, wide enough for him to sit comfortably. Unless someone deliberately stood below the tree and looked up, he was completely hidden from the ground. Within five minutes, Brogan was ensconced, his pack tied to the branch above, within easy reaching distance.

Even though he was dead tired, before he allowed himself the luxury of a precarious nap, he took his battered 10 x 50 Zeiss binoculars and wriggled out on the branch as far as he dared go. Hanging on with one hand, he broke several small branches away and pushed them aside to gain a clear view.

The low hills on either side formed a shallow vee through which a large portion of the vineyard-farm could be seen. From his vantage point in the tree, he could see down past a section of already tented vineyard, across what looked to be the main yard of the farm to a series of low buildings. The main yard was surrounded by five shedlike barns and one Georgian-style house set off to one side. The sheds were metal one-story structures, windowless and arranged in a wide rectangle. As he watched, a green-colored panel van drove out of the yard and disappeared along the drive. Other than that, the yard was empty of life as far as he could tell, but a long green lorry-trailer combination was parked against one of the buildings. The trailer was side on to him, and with difficulty he spelled out the name printed on the side . . . "Mists of Tralee" . . . something or other, probably vineyards.

"Mists of Tralee," he snorted. Damned picturesque. He could almost hear Bing Crosby in the background. A large helicopter squatted next to the house. It was painted the same green color as the lorry and the trailer.

The vineyard itself was surrounded by the electrified fence. What vines remained uncovered appeared to be planted in rows spaced approximately five feet apart, and except for the curvature of the land into hills and valleys, each row ran arrow straight to a main aisle that appeared to bisect each section. Narrower aisles paralleled it on either side.

There was nothing else that could possibly arouse suspicion. His attention was attracted to the fence nearest him again, and he noticed that it appeared to be mounted on an earthen ramp of some kind. The fence was generally two to three feet above the level of the surrounding terrain. For a few moments he puzzled over the significance of this before the explanation came to him. The owners of the farm had taken advantage of the ancient stone fences that must have once encircled part of the present farm. In this boggy country, after a few decades, the stone fences would begin to sink into the soft earth of their own weight until they were little more than grassy mounds. He had seen similar mounds tracing other ancient fences in parts of Great Britain and New England.

Having seen all that he could for the moment, Brogan quickly drew a sketch map, then crawled back to his resting place, shoved his binoculars into the pack and settled back with a cigarette to think.

The previous evening had certainly been strange, to say the least. Strain had called his bluff neatly enough. The warning was plain: No more interference, especially unofficial interference, in Irish affairs. He had been played like a fish on a string, and he knew it.

Brogan finished the cigarette and stubbed it out, started to flick it away, then thought better of it, and stuck it into his pocket instead. There was no special reason for doing so; but of a sudden, the habit of caution was once again asserting itself. Grinning to himself, he settled back. He hadn't done anything like that since his army service in Vietnam. In any event, his friend Strain was in for one hell of a surprise.

The afternoon was heavy with the scent of the new grass and the mild warmth of the Irish summer. He set the alarm on his wrist watch for midnight and resettled himself into a more comfortable position with his jacket bunched beneath his head. In minutes he was asleep.

* * *

It was pitch-black when the watch alarm woke him. He shuddered in the damp coolness of the night, struggled into his jacket, then lowered the pack and climbed down after it. The sky was heavily overcast and there was the smell of rain in the air. Brogan took the binoculars out of the pack and moved forward to the crest of the hill, where he lay down in the damp grass to search along the line of the fence. The darkness was so complete that very little beyond vague shapes could be seen. Off in the distance, at least a mile away, he thought he could detect a spot of light, probably from the farm buildings.

He got up and went back to the tree, where he peeled off his clothes down to bare skin and, shivering in the coolness, fumbled open the straps on the pack and removed the tight-fitting one-piece coverall and struggled into it.

The suit, borrowed from the Army, was composed of several layers of mylar plastic over a nylon underpiece. On the chest were mounted two thin ventilation flaps, which he unzipped and folded back to fasten onto their velcro strips for the moment. He added a pair of boots of the same material, and a nylon hood with a face plate that attached to the neck of the suit. He left the face plate open for the moment and removed a rectangular plastic box from the pack and fitted it to the belt. From the box, a small earphone on a taped lead fitted into the nylon helmet, and a second lead attached to a point just above the face-plate opening. He reached around, snapped the switch and closed the face plate. Immediately, an eye-shaped piece set into the plastic began to glow a pale green, and the surrounding details of the land jumped out of the night. He turned carefully, surveying the ground about him and the tree. The view was in shades of green and white, but quite clear, nevertheless. He touched a stud on the helmet and the view blacked out.

Satisfied, he turned it on again, knelt and began shoving his clothes into the pack. The camera was removed from its metal case, slung around his neck and fastened with a band across the front of the suit so that it rested snugly against his chest on a draw-tight line. Picking up the pack frame, he started for the fence.

He had spent several hours on the plane from Washington to London going over the satellite photos. The oddity that struck him was that, although the farm was located in the middle of open Irish countryside, there were no special security precautions in evidence. The whole farm was accessible to wandering hikers and tourists. The covering nylon cheesecloth accounted for some of the camouflage, but there had to be something beyond the electrified fence and a few guards to keep the curious away. A vineyard in Ireland was certainly enough to attract attention. Accordingly, there had been two reasons for his going first to Aldershot; the most important was to find a place where Sandra could be completely safe. But also, an old and close friend, Colonel Winston Saunders, was a specialist in guerrilla warfare and insurgency activities. His current assignment was testing new counterinsurgency techniques and equipment. He had treated Brogan to a restricted showing, one day a year previously, of some of the latest electronic personnel-detection gadgetry, and the one item that had impressed Brogan most was the suit that he was now wearing.

The Americans had made great strides in electronic and chemical detection of hostile personnel, based on their experiences in Indochina. Saunders had shown him some of the various means to detect humans by the use of infrared, ultraviolet and seismic detectors that measured heartbeats and footfalls. The human body emitted 502 chemicals into the atmosphere in the form of gases and particulate matter every second of life. A number of these chemicals were detectable by instruments, chemical sniffers, such as infrared and ultraviolet instrumentation and mass spectrophotometers. The suit he was wearing was designed to prevent any of the chemicals that the human body emitted from reaching the atmosphere—all were captured by chemical and micropore filters built into the suit. The mylar covering of the suit was so constructed that it took on the temperature of the surrounding air, insulating body heat with almost one hundred per cent efficiency, thus making him invisible to infrared detection techniques.

When Brogan had been unable to find any signs of a security system beyond guards at the gate, he decided to gamble that some type of personnel-detecting sensors had been located about the perimeter of the farm. A flourishing black market in such instrumentation had developed in the wake of the Vietnam war in addition to the civilian versions available for industrial security purposes.

Brogan reached the fence and lay down full length behind the mound and carefully raised his head. With the infrared system in operation, he searched the perimeter; then, leaving the pack, he moved along the fence for several hundred yards in either direction, carefully examining the ground between the mound and the first row of vines until satisfied that the immediate area was clear of both guards and personnel detectors.

His heart was beating faster now with excitement, satisfaction and a touch of euphoria at the thought of finding both opium poppies and processing laboratory together. That bit of luck had tremendously simplified his job, and it began to look as if things might finally be going his way. Returning to where he had left his pack, he drew out the two insulated battery jumper cables and a pair of wire cutters.

The first strand of electrified wire was mounted less than ten inches above the top of the mound. He squeezed the heavy alligator clips open and attached both ends to the bare wire three feet apart and cut through the strand.

To provide a margin of safety, Brogan repeated the process on the second strand, thus making a hole three feet wide by two feet high. Quickly he wriggled through and rolled down the other side of the mound. He got to his knees and unhooked the seismic sensor detector from his belt, switched it on and attached the lead to his helmet. A steady hum indicated that an area at least one hundred feet in diameter was clear—in either direction, ample margin. Brogan resettled the detector on his belt, took a quick look in either direction, then trotted across the open ground to the first row of vines and wriggled through.

Once there, he took a deep breath and settled down to take stock. Surrounding him now were row on row of horizontally strung grapevines. This early in June, the vines were just beginning to show the first clusters of immature grapes. The night was quiet with the supernatural hush that precedes the advent of a storm of some magnitude. At long intervals, the low muttering of thunder could be heard over the horizon.

He had come through the fence at a point almost opposite the main part of the farm. The satellite photos had shown the farm buildings to be located almost in the center of the vineyard. To his right, about four hundred yards, the main aisle through the rows ran straight to the buildings. Two smaller access rows paralleled this main aisle and were intersected by other feeder aisles running in perpendicular fashion to the main aisle. Each feeder, or secondary, aisle was separated from the next by two hundred or so yards. Brogan had planned on staying well away from any of the aisles in the likely event guards were posted or made circuits through the vineyards at night, by crawling beneath the vines. But their density made that almost impossible. Accordingly and very carefully, he moved off to his left to find the nearest secondary aisle.

It took him ten minutes of cautious travel before he found the first one, almost a roadway eight feet wide. Twice the sensors had reported seismic detectors ahead, forcing him to make elaborate detours.

One hundred yards into the vineyard he spotted the first of the poppy plants under the beginning of the nylon tenting. A huge grin spread over his face as he got down on hands and knees first to stare at the weird greenish outline of the obscene petal-less plant, then to carefully examine the long stalk with its bulbous pod at the top. There were no petals in evidence, merely a fringe of what appeared to be immature leaves: an exact duplicate of the plants he had seen in Iran.

The lowest wire strand supporting the bottom branch of the vine was twenty-four inches above the soil bed, and the poppy plant was set forward a few inches. As these poppies had a tendency to have shorter stalks, or so he had observed in Iran, it was well placed to obtain the maximum amount of filtered sunlight. Each plant was spaced six inches from its neighbor in the approved fashion of the experienced grower. Brogan sat back on his heels and contemplated the pod in his hand. Inordinately pleased with himself, he opened the face plate and shook the pod. A slight rattling told him it was nearing maturity.

Brogan got up and moved down the row to the end. As he had expected, the first plant nearest the aisle was smaller than the rest, as if traffic had slowed its growth. Carefully he dug it out, folded it carefully into a plastic bag and put in into his pack. Then he photographed several locations along the row as additional supporting evidence.

For the next half hour, Brogan moved through the vines, measuring the extent of the planting until he had gained a fair assessment of the crop. So far, the plants he had seen were not ripe; yet, if the shipment captured earlier in the month had come from here, at least one area had already been harvested. By planting at different times of the year, it would be possible to harvest two or three or even four crops. The increased temperatures produced by the nylon netting, he guessed, probably extended the growing season by at least two, and possibly three, additional months.

Brogan hunkered down and thought about it. Since finding the first plant, he had explored roughly twenty rows. The sowing appeared to be consistent, each plant approximately six inches apart. Each row was two hundred yards long, which meant an average of 1,200 plants per row. He had no idea how many rows to a section, but two hundred was a safe enough bet, and two hundred rows equaled 240,000 plants. Now, if each plant averaged five grams of opium when mature, he laboriously calculated that there were potentially 1,200,000 grams of opium, which could be processed at a ratio of ten to one into morphine. The synthesis from morphine to heroin was one to one, so there were nearly 120 kilos of pure heroin in this one section alone, and he had counted twelve sections earlier in the day, and he was certain there were additional sections beyond the hills.

The figures were staggering. At a conservative estimate, there were approximately 1,500 kilograms of pure heroin on this farm, more than enough to supply the illicit needs of the entire East Coast of the United States for one year; at today's prices, almost $5 billion. The extent of the involvement far exceeded his wildest imaginings. Almost 1,500 kilos of pure, high-grade heroin from just one farm. Good God, one year's operation, and the entire location could be abandoned if need be. Nine or ten such farms scattered around the world, all impervious to detection by satellite, could outproduce the Middle East and Southeast Asia combined at their highest output in the early 1970s.

Brogan swallowed hard. He had come looking for a small processing laboratory, hoping he could trace back from there to the source, and he had stumbled into a self-contained operation on a scale beyond what he would ever have believed possible. Earlier, staring at the nylon netting, a feeling of exultation had possessed him as he realized that poppies were being grown beneath it. Now that he had stumbled into something far greater than he had anticipated, he was just plain scared to death.

Brogan shivered, then started as a clink of metal brought him up short. For a long moment he could see or hear nothing; then, almost simultaneously, he heard a boot scuffing across loose-packed soil and saw the vague outline of a body two rows over. He froze into absolute immobility, barely daring to turn his head as the guard moved along the row.

The guard halted almost opposite him, struck a match and lit a cigarette, then moved on toward the aisle. Brogan slowly exhaled a relieved breath and, after the man was out of sight, moved carefully away and deeper into the sheltering vines. Once the seismic detector alarm buzzed softly, forcing him into a wide detour. His plan had originally been to work his way down to the main yard, to search for the acetic anhydride source. But now, having discovered that the petal-less poppy was in fact being cultivated on the premises, he discarded that as unnecessary. The plants he had collected would be sufficient to move both INCC and Strain to action as well as tie this source into the Iranian garden.

He still wanted a quick look at the layout of the center area before he left, but discretion was the better part of valor. Exploration of that area was better left to armed police and troops. With some regret mingled with relief, he began moving in the direction of the fence.

It had begun to rain, a slow drizzle at first that gradually increased until it had become a steady downpour. Thunder clattered about and intermittent lightning flashes lit the vines, producing a haunted jungle of fleshy leaves and muddy soil. Alternately cursing and blessing the rain that reduced visibility in the infrared by cooling everything to an even temperature, it did have the advantage of protecting him even more from sharp-eyed guards.

The rain was showing no sign of slackening by the time he reached the end of the vineyard half an hour later. He crept carefully up to the last row of vines and hunched back into its cover as best he could to study what little he could see of the fence.

He pushed the hood back and listened carefully, but the only sounds were those of the rain spattering on the vines. The break in the fence lay to his right, if he remembered correctly, and he worked his way down the row, wishing he dared risk a light on the uneven ground. He stumbled twice on the plowed dirt between the rows and muttered under his breath. It was only the sibilant rush of wet leaves that caused him to duck to one side in time to sense rather than see the rifle butt slash past his head. The blurred silhouette of a guard swung the rifle toward his head in an overhand thrust a second time, but Brogan was facing his attacker and ready. His left foot slid forward at a narrow angle to the attacker as he thrust his right fist high over his head in an upward block that deflected the clubbed rifle. He hooked his right hand over the man's wrist and yanked down, throwing him off balance to meet a savage roundhouse knee to the midsection. He smashed his left fist into the man's rib cage, stepped up sharply with his left knee, catching the base of the spine with a jolt and delivered a final roundhouse kick to the groin. The guard collapsed without a sound. Brogan kicked him once at the base of the skull for good measure and dropped down into the dirt beside him for a careful look around to see if the fool had alerted anyone else. Five years with the INCC, his thoughts came in a rush, and this was the first time that he had ever had to use any of the karate that had been so laboriously pounded into him. Nothing happened, no rush of guards, no gunshots or yells to alert others. Apparently, the guard had stumbled across him by accident.

Brogan decided quickly that retreat, damned fast retreat, was the next order of business, and he sprinted down the fence until he found the break, wriggled out, grabbed up his pack and scurried for the relative safety of his tree, not bothering to waste time concealing evidence of his egress. When they found the guard they would know what had happened, and now minutes were damned precious.

13

The first hour after dawn found Brogan wearily plodding along an old country track that meandered north to the village of Athea in County Limerick, some seven miles beyond the farm. The rain had died away to thin drizzle an hour before, and Brogan was shivering and soaking wet. He had shed the uncomfortable infiltration suit, preferring the clean rain to its sweat-bath atmosphere. It was folded away into the bottom of his pack along with the camera and helmet. The film cartridges were zipped into his jacket pocket and he patted them for reassurance.

As he trudged along the muddy track his reluctance to enter the village grew; his presence so early in the morning would be certain to attract unwelcome attention. So far, he was certain that the darkness and rain were hampering the search for him by preventing the use of that damnable helicopter.

There was little choice in his route, he knew. The long hike back to his car over the open hills was out of the question, and Abbeyfeale, the nearest other village, was too damned close to the farm and would be the first place they would look. There were a few scattered farmhouses about, but he preferred to stay clear of them. They would certainly be checked quickly, and he had no wish to expose any of the local people to possible harm. Athea at least offered the sanctuary of a telephone and post office; and with what he was carrying in his pack, if Strain could not now be convinced that he had to move immediately, then he was a damned fool—and unhappily, he himself could wind up quite dead. His elation at finding irrefutable confirmation of his suspicions was still high, although as the hours wore on through dawn, caution was beginning to reassert itself.

Brogan trudged over the final bracken-covered crest to see the tiny village nestled into a fold in the hills below him. In all, it was no more than a three-street-wide collection of houses along a narrow macadamized main road winding slowly through the valley. An occasional farm could be seen through the mist, straggling up into the hills beyond the village. There was no indication of any undue excitement in the village itself: one or two cars and very few people on the streets. His watch showed eight-thirty, early, yet not too early to call Strain and ruin his day.

A few minutes later, he was walking slowly down the main street, conscious of curious eyes following him from windows along the way. Hikers should be no stranger to this most beautiful part of Ireland, and he was trying as hard as he could to act the part. Certainly his wet, dirty clothes and soggy pack were in character. The village was typical of rural Ireland: narrow streets lined with whitewashed stone and brick houses, a few converted to shops. At the far end of the street, an old petrol station rested with a weary air of somnolence. Near the center of the village the road widened and a white, gable-roofed building sported a sign proclaiming itself an inn, the name of which had long since weathered away. Directly across the road from the inn was the local post office, and Brogan turned off and pushed through the battered screen door.

The building was, in fact, a combination grocery and post office, the area devoted to the mail being located in a small wire cage at the back of the store. Brogan leaned his pack against the counter and bought a mailing carton and some string from the old woman who doubled as grocery clerk and postmistress. He scribbled a quick note, then dropped it and the film cartridge into the mailing carton, added the wilted poppy and sealed and wrapped it securely with string. He hesitated a moment, then addressed it to himself at his office in London. A little outside pressure on Strain at this point might just do the trick. He took the package to the wire cage, bought the proper amount of postage and watched the old woman tuck it into a mailbag. The postal schedule indicated that it would be on its way before noon.

Brogan glanced around the store and found the telephone on the back wall. His first call was to Sandra. There were a few moments' wait as the operator put through the connection to Aldershot, then a woman's voice answered after several long rings.

"Hello, Sandra?"

"Who?"

"Sandra . . . ? This is Cole . . ."

"Who? Cole? Cole, am I certainly glad to hear you. This is Yvonne. Where are you?"

Yvonne was Saunders' wife, and at the relief in her voice Brogan felt a moment's apprehension. "Is Sandra there, Yvonne?" He was practically shouting in an effort to make himself understood.

"Yes, yes she is. Just a moment."

Faintly he could hear Yvonne calling to Sandra, and then the click as an extension phone was lifted from the receiver.

"Cole? Cole is that you?"

Brogan laughed in relief. "Yeah, it's me. How've you been?"

"Never mind that. Are you all right? Where are you?"

Brogan laughed again as relief overpowered him for a moment, making it difficult to speak. "I'm perfectly fine. I'm in Ireland, a little town called Athea, in Limerick. I found what I wanted and I've put films and samples in the mail to the office. They should be there tomorrow at the latest. Is Winslow still there with you?"

"Cole, you mean that you really did find . . . samples of what . . . ?" She paused for a moment as realization dawned. "Cole, do you mean that you found . . . ?"

"Hold on," Brogan cut her off quickly. "Don't forget this is an open line. Yes, they really are there. Look, is Winslow still there?" he repeated.

"Winslow? Oh, no, he had to go back to London yesterday. There is a military policeman outside . . ."

"Okay, then, listen to me carefully. I want you to call Winslow to come and get you. He is to take you right back to London, to the office. I want you to go directly to Vandervoort and tell him that I mailed the films and samples to myself. But tell him not to wait for them. You have to convince him to call Strain right away and put the pressure on for an immediate investigation."

He glanced quickly around, but the old woman was at the front of the store busy with some stock. "Do you think you can do that?"

"Cole, I don't know. Vandervoort isn't likely to listen . . ."

"Look, Sandi," Brogan interrupted. "I know it won't be easy. But you have to do it. Pound it into that stubborn Dutchman's head with a club if you have to; go to the director if everything else fails. But get them to put the pressure on Strain. There are some politics tied up with this, and I don't even pretend to understand what's involved. But our only chance is to create a big enough fuss. Do you understand?"

Sandra was silent a moment. "Are you saying that someone is pressuring what's his name . . . Strain . . . to do nothing. And that the only way to get him to act is to put more pressure on him from London?"

"Exactly. I can't tell you any more than that now, but that's the situation in a nutshell. How fast can you get Winslow out to pick you up and get back to London?"

"Possibly by this afternoon sometime. It depends on whether or not I can find him . . ."

"Okay, do your best; but no one except Winslow. I think he understands the seriousness of the situation, even if he doesn't know exactly what's going on. I'm going to put through a call to Strain now, but if I get any co-operation at all I have a feeling it will be damned little, so we have to move as fast as possible or else these people are going to run."

"I understand, Cole." Sandra's voice wavered a bit. "I'll do whatever I can. Please take care of yourself. When will I see you again?"

"I don't know, honey. I honestly don't at this point. It depends on how much luck you have with Vandervoort and how much I have with Strain."

Sandra was silent for a long moment. Then, "Cole, I love you. Please be careful."

Brogan took a deep breath. "I love you too. Be careful going into London and get to the office as fast as possible."

Brogan hung up and waited beside the telephone for a moment until the operator rang back and he deposited the fifteen ten-pence pieces requested.

He then had her put through a call to Strain's office in Dublin. Wearily, he shifted from foot to foot as he waited for the connection to complete.

Strain's secretary came on the line and he asked for Strain, giving his name. The secretary hesitated a moment, then asked him to wait. Within seconds, Strain was on the line.

"Cole! Where are you, old boy? Are you in Ireland again?" His voice was friendly enough, but underneath Brogan detected an edge of irritation.

"Hello, Brian. Yes, I am in Ireland." He took a deep breath. "In fact, I never left."

"Oh . . ."

"Yeah, and you probably are not going to like what I have to tell you either, but . . . I have been out to that farm we talked about, and found it just as I said it would be."

"You what . . ." Strain shouted. "By God, with what authority do you . . . ?"

"Hold it, hold it," Brogan cut in. "By no authority, and you know it. So let's cut the nonsense and get down to business."

The old woman had worked her way back to the postal cage, where she was pretending to be busy. Brogan swung about and cradled the phone between his shoulder and chin and leaned against the wall to muffle the conversation. Miffed, the old woman moved away again.

"Look, whether I have your permission or not, I have been to that damned farm and found exactly the setup I told you I would find," Brogan growled. "And more beyond that. Those bastards are actually growing poppies, and there is no mistake about it. I figured that they have the capacity for producing nearly fifteen hundred kilos of heroin per harvest."

"Fifteen hundred kilos!" Strain's voice was incredulous. "That's ridiculous."

"The hell it is. And I have photographic proof of what I say. As well as samples. Damn it all, Strain, can't I get anything through to you?"

"You say you have photographic proof . . . ?"

"And some actual samples of the plants. There is no doubt

about it. These are the same damned plants I saw in Iran, and with the setup they have"—he held the phone closer and lowered his voice—"they can revive the heroin market in North America almost on their own. And God knows how many other producing units like this are scattered around the world."

"Where are you now?" Strain asked after a moment's silence.

"In a small village called Athea, about seven miles north of the farm. One of the guards tripped over me and I had to clobber him. So it's a damned cinch that they know someone has been inside during the night. I didn't dare head back to my car, so I hiked north to call you . . . and Vandervoort," he added maliciously. "If you intend to do anything about this, then you had better get a move on quick. It probably won't take them more than a day to clear out."

"You say you have already spoken to Vandervoort?"

"Yeah," Brogan lied. "I told him what I found and that proof is on its way to him. You can expect a call sometime this afternoon urging you to get on with it and stop stalling."

"Damn you, Brogan!" Strain snarled. "No one is stalling. What did you tell Vandervoort?"

"Exactly what I've told you."

"Then, no one else has seen this proof?" Strain persisted.

Brogan shook his head. "No, not yet anyway. But the films and the plants have been mailed to Vandervoort. INCC will have them by tomorrow at the latest, in addition to what I'll show him when he arrives . . . you too, if you can get your ass out here with some cops in the next couple of hours."

"You mailed them? From where? Athea?"

"That's right. And there's a mail pickup at noon. He'll have them by tomorrow morning."

Strain was silent for several moments, and Brogan fancied that he could hear the wheels turning. If he was right, this was just the pressure needed to make Strain act.

"All right. Tell me what happened and what you saw."

"Okay, but you call me back at this number. It's a pay phone and I'm running out of money." He gave Strain the number and hung up. A few moments later the phone rang and Brogan picked it up, receiving, as he did so, a nasty look from the old woman at this usurpation of her authority.

"It's for me, dear," he called out. "Strain? All right, here it is . . ."

For the next fifteen minutes Brogan went over in detail everything he had done since he had left Strain the night before. He described the layout of the farm as thoroughly as he could and the method by which he had derived his estimate of the number of poppy plants that could be produced. In so many words, he left the impression that he had also been able to photograph the processing laboratories and their equipment.

"Well, I would say that that puts the cap on it," Strain said calmly when he had finished. "The evidence is certainly overwhelming . . . in view of the fact that you have photographs and plant samples, or so you claim."

Brogan chuckled. "You never give up, do you. I have them, don't worry about that. And, as I said earlier, unless you want to be left holding the bag, you had better get busy."

"Yes," Strain agreed, "I guess I had better. I think you had better stay where you are. Within half an hour I will have police on the way. They will pick you up in the village and I will meet you at the farm. Where in the village are you?"

"Don't worry about that. This place is so damned small it doesn't make any difference. Right now I'm at the post office."

"All right. Stay there, then, until the police arrive. I will instruct my office to put through the call from your Mr. Vandervoort as soon as it comes in."

"Good enough. See you in a couple of hours."

Brogan hung up and walked back to the front counter, where he retrieved his pack. He nodded to the old woman, who ignored him, and feeling much better than half an hour before, he went across the street to the inn for a well-earned breakfast.

At nine-thirty, Brogan walked slowly back across the street to the post office and sat down in a rickety wooden armchair outside the front door to wait for Strain's policemen to show. A good-sized breakfast of eggs, bacon, porridge and coffee had produced a comfortably stuffed feeling that left him at peace with the world. He had done his job in spite of considerable discouragement, and done it well, and he leaned back to bask in contentment and self-congratulation.

The drizzle had stopped completely and the morning mist was beginning to thin, allowing the air to warm slightly. Brogan watched the main road of the village leading south to the hills. In less than an hour, if everything went right, the police would have arrested everyone on the farm, and that would end at least this phase of the syndicate operations. The next step would be to find out just how widespread the syndicate was. He might even consider rejoining INCC . . . under considerably changed circumstances, of course. He felt in his jacket pocket for a cigarette and found only an empty pack. With a lazy groan, he got up and went inside the store and asked the surly old woman for a package of Camels. When she said she did not have them, he settled for a packet of Players.

As he slit open the packet with a thumbnail, he heard a motor vehicle changing gears as it entered the town and he stepped to the window. He extracted and lit a cigarette as the vehicle, a dark-green Bedford van, came to a stop in front of the store and two policemen carrying shotguns got out. They were in proper uniform, but something about the way they were acting did not ring true. As he watched, it occurred to him to wonder why they had to carry shotguns to pick him up—guns were as anathema to the Irish constabulary as the British . . . then it registered on him that the van was dark green and not the deep blue of the Irish police. He looked more closely at the truck; the side panel had been hastily repainted—repainted to mark out a name. Brogan began to edge toward the back of the store just as one of them waved at the post office-store combination and the other pointed to his pack.

Cursing, Brogan turned and ran. The old woman came around the counter from her postal cage with a surprised look on her face, but Brogan pushed her aside and ducked inside to snatch the mailing carton from the mailbag. To the accompaniment of her screams, he shoved through the back door and found himself inside a storeroom with the door to the outside locked. He kicked once, twice, and it burst open as the bell over the front entrance jingled; still cursing, he sprinted across the tiny garden and vaulted the high fence. He landed heavily in a muddy alley and staggered to his feet in time to see a lorry turning out into a side street at the end of the alley. Brogan raced after it and, as it completed the turn into the street, jumped and pulled himself up and over the tailboard and under the canvas cover. He hunched down, as the lorry accelerated up the street, to watch the end of the alley. But the lorry turned again before anyone showed at the street entrance.

Brogan thought furiously, trying to reconstruct the layout of the town in his mind. The village, seen from the vantage point of the hills, consisted of three narrow streets running parallel to each other with the main street in the center. He had come out the back of the store facing the north side of the town, which placed him now on the south street of the village. Through the gaps in the houses and shops, he could see the misty green loom of the open hills. The safety they offered was tenuous at best, and therefore usable only as a last resort.

The lorry began to slow for the curve that led back onto the main road. Brogan glanced over the tailgate again to see an empty street, and as the lorry began its turn he clambered over the back and dropped to the pavement. He got to his feet, brushed himself off and walked methodically to a dingy café a hundred feet away and pushed open the door. A tiny bell jingled, and a moment later a smiling, round-faced girl pushed through the curtain from the back and wished him a good morning.

Brogan ordered a cup of coffee and took it over to the front window. He arranged a chair at a table from where he could look out but not be seen from the street, and sat down to contemplate the mess in which he now found himself. He found his hands were shaking so badly in response to the delayed shock that he could not hold the coffee cup. Abruptly, he put it down and fumbled for a cigarette.

Those two men certainly had not been police; where they had come from and how they had found him, he had no time to worry about now. The village was small enough that, even if they searched every building, it would not take them longer than an hour to find him. The entire village was surrounded by open fields leading to the hills, and no matter which way he ran, they would have him before he had gone half a mile. Yet he had to move!

He took out the parcel and turned it over in his hands. It had to get through to Vandervoort somehow . . . Could he persuade the girl to hide him?

He glanced around the café. It was rather dark and drab but clean in contrast to the appearance of the other structures on this back street. There were four tables, all nicely polished, with cane-back chairs and several framed photographs of hurling teams on the walls. The counter was a simple bench mounted on high legs, and beyond was a green-curtained alcove that contained the kitchen and probably meager living quarters as well. No good. Someone might have seen him jumping from the truck, and, besides, the place was so small he doubted if there was room to hide a mouse, let alone a man.

A phone was mounted on the wall but there was no dial. Evidently, the village had not yet received direct dialing, and all calls would have to be made through a central switchboard, in which case the first thing the phony police would have done, after chasing him out the back door of the post office, was to instruct the switchboard to pinpoint any outgoing calls from the village.

As the minutes slipped by, he had about arrived at the conclusion that a run for the hills was better than waiting for them to come and collect him, when a motorcycle rider turned down the narrow alley beside the café. A moment later a young man came in through the back, pulling off his helmet and gloves. He called out a greeting to the girl and sat down at the bar, joking with her. The room was suddenly cheery with her laughter, and grinning in response to renewed hope, Brogan dropped some coins on the table and hurried out.

He slipped around into the alley and trotted down to where the motorcycle was parked next to the rear door. It was a 350cc Kawasaki Enduro model for both street and off-track use. Luck was beginning to grant him a few favors again. Brogan kicked the stand up and wheeled it down to the bend of the alley, lifted the seat and fumbled along the ignition wires until he found the tee-joint. He examined both black leads into the connector, yanked one loose, and stamped down on the starter. The motor turned over with a mumble. Swearing, he jammed the lead back into the connector and pulled the other one. As he looked up, he caught sight of a middle-aged man hesitating across the road.

"Uh oh," he muttered, and kicked the starter down a second time. The engine, still hot, caught immediately. Brogan slammed the seat down, vaulted onto the bike and roared down the alley as the man limped toward him, motioning him to stop and shouting something about a thief. He toed the clutch into second as he hit the street and accelerated away. Behind him, the café door was flung open and the cycle's owner bolted into the street, screaming with anger. Brogan caught a glimpse of a uniform racing out of an alley ahead, but before the shotgun could be swung up, Brogan swerved and the man jumped for safety. He cut back and took the turn onto the main street dangerously fast as the shotgun boomed, and with a distinctive squeal the pellets sliced over his head as the shot went high; then he was into third gear and the street dipped and curved slightly coming out of the north end of the village, and he was out of range before a second shot could be fired.

He was doing well over eighty as he came up and over the first hill beyond the village and started down a long slope that led straight as an arrow to more hills beyond. With a groan, he twisted the grip as far as it would go and rocketed down the narrow tarmac road. The wind blasted his face and he had to squint, so that he could barely see the road. It would take them less than two minutes to get after him, and he needed those hills.

Brogan had taken the only road north from the village, and it led to Carrigkery, a straight run of some six miles or so, if he remembered the map correctly. Beyond Carrigkery another four miles was the village of Ardagh, and finally the junction with Highway T-28. But he was as certain as he had ever been of anything that if he was not off the road long before he reached Carrigkery, he would never make it to the junction.

Ahead now, the road began to climb into the hills. The roar of the cycle's powerful engine was lost in the wind whipping his ears. He risked a glance behind and saw the van just clearing the first hill at least two miles behind. The road narrowed to one lane as he crested a small rise, then became a mixture of gravel and tarmac. The road shot away on either side as he crouched low, fighting the handlebars. In spite of the obvious danger of staying on the road any longer than absolutely necessary, stone fencing on either side and fields falling away to tangles of thickets and ponds precluded any other choice.

A further few minutes of furious riding brought him to a small creek shouldering its way through the thickets to flow under a tiny bridge. Beyond, the road climbed abruptly through a narrow pass between two high hills. Just past the bridge, he spotted a narrow track that crossed the road and angled off northwest and southeast.

He braked carefully to a stop, turned the bike around and rode quickly back to the bridge, then skidded the cycle onto the turning leading southeast for a short distance before he made a narrow circle through the field and rode back to the bridge, where he dismounted. Swearing at the weight of the bike, he manhandled it over the verge so as not to leave any marks in the dust and wheeled it carefully down through the grass and weeds and into the creek. He backed the cycle under the bridge and crouched down beside it in the icy water.

A few moments later, heavy wheels thundered over the bridge above his head and the sound of the lorry dwindled in the distance. He waited a moment to make sure that no other vehicles were following, then pushed the bike out from under the bridge. Still in the stream, he climbed on, started it up and gunned the cycle straight upstream as fast as he could go until the banks were low enough to permit him to ride up and over into the fields. He headed the bike for a small copse of woods several hundred yards from the road, where he stopped to wait until the van came slowly back along the road.

It stopped on the bridge, and a man in uniform jumped out and ran back to the track. Brogan held his breath, then the distant figure waved at the road running southeast, as

Brogan hoped he would, and the van backed and swung off the bridge. The man hopped aboard as it went past and the van picked up speed, jolted down the road and over a low hillock and was lost to view.

Brogan let out an explosive sigh of relief, turned the cycle out of the trees and rode as fast as he could for the crest of the hills to the west.

14

The cycle slithered abruptly to the right, the front wheel cracked against a half-buried rock, and Brogan was jolted out of the saddle to land stunned on the soggy turf. The cycle slipped sideways, started to rear up as the clutch disengaged and crashed to the ground ten feet away.

After a few moments, Brogan sat up with a groan. He drew his knees up and ducked his head down until the surge of nausea passed.

Shortly after he had turned off the road, the sky had darkened and the drizzle had begun again, soaking the already peaty turf still further. The cycle's tires were not designed for this type of terrain, and he had fallen twice already. Stiffly, he got to his feet and limped to where the bike lay on its side, the front wheel turned half under. He struggled to bring it upright, then dragged it backwards until he could rest the kick stand on the treacherous rock that had thrown him. One of the fender braces was buckled, jamming the fender down onto the tire. Swearing in a dull monotone, he found the rudimentary tool kit under the seat and used the screw driver and universal wrench to pry the fender far enough away from the tire for it to spin freely. Brogan sank down on his haunches beside the cycle and dug out the crushed packet, and shielding a cigarette from the drizzle with a cupped hand, lit it and gave in for a few moments to his exhaustion. The combined effects of a full night's driving, a full day and night's hiking, and now three falls, had left him aching in muscles he had not known he possessed. He had been lucky so far that he had gained nothing beyond a turned ankle and a bruised shoulder.

He looked around at the grass and moss-covered hills, barren of tree or bush, and at the lowering gray sky, and was once again grateful for the unpredictable Irish weather that kept the helicopter from being pressed into the search he knew must be going on for him. He had no clear plan other than to put as much distance between himself and Athea in the most unlikely direction as possible. The car was south and east, and if he could reach that, he stood a good chance of remaining safe until Strain got his police onto the farm grounds. But until then, this barren hillside overlooking a mist-shrouded valley through which ran a main highway was no place to wait. He was soaking wet and, in his exhausted state, already risking pneumonia. Reluctantly, he stood up and started the cycle's engine. For now, he was better off staying in the hills and away from the road.

* * *

Just off the main road and inside a fringe of trees lining the golf course north of Tralee, Brogan had been waiting for almost an hour for darkness to fall and watching Highway T-28, which led into the city. Traffic was light, and so far no police cars or strange green-panel vans with the sides painted over were in evidence. He had spent the time rewiring the motorcycle's ignition circuits to make the head and tail lights work without the ignition key.

By nine-thirty he felt it was dark enough to start. He ground the cigarette out, stretched, then kicked the bike into life, bumped down through the drainage ditch and up onto the paved road. The bike ran smoothly enough after the hard day's riding in the roundabout way down from the north. Even though it had been years since he had ridden a motorcycle as a teen-ager in California, he had managed the cross-country trip well enough, he thought, with some conceit.

The traffic grew heavier as he neared the city center, and he began to feel extremely exposed. The fuel in the cycle's tank was dwindling fast, which posed an immediate problem, as his wallet was still in the pack, which he had last seen leaning against the wall of the post office thirty miles north in Athea. He had thirty pence in change from the cigarettes, and if he used that to buy gas, there would be nothing left for food and he was ravenous—not that thirty pence would buy much more than a few candy bars.

A boulevard led off to the east to skirt the main section of town, and Brogan swung onto it and rode along for several miles as it faded from residential to shops to industrial and back to shops again. By ten o'clock night had settled down completely, and so had the level of gas in the cycle's tank. He spotted a collection of small shops ahead and, to their side, a narrow, deep car park. This was as good a place as any, he decided, and idled the cycle to the edge of the road.

The street was empty in both directions and all the shops appeared closed. The few houses along the way were lit but tightly curtained. Brogan took a deep breath and walked the cycle back into the shadows of the car park.

He parked the bike and scouted along the back fence until he found a relatively clean soft-drink bottle. He chose a late-model Hillman parked in the deepest shadows, crawled under the back and scrunched around until he could reach the gas tank. With his penknife, he managed to poke a small hole where the metal of the tank curved to seat a restraining strap. After much swearing and a sleeve soaked with gasoline, he got the bottle filled. He scrambled out and dumped the petrol into the cycle's tank. The performance was repeated several times until the tank was reasonably full.

He cleaned the mud off his clothes as best he could and, having calmed down to the point where he no longer felt any animosity toward the car he had just drained of its fuel, he wrote down the registration number. Assuming he got out of this alive, the least INCC could do would be to repair the damage. As an afterthought, he also noted down the motorcycle's number. A few minutes later, he carefully edged the bike out to the deserted street and started the engine. At the next intersection he turned south and kept on going until he came to a roundabout, where signs pointed to Highway T-28. Brogan spotted a post box ahead and drew over to the side of the street and dropped the somewhat bedraggled package into the box. A few minutes later he was heading east out of Tralee, on T-28, munching one of the four candy bars his thirty pence had bought.

* * *

Brogan burrowed deeper into the straw, sneezed at the dust he stirred, and sat up to stare dully about in the gloom of the old barn. A faint gray light that did little more than suggest dawn filtered through the single dirty window near the door. He was tired and he was sore and the night spent in the clammy straw had not helped either condition.

Reluctantly, he got up and stumbled over to the door and shoved it open a crack. Steel-gray rain pelted down with a vengeance, and a cool wind blew in bringing a breath of fresh air to the stuffy dampness of the barn's interior. Brogan took a deep breath and stepped back inside. He peeled off his clothes and went out into the stinging rain to let its refreshing chill wash the dirt and sweat of two nights and days from him.

He used his shirt to dry himself, then built a small fire of straw and broken wood. While he sat staring at the flames, he munched the last of the candy bars.

A hell of a fix, he thought to himself. Unable, because of sheer exhaustion, to ride any further the night before, the loom of the barn against the night sky had been heaven-sent. He dressed and wandered over to stare through the window. The rain fell in long slanting streamers with vicious force, as if it wished to wash all traces of human habitation from the famed emerald hills of Kerry. Through the driving rain Brogan could see an occasional vehicle passing on the distant highway below. Beyond, he could barely make out the faint loom of hills separating the inland of County Kerry from the coastal area around Castlemaine Harbor some twenty miles southwest.

With his pack containing all his money as well as his pistol abandoned outside the Athea post office, he was in no position to threaten anyone overtly. His main danger to the syndicate came from what he knew, but by now Strain's people should have dealt with them. When the rain let up, he intended to ride north to his car and return to Dublin, where he could call Vandervoort and Sandra from Strain's office.

Brogan wandered about the empty barn, poking into corners,

snooping around for something useful; the only thing he turned up was a broken broom and a rusty piece of a sickle blade. He was wasting time, he knew, but he dared not ride in the rain. Without even so much as a raincoat, the first policeman who passed on the highway was bound to stop him to find out why he didn't have sense enough to stay in out of the rain.

He walked out under the overhang of the roof and stood watching the rain. Except for the highway and an occasional car, there was no other sign of human habitation as far as he could see. It was as if the rain was a shroud for all of the dead—men and dreams—of Ireland's past. It had been the same all down the western coast; mile after mile of empty land, marked here and there with weathered traces of crumbled or sunken stone fences, grassy mounds that had once been farm outbuildings, a ragged pile of mortared stone all that remained of a farmhouse. Famine and emigration had emptied the countryside of half its population, and still, a century later, the nation had not recovered. Shrugging, he turned back inside and leaned against the window, railing inwardly at the rain which forced him into inactivity. On the highway below, a brief flurry of traffic attracted his attention. The road led down a long, steep hill toward Killarney, but even so, there had not been a great deal of activity, probably because of the storm. A slow-moving lorry-trailer combination cleared the top of the grade and started down the far side, gathering speed as it went. The trailer was painted emerald green, and drawn in distinctive yellow letters on its side . . . "Mists of Tralee."

Brogan swore in surprise. The green lorry was already halfway down the grade, disappearing around the bend with the dull grinding noise of its engine floating back as Brogan yanked open the door and scrambled down the hill. The rain flurried to soak his jacket and levis, but he was too angry to notice. The truck rounded the bend and disappeared, and Brogan stopped, swearing volubly. After a moment he turned and trudged back up the hill toward the barn, wondering.

Sixty feet or so from the door, an outcropping of rock forced the path to turn away to higher ground. Glancing down the sweep of highway to the west from this meager vantage point,

Brogan spotted a second green-painted lorry beginning the long climb to the summit. Not even daring to hope, he climbed quickly up on the rock and watched until, reaching into a long curve, the trailer showed enough side panel for Brogan to pick out a flash of yellow.

Stunned, he stared at the distant lorry-trailer as the rain beat down harder, obscuring the highway, and wondered what the hell had happened. How in the name of God had they . . . where in hell was Strain . . . ? Suddenly, Brogan went cold, far colder than the effect of the driving rain, as the realization of what had happened broke the enthrallment, galvanizing him. He ran for the barn.

He rooted through the debris he had turned over earlier until he found the broken sickle blade and the broom handle. He snapped the broom handle over his knee to provide a piece of wood six inches long, and with the nylon hood tie from his jacket, he bound the rusty blade to the wooden handle to form a rough but serviceable knife, which he stuck into his jacket pocket. Then he wheeled the motorcycle to the doorway, started it up and rode gingerly down the muddy path to the highway. A quick glance as he passed the outcropping showed him that the lorry was less than halfway up the steep grade and moving very slowly, with no other vehicles in sight.

Accordingly, he took the bike out onto the slippery pavement as if the mud did not exist and blasted straight down the hill, wincing at the angry pain in his upper thighs and crotch. Just below the crest of the hill a sharp, right-angled curve hid the crest. Brogan slowed the bike, cut sharply across the highway and slid off as it crossed the verge. The bike slithered down the rise, jumped the narrow, rain-wet ditch and buried itself in the thick bushes. The motor sputtered once and died. After making sure that the bike was well hidden from the road, Brogan pushed partway into the dripping bushes and, moments later, caught the sound of the lorry's engine changing down for the last time below the crest.

The lorry cab edged into view and ground past at a walking pace. Brogan could clearly see the driver's bored expression as he lounged back in the seat, one hand on the wheel and the other on the gearshift lever—the driver and only the driver.

There was no guard, as he had half expected, nor was a car following, as the view from the top of the rock outcropping had shown him.

As the lorry passed the stand of bushes, Brogan sprang out and sprinted along the trailer, jumped for the running board of the cab and grabbed desperately at the door handle. His muddy boots slipped on the grated metal and he threw himself forward with his last ounce of strength and yanked down on the handle. The door wrenched open and he had just time enough to shift his balance, snatch the makeshift knife from his pocket and throw himself into the cab, where he stretched full length across the seat and jabbed the sharp point of the sickle blade under the startled driver's chin.

For a moment, too winded to say or do anything more, he lay across the seat, then the door banged painfully against his legs. He kicked it open and drew himself inside, careful to keep the blade pressed against the driver's throat.

"Don't do anything but drive . . . or this goes right through your windpipe," he managed to gasp.

The truck by now was almost to the crest and veering dangerously toward the shoulder. He punctuated the threat with a jab, and hastily the driver straightened the lorry. Brogan set one knee on the edge of the seat and watched the road. "There, to the left . . . up that track."

The engine roared as the driver swung off the road and onto the slippery mud of the track.

"It's worth your life if this thing gets stuck," Brogan warned.

The lorry struggled up the slippery embankment, wheels spinning on the wet mud and rock. Frantically, the driver downshifted until the lorry was in first gear. The wheels spun again, cut through the mud to the firmer soil beneath and lurched forward. The driver's face was covered with perspiration and his hands were shaking on the wheel.

Brogan had him stop in front of the barn, then reverse the lorry around until it was pointing back down the track. "Brakes," he growled, and the driver set the emergency brakes on the lorry and trailer.

"All right, follow me out of the cab, slowly."

The driver stared wildly at him, then down at the makeshift

knife. Brogan pushed open the door and backed out, free hand grasping the driver's jacket, until they were both standing on the ground next to the cab. Brogan spun him around, kicked his feet apart and pushed him forward against the cab door. Satisfied that the man was unarmed, Brogan punched him hard above the kidneys. The driver dropped to his knees with a scream, and at the same time Brogan grabbed a handful of hair and jerked his head back. The man's throat was fully exposed, and Brogan raised the blade until it came down into his line of vision. The driver's eyes, pupils dilated in terror, rolled from him to the blade and back again.

Brogan set the point against his throat. "Where were you going?" he asked softly.

The driver swallowed and moved his lips but could manage only a heavy croaking sound. Brogan lifted the blade a bit and asked again. "Where were you going?"

"West . . . to Cork . . ."

"Where in Cork?" Brogan prompted with undeceptive gentleness.

"Pier 23 . . . some kind ship . . . man named Angelo."

Brogan nodded. "What are you carrying?"

The driver shook his head but, as the knife approached his throat again, said quickly, "Wine . . . just wine. Take it . . ."

"This isn't a hijacking, fella, and you aren't carrying just wine, are you?" he asked with a smile.

"Just wine . . . that's all."

"Just wine?" Brogan smiled again. "What about the heroin?"

The driver stared at him in surprise, forgetting his fear until Brogan jabbed him lightly with the knife.

"That's right. Heroin. What were you going to do with the heroin after you delivered the truck to Angelo?"

"Nothing . . . just deliver . . . I got nothing to do with that stuff."

"Don't give me that crap," Brogan snapped. "You aren't Irish. You're an American or a Canadian. And there's no reason to import truck drivers unless the cargo is very special . . . is there? Now, what were you going to do with the heroin?"

The man shook his head as much as the knife would allow. "Nothing, so help me God. I was supposed to take it to Angelo.

He does the rest. I don't even know where in the truck the stuff is hid or how much there is."

Brogan pressed the blade harder.

"So help me, I don't," the man whispered. "My God. I'd tell you if I did . . ."

"What about the police raid?"

Surprise showed in the man's eyes again.

"Police raid," Brogan prodded.

"What police? . . . there was no raid . . ."

"Damn it," Brogan swore and yanked the terrified man to his feet, then shoved him toward the barn. The man stumbled and fell through the door, but Brogan grabbed him by the collar and pulled him up again and hit him hard with a roundhouse knee to the midsection. The driver folded with a gasp and Brogan hit him behind the ear, hard, with his fist, and he collapsed in a heap, unconscious.

Brogan stood above the prostrate body, breathing hard, and stared down at the upturned face smeared with mud. He recognized him now as one of the men in London, the one who had gone out the back door of the boutique on Knightsbridge. He unwrapped the nylon line from the makeshift knife and tied him securely, both arms on either side of a stone pillar supporting the roof. It would be a long time before he got loose.

Then he walked thoughtfully out to the truck, wondering, now that he had it, what the hell he was going to do with it. The barn was too small to drive it inside, and besides, as soon as the syndicate discovered it was missing they would be out in force, backtracking along the route. And the barn on the hill was just too obvious to pass up. Yet, where could he take it? Tralee was out. If the truck disappeared in this area, it would be the first place they'd search.

He rummaged through the glove box and seat pockets until he found a map of southern Ireland. After a few minutes' study, he concluded that he had a choice of three routes: west to Tralee, south to Killarney and Bantry Bay, and finally, east to the Cork area. All three directions were on main roads, and main roads were going to become damned dangerous very shortly. Bantry Bay and Killarney were the closest, but they were also the most logical. Besides, there was only one main road through MacGillicuddy's Reek's, and that was T-65. The few supplementary roads displayed on the map would be little more than tracks in some places, and he doubted that he could manage the heavy lorry over those hills on anything but a main road. In effect, that left only Cork, some eighty-five miles distant.

Brogan studied the map carefully, noting the series of secondary roads that led in an easterly direction to Cork. They would not move the heroin without some system of checkpoints along the way, and it would not take the syndicate long to realize that he was neither moving west to Tralee nor south to Bantry Bay. Within two hours at the outside, he could expect them to be concentrating their search along Highway T-28. But the web of secondary roads ought to provide a slight chance. The distance to Cork was too great to offer any reliable odds, but if he could find a town large enough to have a sizable police force, he just might stand a chance. Highway T-28 ended at Castleisland, a town with a population of less than a thousand. The next town west on the secondary road, L-9, was Kantur, again a village, and beyond that, nearly sixty miles distant, was Mallow. Mallow had a small airfield, and the population of five thousand just might require four or five policemen, enough anyway to hold out until reinforcements could arrive from Cork, providing he was able to convince the Mallow police of the seriousness of the situation.

Brogan considered the route. It was on a link road, which meant that it should at least be paved and therefore wouldn't be knee-deep in mud. The distance he would have to go on T-28 was very short, no more than eight miles. The area between Castleisland and Mallow was full of hills, thus increasing his chances—as long as the rain held. So, all things considered, Mallow might just provide his best chance.

He went back to the barn, where he found the lorry driver regaining consciousness. As he bent down to go through his pockets, the man began cursing him. Brogan cuffed him alongside the head. When that didn't stop the flow of profanity, Brogan hit him harder. Without a word then, he extracted the man's wallet and found thirty pounds in notes.

At the door, he turned. "As soon as I can, I'll get word to the police to come and cut you loose. Until then . . . be a good boy."

Laughing as the cursing began again, Brogan slammed the door shut, walked down to the lorry and climbed aboard. He had a bit of difficulty until he discovered that the trailer's brakes were on a different system than the lorry's. The engine started easily enough and Brogan eased the engine into gear and edged gingerly down the muddy track to the highway. The road was clear in both directions and he drove onto the pavement and turned east on T-28.

The lorry ran easily down the long grade and Brogan found that it needed no more than a slight touch on the brakes to keep the speed from becoming excessive. He wished that there had been time to examine the load, but he did not dare risk the time. The rear door was secured with a heavy padlock and sealed, and it would have taken too much valuable time to break it open.

Commissioner Brian Strain, my very good friend, he thought bitterly. Girls, parties, good times. Sure, someone had been pressuring Strain to keep the lid on, his mouth shut and his ministry inactive in the face of the evidence Brogan had presented to him. He had done so because he was part of the heroin syndicate. There hadn't been any raid, nor would there ever have been. Why had the phony cops shown so fast? Because he had told Strain exactly where he was. If they had gotten him, there would have been no one left to threaten the syndicate heroin operation. Brogan would have been dead, the evidence in the form of photographs and the sample plants destroyed, and he would have been discredited by INCC, who had ignored his findings all along. He would have met with an unfortunate accident, probably somewhere outside the country, and everything he had done, all the circumstantial evidence he had gathered, would have been filed away under *C* for crackpot and forgotten.

But he was still alive and the packet containing the films and the poppy samples was safely on its way to London. Even Strain could not stop that now . . . "Oh, hell!" he roared in anger, then broke into uncontrollable laughter at the way he had been neatly boxed.

Strain was the Assistant Commissioner of Customs and, as such, he had the authority to order all packages entering or leaving the country held for inspection . . . personal inspection if needed. As soon as his phony policemen searched the post office and found the package missing, they would have notified Strain immediately and he simply would have put in a call to the postal authorities to hold any packages addressed to London for his inspection. Not only were the chances very good that he had the package by now, but he also would know exactly from where it had been mailed and at approximately what time.

Damned and double damned, and nothing he could do about it. Without his passport, credentials, pistol, and with little money, he was completely isolated.

The rain beat fiercely against the lorry's windscreen for a moment, as if it too felt his anger. The rain was a shroud, all right, he thought—not for Ireland, but for him. And even the hope that Sandra had been able to convince Vandervoort to act without the evidence contained in the packet was now dead. There had been no raid and the syndicate was moving heroin, probably clearing up in case he managed to slip past them again. For Christ's sake, he was sitting in their damned truck, wasn't he? "Strain, you bastard," he snarled aloud.

As the lorry came down off the grade, Brogan jammed the accelerator pedal to the floor and the lorry gathered speed. A banked curve showed ahead and the unit swung easily into the curve, picking up speed until the speedometer was hovering near eighty. The road was rain-slick and Brogan could feel the trailer begin to fishtail at every bump. Nursing the wheel, he kept the speed as high as he dared.

Castleisland was in sight in a few minutes, and Brogan slowed enough to meet the speed limit and pushed on through the small town, anxious that the first lorry might have halted to wait for him. On the east side of the village the highway turned south. Brogan slowed for the traffic circle, slipped into it and bore around to the far side, where a small sign pointed to Kantur and gave the distance as thirty-two miles.

Five miles east of Castleisland the road began to worsen until it was little more than a single-lane road. The term "paving" was a joke, but what little there was at least served to keep the mud down. In places, Brogan was forced to slow the truck to less than ten miles an hour. In all, it took nearly sixty minutes to reach the tiny crossroads village of Scartaglin. Cursing the Republic's highway-maintenance department, he slowed the lorry and stopped it outside the village pub. As he climbed down, he noticed one or two children running to see what was happening, and as an afterthought, he reached in and pulled the keys from the ignition and locked the door. The owner of the pub came to the door and waited with arms folded as Brogan walked up.

"We are not open for another two hours yet," he scowled, his voice full of the broad accents of Ivernia. Obviously he did not approve of lorry drivers who stopped in out-of-the-way villages to take a drink.

Brogan smiled what he hoped was a friendly smile and nodded. "Yeah, I know. But I need to use a telephone."

His face lightened a little at that. "Well, in that case, you're welcome to use mine. Just inside the door there."

As he followed Brogan inside, he pointed to the phone on the wall—direct dial, Brogan noted with relief.

"You're a Yank, aren't you? Driving for that crazy man who owns the Mists of Tralee farm." He shook his head. "Trying to make wine in Ireland. He must be daft."

Brogan swung around to face him. "Do you know the owner?"

The barman smiled widely. "Know *of* him, that is. Never met him. Some say he's a politician in Dublin. He's something to do with the government. Imagine, him thinking he can grow grapes under tents," and he laughed expansively.

So he had something to do with the government, Brogan thought as he dug a ten-pound Irish note out of the wallet he had lifted from the driver.

"Can you give me change for the telephone, about three pounds' worth, and fix some bacon-and-egg sandwiches and coffee for me? I haven't had any breakfast yet."

The barman nodded. "Take about ten minutes, but I don't

have that much change this early. Call the operator, tell her to put your call through. You can pay me when you leave."

"Great, thanks for the help, and look, put the sandwiches and coffee in a bag, will you? I'm running behind schedule."

The barman handed him a five-pence piece and nodded. Brogan dialed the operator and deposited the coin, explained how to charge the call and asked for the London number of INCC headquarters.

15

"Cole, I've been trying to telephone you everywhere . . . What's happened? Where are you? Are you all right?"

"Easy, Sandi, slow down, I'm okay now. Has Vandervoort gotten anything started yet?"

"Cole, I want to know where you are, right this very minute. Otherwise, I won't tell you a thing!"

Brogan laughed happily. "Stubborn woman! All right, you win. Our friend Strain turns out to be hand-in-glove with the syndicate. He sent some of his gunmen after me."

Brogan heard Sandra gasp. "It's all right," he added hastily. "They couldn't catch me. When I'm scared I run faster than an Olympic sprinter."

"But how . . . Strain? How can he . . . ?"

"Right after I finished talking to you yesterday, I called Strain and told him what I had found. He told me to stay put, that he was sending some police to take me back to the farm, where he would meet me. He sent police all right; but they weren't *police,* just his people dressed up in uniforms. I got away. It's as simple as that."

"Cole, tell me the truth. Are you all right?"

"Of course I am. If I wasn't, I wouldn't be talking to you, would I?"

Sandra thought that over for a moment. "All right, then, where are you now?"

"I'm in a little village called Scartaglin, east of Tralee about thirty or so miles. I managed to hijack one of their lorries a little while ago. Damned thing's loaded with heroin . . . I hope. Apparently they thought they had me finished off and that it was safe to move. Either that or they are clearing out and couldn't resist this last shipment. Anyway, they pushed their luck a little too far this time. I'm going to take the lorry to Mallow. There should be a big enough police force there to hang on to it in case they try a power play. Now, what about Vandervoort?"

Sandra's voice was thin and distant over the phone, and Brogan realized that she was close to tears. "I don't know, Cole, I honestly don't. He listened to me, very politely. Then he took me up to the director and had me repeat your story. Neither one of them seemed to be paying much attention. The director said that they would wait for your package to arrive. I've been watching the mail all day and it still hasn't come."

"Damn, damn, damn!" Brogan pounded the wall in frustration.

"Cole, what's wrong? What's the matter?"

Brogan managed a semicoherent explanation of his fears concerning the package, concluding, "If it hasn't arrived by now, then it never will. Sandra," he said forcefully, "you've got to make Vandervoort move anyway. Strain is tied in with the syndicate somehow; I'm one hundred per cent certain of that. Anything I do from this end is automatically blocked unless I get through with that lorry. And that's a damned long shot. Vandervoort has got to act—and fast!"

He took a deep breath to calm himself and nodded absently to the barman as he came back with a paper sack containing the sandwiches and coffee.

"Cole, tell me what to do. Vandervoort is not going to take any action until he sees your proof. I'm certain of that. I don't know what else there is to do . . ." Sandra started to sob openly.

"Hey, just a minute," Brogan cut in. "Stop bawling. You can't help that way. But there is something you can do. I don't know why I didn't think of this sooner. Call Charlie in Washington. Lay out the situation to him. Make him understand the urgency. Maybe he can get someone to act from that end. But make sure he understands that Strain is involved up to his neck with the syndicate. Tell him to go directly to the Irish Home Office, and the higher up the better."

"I'll do my best," Sandra sniffled. "But I don't know . . .

What are you going to be doing . . . Cole? Leave that damned silly lorry and get out of there . . . !"

"Sandi, I wouldn't do that if I could. For one thing, where am I going to go? I'm in the middle of Ireland with no other transportation except the lorry. No, I can't leave it. As soon as I hang up I'm going on to Mallow. If all else fails and I get through, a load of heroin ought to stir something up. Look, Sandi, I've spent too much time here, as it is. Get through to Charlie and then go back and work on Vandervoort some more. Tell him I've got a truck full of the stuff and he's going to look like a damned fool if I bring it in without his help."

"Cole, now wait a minute . . ." Sandra started to protest angrily, but Brogan blew a kiss through the phone and hung up, his face grim. He hurried to the counter, peeled off a ten-pound note and grabbed up the sandwiches. "That ought to cover the phone call . . ." Surprised, the barman did not even have time to object before Brogan was gone.

Outside, he shooed the children away from the lorry, unlocked the door and climbed inside. The engine started immediately and he swung onto the road and barreled through the town, pushing fifty by the time he reached the outskirts. He dug open the bag with one hand, fished out a sandwich and, munching mechanically, began the long struggle to again keep the lorry on the miserable road.

* * *

The road wound down and along the eastern fringes of the Mullaghareirk Mountains, lowering and ugly under the cloud-covered sky. As he drove eastward, the road worsened rapidly until all traces of paving died away, leaving a deeply rutted gravel surface that slowed him to less than twenty miles an hour. There were still almost fifty miles to where the Link road joined T-30, twelve miles or so west of Mallow . . . Brogan dared stretch his luck on a main highway no further than that. But if this road got any worse, he knew he would be forced to turn south and join Highway T-30 at a point more than thirty miles west of Mallow, whether he wanted to or not. If the rain and heavy cloud cover continued, anyone searching for him would be restricted to surface vehicles, and the longer he stayed on the back roads, the less chance of being spotted.

But Brogan's luck seemed to have finally run out. It was shortly after noon and he had just passed through the tiny village of Newmarket when the rain stopped—for good this time. The road, which had improved on the approaches to the village, worsened on the far side, forcing him to a crawl again. As the afternoon began to lengthen, the cloud cover withdrew until first the mountain slopes and then the peaks were clear and the afternoon sunshine broke through the haze in a burst of Irish gold.

He saw the helicopter before he heard it—a bright pinpoint that came slipping down the long flank of the sunlit hill and skimmed across the wet fields of the deserted valley toward the road, where it pulled into a tight orbit around the lorry. Satisfied that it had located its quarry, the copter roared off half a mile and settled carefully down into the middle of the road.

It was the Sikorsky passenger helicopter that he had seen two days before on the farm. As its blades braked to a halt, the cabin door slid open and three armed men stepped out. One of them raised his rifle and fired. Brogan flinched but the bullet punched a neat little hole in the glass on the passenger side and literally exploded inside the padded seatback, spraying foam rubber and plastic around the cab. The stink of melted rubber pervaded the cab instantly, and if the shot had been meant to serve as a warning, Brogan thought, it had been highly effective. He flipped on the brake lights and slowed the lorry to a walking pace.

As the truck drew nearer, Brogan could see that the face behind the rifle muzzle was calm and confident. The other two men leaned against the helicopter's fuselage, their weapons cradled. There was nothing else that he could do. A narrow stone wall lined one side of the road and a small creek ran through the field not far away on the other. So he halted the lorry twenty feet from the copter, drew a deep breath, shoved open the door and stepped down with his hands behind his head and waited.

The man with the raised rifle lowered it to Brogan's midsection. The other two men grinned at each other, and one of them banged on the helicopter's side.

"Good afternoon, Mr. Brogan," a thin, dapperly dressed individual greeted him as he stepped down. "You seem to have led us quite a chase." There was a faint smile on his face but no answering humor in his eyes. He stopped in front of Brogan.

"My name is MacArthur. I see that you have our truck. Still in sound condition, I trust?" Brogan, in spite of being scared stiff, could tell that the man was enjoying himself. MacArthur motioned to one of the men, who trotted around the back of the trailer. Brogan heard the doors being opened, and MacArthur studied Brogan minutely until the man returned, nodded and handed him a cardboard wine carton.

"So the seals are still in place," he observed. "What was the matter, Mr. Brogan? You did not check the cargo? Was your curiosity not sufficiently aroused? It seems to have been piqued by just about everything else."

Brogan grinned but did not reply. He was not certain that his bravado could be extended any further. To hide his shaking knees, he shifted from one foot to the other. MacArthur motioned again and the man who had checked the seals yanked Brogan's arms down in front and fastened on a pair of handcuffs.

"Tightly now." MacArthur laughed and the gunman complied, squeezing the cuffs tightly together, cutting the circulation in his wrists instantly. He handed the keys to MacArthur, who turned back to the helicopter. Two of the guards climbed into the lorry and started the engine. The other guard pushed Brogan into the helicopter and jostled him down the aisle and into a rearward-facing seat in the back of the cabin. Then he sat down opposite and laid his cut-down Browning shotgun across his lap so that it was pointing at Brogan's chest. MacArthur placed the carton in a front seat and walked down the aisle. He gave Brogan a grin full of hard confidence, then jerked his thumb at the pilot, who had turned to watch from the cockpit.

The engines started with a whine, caught, and the two big

turbines spun the blades up to speed. The beat changed as the pilot increased pitch, and a moment later the helicopter went up like an express elevator. Below, Brogan could see the lorry grind forward until it was lost to view as the copter swung west by north and headed out over the empty meadows toward the mountains.

The helicopter flashed across the wet fields, which had become golden-green in the late-afternoon sun. A tiny dirt track, no more than a thread, ran along the foot of the mountains and a herd of sheep strayed along the lower slopes. The copter reached cruising altitude and the harsh whine of the turbines slid down to a muted roar. MacArthur glanced across the aisle at him, nodded absently to the guard and opened his briefcase on the seat in front of him. For some minutes he busied himself with a sheaf of papers while Brogan watched the misty green hills unroll beneath, bitterly contemplating the terrible luck—and his own stupidity—that had dogged him for the past three days.

It was pure luck—good on the syndicate's part and bad on his part—that the skies had cleared enough for the helicopter to go aloft, and even more luck that they found him at all. He had relied on Vandervoort, expecting him to move quickly after the package had arrived. But then he had not allowed for the possibility that the package might not arrive. In view of Vandervoort's past unwillingness to take his word for anything, that had been stupid. Then he had put his reliance in Strain, only to find that he was deeply involved in the syndicate's operation. That was careless. And finally, he had been hoping that the fickle Irish weather, never famed for clear skies, would hold an hour or two more until he reached Mallow. That was ridiculous.

"I have certain questions for you, Mr. Brogan," MacArthur said and snapped his briefcase closed.

Brogan glanced at him but did not answer.

"Mr. Brogan," he said patiently, "I hope you understand that nothing will be served by any refusal on your part to cooperate. It can only cause you much pain."

Brogan turned away and MacArthur said sharply, "You do understand, don't you? While there is not much room in a helicopter, Connor here can still inflict a great deal of pain. Show him, Connor," he said quickly.

There was not even time to turn his head before Connor kicked him hard across the shin. Brogan gasped and Connor hit him a staggering blow on the chest, driving the wind from his lungs. He retched and doubled up, but Connor yanked his head back by the hair and smashed a solid fist against his cheekbone, then let him drop half onto the floor.

MacArthur waited calmly while he recovered his breath and struggled back up onto the seat. "You see, Mr. Brogan, a great deal of pain."

Brogan, gasping for air, forced himself into a sitting position. His chest felt as if the rib cage had been shattered with a sledge hammer. Every breath was agony, yet his laboring lungs demanded more air. Vying for attention was his leg, where Connor's heavy boot had most probably peeled a long strip of skin away. Strangely enough, his face had not yet begun to hurt, even though a thin line of blood was dribbling from his mouth and his jaw refused to work properly.

MacArthur smiled at him. "Connor spent several years with the IRA Provisionals in the North, and you might say that he is a specialist in obtaining information. Sometimes his methods do seem a little heavy-handed, but they work . . . quite well."

Brogan spat a gobbet of blood on the floor, narrowly missing Connor's boot.

"You son of a bitch," he muttered and braced himself for the next blow, but MacArthur shook his head.

"That bastard can kill me," Brogan said between gasps, "but that won't get you any information."

MacArthur considered a moment, then reached for his briefcase. He placed it on his lap, turned it so that Brogan could see, and opened the top. Several plastic pockets were attached to the lining and contained a series of vials and two hypodermic syringes.

"That is true, Mr. Brogan. However, Connor and I have been together for some years now. If he fails to elicit the correct responses to my questions, then it is my turn. The correct dosage of scopalamine never fails to do the trick. Now, Connor . . ."

Connor handed the shotgun across the cabin to MacArthur and caught Brogan a stinging blow on the backswing. His head thudded back against the seat and Connor swung his foot at the other leg. Brogan was ready for him this time and, as he shifted, his own boot came up swiftly to catch Connor just below the kneecap. The man stumbled back and Brogan followed up with a kick to the groin, which Connor, twisting desperately, took on his thigh. Brogan was half out of the seat when MacArthur hit him in the side with the shotgun stock, knocking him against the window. Connor staggered up and hit him twice, fore- and backhand across the face, then once hard, in the stomach. Brogan thudded to the cabin floor and Connor, swearing like a madman, kicked him several times before MacArthur could push him away.

"You ass! We don't want him dead yet! Sit down and take hold of yourself!"

Connor staggered back to his seat, grabbing the shotgun from MacArthur, who bent over Brogan and rolled him around to where he could examine his injuries. Brogan was unconscious and bleeding from the nose and mouth. One eye was beginning to swell badly and the leg of his jeans was soaked with blood. MacArthur examined the leg and satisfied himself that it was not broken, then looked over at Connor.

"Stupid! That's what you are, stupid! Use your head. This man is dangerous. He's managed to hide from us for three days after breaking into the farm. He killed Marcy and he managed to get hold of that truck somehow." MacArthur took a deep breath. "Now, put him back in the seat and keep yourself under control. And don't let him hit you again," he finished witheringly.

The Slieve Mish Mountains were in sight below before Brogan revived. He groaned several times and Connor shoved him back into the seat as he started to slide to the floor. With the help of a wet towel and some brandy, they managed to bring him awake and sitting up of his own accord.

It was as if he were staring at them through a dark tunnel. As they talked, their voices echoed around and around in his brain and nothing would stay in focus. When he rubbed a hand across his forehead, he found it covered with sweat, and only then did he realize he was both feverish and nauseated. MacArthur pried his mouth open and forced another long swallow of brandy down his throat. The shock of the liquor cleared away some of the disorientation, and as MacArthur started to peel back an eyelid, Brogan shook him off irritably.

MacArthur sat back and studied him for a moment, as if trying to determine whether or not he was fully conscious.

"Well, Mr. Brogan," he said after a moment. "You have returned to us. I was not sure that you would. Connor lost his temper and almost beat you to death."

Brogan had no trouble believing him. His body was an amazing assortment of aches and needlelike pains, and he could barely see through his swelling left eye. He had taken most of Connor's kicks on his arms until he lost consciousness, but two or three had landed on his ribs and back.

"Now, Mr. Brogan, are you ready to answer my questions?"

Brogan leaned his head back against the seat and shut his eyes. "Hell, . . . I . . . if you . . . keep . . . bastard off . . ."

"All right, then, but remember we still have the drugs to work with if you don't co-operate. And I can make the administration and the effects much more painful than Connor's tender ministrations—much more painful than you would believe possible."

Brogan nodded as if too dazed and weak to resist further.

"That is much better. Much better. I do not mind admitting that you have caused us a great deal of trouble with your resourcefulness. Now, from what you told Mr. Strain several days ago, your attention was first drawn to Ireland and the farm by information supplied to you from the American Bureau of Narcotics and Dangerous Drugs. Is that correct?"

When Brogan did not answer, a pained expression worked its way across MacArthur's face.

"Come now, Mr. Brogan. You are making things very difficult for yourself."

He waited patiently for several moments, and when Brogan still did not answer, he reached over and opened his attaché case again, turning it so that Brogan could see the syringes and vials of amber-colored fluid. He selected a syringe, filled it from one of the bottles, then depressed the plunger to squirt the excess from the barrel. Brogan eyed the amber drops which had fallen onto his arm.

"All right," he mumbled. There was absolutely no doubt in his mind as to the outcome of this helicopter ride for himself, and nothing would be gained by being drugged into immobility.

"That is much better, Mr. Brogan," MacArthur nodded. He replaced the syringe in the briefcase but did not close the cover. "The questioning process, as I said before, can be very painful, and the side effects protracted and severe."

Brogan snorted and eased his head around. "Side effects . . . are the least of my concerns . . ."

MacArthur smiled but said nothing.

"Now, Mr. Brogan, the question once again. The information was first supplied to you by BNDD in Washington . . ."

Brogan nodded his aching head as much as the cramped neck muscles would allow.

"And you were once employed by BNDD several years ago?"

Brogan nodded again and closed his eyes. ". . . very thorough."

"Oh yes, Mr. Brogan. We even know that you resigned from BNDD . . ." (he held up a hand) ". . . but that was only to cover up the fact that you had overstepped your authority in apprehending a drug dealer who was under surveillance by another agent. In fact, you were fired."

". . . bastard drugged, raped . . . killed a fifteen-year-old . . . girl."

"And she was the daughter of a close friend, and so you beat him half to death. Yes, we know all about that episode and about your famous temper. But we are not concerned with your past history now. The information that BNDD supplied to you was procured by satellite surveillance, was it not?"

Brogan started to laugh, but choked and broke into a coughing spell. "You bastard . . ."

MacArthur smiled briefly. "Come now, Mr. Brogan, no hard feelings. I do not mind admitting that the satellite surveillance system has become a real obstacle to our operations."

Brogan leaned back and stared at him. "Yeah, it sure as

hell has . . . how much time and money" (he swallowed hard) ". . . spend developing . . . poppy?"

"Let us just say it was a very expensive program, and let it go at that. You can understand, of course, that we are not about to let you or anyone else interfere with our operations."

"If you kill me, INCC . . . going to start checking," he whispered. His throat was full of phlegm and blood, and talking was becoming very difficult.

"But you have resigned, haven't you? Why should they bother . . ."

"Why?" Brogan repeated. "INCC is a bureaucracy . . ." Brogan broke into a coughing spell. MacArthur motioned and Connor yanked his head back and tipped the brandy bottle into his mouth, then used the towel to wipe away the blood and sweat from Brogan's face.

"Bureaucracy hates paperwork . . . not complete. I resigned, didn't sign release forms. They'll look for me."

MacArthur shrugged. "If that is of any real importance. In any event, you will no longer be concerned with what happens, will you?"

"A revenge killing . . . ? Thought the professionals . . . didn't kill for revenge."

"A fallacy, Mr. Brogan. And in your case there are practical considerations, not the least of which is the fact that you know too much." MacArthur glanced at his watch. "Now, time is running short . . . for both of us. The confirmation did come from the satellite surveillance system, did it not?"

"Only confirmed suspicions."

"Then the surveillance is worldwide and not just over suspected growing areas?"

He roused himself with an effort. "No . . . it was accidental."

"What exactly do you mean by that? The satellite system did spot the acetic anhydride source, did it not?"

Brogan smiled, half to himself, and forced his head back so that he could look directly at MacArthur. "Routine maintenance run . . . pure accident . . ."

MacArthur was thunderstruck. "How could . . . the chances are . . ."

Brogan tried to shrug. "Sorry . . ." His head dropped loosely onto his chest. He was slipping in and out of consciousness and it was becoming harder and harder to concentrate. MacArthur had said something, something that was important, something . . . he gave up. The pain of the beating was so intense and his mind so jumbled that it was impossible for him to think clearly.

MacArthur shook his head ruefully. "It looks as if we must revise our estimates of the system's capabilities."

Brogan opened his eyes and stared directly at MacArthur. "Why? Are there other installations?"

MacArthur smiled at him. "Now, now, Mr. Brogan. I will do the questioning. Was there anything else, then, that led you to us?"

"Danish fishing captain. Said the source was somewhere in Ireland . . . I beat hell out of him."

"Captain Hansen?" MacArthur said mockingly. "It seems that he was of more help to us than to you. I note that it was several days afterward that you finally came to Ireland. I assume that you were waiting for confirmation from the satellite."

Brogan shrugged and MacArthur nodded in satisfaction. "I thought so. You see, it was Hansen that led us to you. He identified you later that night. The people we sent to get you could not find your room. They waited for you in the parking garage but you never showed up."

"Christ . . . incompetents on your payroll. Two rooms down hall from Hansen. Saw them in garage . . ."

MacArthur was skeptical. "Do you expect me to believe that?"

"I could care less," he said with a half smile.

MacArthur made a note on his pad. "I think we had better look into that when we get back, Connor. If Mr. Brogan is correct, the incidence of incompetence in our organization seems to be exceedingly high. Unacceptably high," he finished grimly.

"Now, how much did you learn the other night?"

"Only what I told Strain," Brogan replied wearily. "I got inside, got enough on film to stand up in any court, and brought out two poppy samples."

"And of course we have them now. So there will be no

further threats from that quarter. Tell me, you did not seem surprised to find that Mr. Strain is involved."

The pain had eased to the point that it was bearable. The dizziness and nausea had receded. He let his head roll back against the window so that he could see both men. "Not hard to figure. He was the only one who knew that I was in Athea."

"Ah, yes, the only one," MacArthur answered mockingly. "And now, one last question. Did you place a phone call through to London at any time today?" MacArthur stared at him. "Answer truthfully."

"Yeah," Brogan said in resignation, but determined to keep Sandra as uninvolved as possible. "I put a call through to my boss . . . my ex-boss . . . but he wouldn't listen to me."

MacArthur nodded, satisfaction evident on his face. "That confirms our information, then. I have no further questions for you, Mr. Brogan."

Connor glared at Brogan from across the narrow aisle, his eyes full of malice. Brogan ignored him and turned his head to the window, his mind a near blank. For the next ten minutes he stared without seeing as the view below changed gradually from the rolling green hills of Kerry to the deep blue of the coastal waters.

Nothing more was said until MacArthur leaned across the aisle and pointed to a scattering of small islands below.

"The Seven Hogs," he said briefly. Connor grinned at Brogan and licked his lips. MacArthur spoke to him in Gaelic, then went forward to stand in the cabin door, from where he could watch both Brogan and the pilot.

The dull drone of the engine changed to a more insistent whine as the copter began to circle over the westernmost island, losing altitude as it aimed for a point of land on the leeward side.

"This is where we will be leaving you, Mr. Brogan," MacArthur called back. "A special freighter will stand in about midnight to receive a package which we will leave for it. This little change in our routine is dictated by your interference. So we think it only right that you be here to welcome it."

The silent Connor was obviously enjoying the sight of his badly battered face. The best that Brogan could hope for would be a bullet; otherwise, Connor would beat him to death and Brogan was under no illusion that he would be in any hurry to complete the job.

With a half-smile on his face, Connor turned back to watch the landing as the copter settled gingerly toward the shingle beach less than a hundred yards from the water's edge. The bulk of the island was between them and the mainland, but the winds, after the long, two-thousand-mile passage across the North Atlantic, were blowing in directly from the ocean and the copter was being severely jostled. A long streamer of spray came crashing onto the shingle. Just as the copter was about to touch down, the wind caused it to slip to one side and Connor, startled, clutched at the seat arms. The shotgun slid from his lap and he snatched at it.

In desperation, knowing that this was the last chance he would ever be offered, Brogan twisted and flung himself across the aisle. The pilot chose this moment to bring the nose up to counterbalance the pressure of the wind, thus adding to Brogan's momentum, and he crashed into Connor. As they collided, Brogan snapped his elbow back, once, twice, three times into Connor's chest, driving his breath out in three deep whoops. Brogan twisted again and smashed his elbow back a final time, directly into his throat. Without waiting to see the effect, he threw himself to the floor and scrambled for the shotgun.

MacArthur, hearing the struggles, spun around, clawing for his pistol, but the gyrations of the copter threw him off balance long enough for Brogan to bring the shotgun up, clasped between his cuffed hands like a handgun, and pull the trigger. The weapon bucked, spraying shot the length of the cabin. MacArthur screamed and jolted back into the cockpit and against the reserve control column. The nose dropped abruptly, slamming hard against the rock. The blades splintered and the copter did a half-cartwheel onto its side. Brogan was thrown heavily against the cabin wall, then back against the seat, cracking his already abused head hard against the metal rim. An explosion rocked the helicopter and fingers of flame licked down from overhead. A gobbet of burning oil dropped into the cabin.

The helicopter had come to rest on its side, hatchway hard against the rock. The front of the copter was already a mass of flames, which drove Brogan to the rear of the cabin as the oil leak became a steady stream. Any moment now, he realized the flames would find the fuel tanks. He staggered to the emergency exit, now above him near the rear bulkhead, and yanked down on the handle. He pushed the heavy panel upward until it slid down onto the metal side with a thump. The heat from the burning oil was growing more intense by the second. Frantically, he clambered up onto a seat beneath the open hatchway, grasped the edge of the coaming and pulled himself through with what seemed the last possible ounce of strength he possessed. As he rolled over to slide down the side of the copter, he caught a glimpse of Connor struggling into a sitting position in the flame-and-smoke-swirled interior, one hand holding his throat. He stared dazedly around at the flames and then up at Brogan, almost directly over his head. Realizing then what was happening, Connor crawled onto the seat, as Brogan had done, and grasped the edge of the hatch. Deliberately, Brogan smashed the handcuffs down on his blackened fingers where they curled around the metal. With a scream, Connor fell back into the flaming interior and sickened, Brogan turned away and slid down the side. He landed heavily and staggered away, but before he had gone thirty feet, could in fact still hear Connor's screams, the fuel tanks blew up. The concussion smashed him headlong to the shingle.

* * *

Brogan found himself huddled against a rock, some distance from the crash site. Without moving, he peered around him trying to bring the scene in focus. Dusk was settling in and, as he watched, the last glimmer of sun disappeared from the island's peak. The long Atlantic waves were still crashing onto the shingle as regularly as a metronome's beat, a tumble of white, a foaming flood and, finally, a long subsidence that flashed and glinted with silver across the gray rock. The wind was gone and, but for the gentle roar of the ocean, an evening's stillness had settled over the island.

A long column of black smoke still towered straight up into an indigo sky unmarred by a trace of cloud. He was wet and cold and shivering and his wrists ached abominably from the tight handcuffs. Already the skin was swollen and blue, the metal bands almost buried in the flesh. Carefully he got to his feet only to find that his legs would not support his weight. He stumbled and fell hard against the rock as an agonizing scream tore from his lips and he collapsed into a heap, whimpering.

After a long while of semiconsciousness the pain eased, and in the gathering darkness he tried once again. This time his legs held and he staggered forward. His right leg was stiff with blood, but the fact that it would bear his weight indicated that it was not broken. Cautiously, Brogan limped to the helicopter, noting the bloody track on the rock where, semiconscious, he must have crawled away from the blistering heat of the burning aircraft following the explosion.

The aluminum fuselage covering had burned away completely, leaving only the twisted and broken steel members. Only fused metal remained of the cockpit where MacArthur and the pilot had died.

A wave of dizziness washed over him and he dropped down to a sitting position. The remains of the helicopter were still smoldering, and in the radiated heat his uncontrollable shivering gradually stopped. He was unaware of how long he sat there beside the ruined helicopter while the darkness grew, but gradually a heavy beating sound aroused him and he looked up.

For a moment he could see nothing but flashes of light. Then the silhouette of another helicopter took form. He shut his eyes, then opened them once more too unutterably weary to even move. If they were going to kill him, there was nothing further that he could do to prevent it. He had done his best and could do no more. Curiously, he did not feel despair, only a patient acceptance.

The helicopter drifted slowly across the beach, several hundred feet above. An intense beam of white light stabbed down, and Brogan turned his head away from its glare and shut his eyes. When he opened them again, the helicopter was settling down onto the beach. The engines cut off and a hatch slid open. A figure climbed down and, as he turned with a flashlight to help another man, the beam passed over the Irish naval insignia painted on the fuselage.

16

"Wake up, sir, wake up." Brogan opened one eye on a baleful world which insisted upon intruding whenever he fell asleep. He tried the other eye but everything was a dull blur, as the swollen tissues would part only enough to let in a glimmer of light.

The young naval driver shook his arm again and pointed to the Customs House.

"Oh . . . yeah," he mumbled and struggled into a sitting position. He drew a ragged breath, pulled his jacket close, zipped it up and shoved open the door. He was still none too steady on his feet and he leaned against the car for a moment, letting the cold wet wind from the Irish Sea blow away some of the cobwebs. God, but he felt terrible! His leg ached abominably and his ribs felt as if they might come loose with each breath. His head throbbed with the worst headache he had ever experienced.

A policeman moved to intercept him as he started across the walk. "I'm sorry, sir, but no one is allowed in or . . ."

He stopped at the sight of Brogan's face. "I beg your pardon, sir, but are you all right?"

Brogan started to shake his head and thought better of it just in time. "Hell, no," he growled. "I'm ready to die. Who's in charge of this idiot operation?"

"I'm sorry, sir, but this is an official . . ."

"Damn it, boy, don't stand there making conversation," he snapped irritably. "Take me to whoever's in charge . . ." He was interrupted by a shout.

"Brogan . . . Brogan . . . where in hell have you been?" Brogan looked up to see Vandervoort puffing across the pavement like a locomotive. He grabbed Brogan by the arm, not seeing the wave of pain that washed over his face.

"Where in hell have you been for the past three days? We've been looking all over for you . . . My God, you look terrible!"

Brogan pulled his arm away. "Let go of me, you fathead. I'll just bet you've been looking for me."

Brogan spun away and started for the doors, and the startled Vandervoort hesitated a moment, then trotted after him.

"What's going on here," Brogan demanded as he pushed through the doors and into the main vestibule. "Have you bastards finally decided that I knew what I was talking about?"

Vandervoort had stopped just inside the door. His face broke into a grin and he took out his pipe. Brogan was almost to the lift before he noticed that Vandervoort was missing. He turned and stalked back.

"Well, have you . . . ?"

"Have we what?" Vandervoort asked blandly.

"God damn it. Have you decided I know . . . I knew what I was talking about when . . ."

"Knew it all along." Vandervoort chuckled and blew out the match.

For a moment Brogan was speechless. When he found his voice again, he treated Vandervoort, several policemen and the few bystanders to a display of the choicest profanity they had heard in years. Two of the policemen grinned and nodded to each other in admiration when he finished.

"Now, now," Vandervoort said in a soothing voice. "We merely took advantage of your own stubbornness, you know. The more you are balked, the harder you try. And in any case, if INCC had supported your investigation and backed you, why, the syndicate would have closed down the operation a week ago. As it was, they thought you had quit or been fired and were merely working on your own and so continued with their operations. I must admit, though, that you moved even faster than we anticipated, and we were not able to cover as we had planned."

"What the hell . . . you mean to tell me that you had . . ."

Vandervoort nodded happily. "Strain has been suspected of, shall we say, outside activities, for a long time. But when dealing with a man in a position as high as his, the police have to move very circumspectly, and of course they had no idea that he was involved in drugs. There was no way to tie him to that farm which you located, no hard evidence of any kind to tie him to the syndicate. But there is a great deal of circumstantial evidence, which unfortunately will not be strong enough to stand up in court on its own. We suspect that he is somewhere in the middle echelons of the syndicate's management structure, but just where, we do not know. That is why we want him, and badly."

This time, in spite of the thumping headache, Brogan shook his head in amazement. "In other words, you set me up for all this. You . . ."

"Careful, now. As I have told you many times, that is no way to talk to your superiors. If you weren't such a cowboy, you would have been in very little danger."

Too choked with anger to say anything else, Brogan swung around and bumped into a middle-aged man standing behind him.

"Ah, Inspector Calhoun." Vandervoort smiled. "I would like you to meet my assistant, Inspector Cole Brogan. Cole, this is Inspector Michael Calhoun of the Dublin police force."

Brogan snarled and stalked past. Vandervoort gathered up the surprised inspector and followed as Brogan hurried into a waiting elevator car and punched the button for the third floor. Vandervoort caught the door and they crowded in.

"Now, Cole, it really is your own fault, you know. If you had let us know what you were up to we could have made it a good bit easier for you, especially after you found out that Mr. Strain was part and parcel of the operation."

Brogan gave him a withering glare but kept still. Vandervoort smiled at the inspector. "A bit headstrong sometimes."

Calhoun shook his head. "I daresay. He really is an Inspector . . . ?"

"The hell I am. Ex-inspector . . ."

"Ah, yes, about that. Somehow your letter of resignation was lost. It was never processed, and so it seems . . ."

"Shove it up . . ."

Vandervoort broke into a rumbling laugh, and Brogan choked and subsided.

The doors slid open and Brogan charged out as fast as his limp would allow and down the corridor to Strain's office.

"I was right and you wouldn't . . ."

"Knew it all along," Vandervoort called after him, but Brogan pushed past the Dublin policeman, who jumped too late to intercept him.

"Here now, you . . ."

"It's all right, Constable," Calhoun said, shaking his head in wonderment. "Let him go."

Brogan stopped in the outer office and glared around. Strain's secretary was seated at her desk, snuffling into a crumpled handkerchief. A uniformed policeman stood by the door to the inner office and Brogan pushed past him and into the room. Several men in plainclothes were examining the books and contents of Strain's desk. Everything was neat and tidy, exactly as it had been two days before, except where the police had piled papers on the conference table for the man with the camera to photograph.

"What time did you get here?" Brogan demanded, swinging around to confront Calhoun.

Calhoun glanced at his watch. "I'd say about six-thirty last night, less than fifteen minutes after we received the call from the Navy."

"Six-thirty. Hell, he would have been gone for almost an hour by that time."

"A little more than that, I'm afraid. Mr. Strain left about eleven o'clock in the morning. He told his secretary that he was attending a meeting, and that's the last she saw of him."

Brogan nodded. "Christ! Eleven o'clock. That gives him a seven-hour start." He pulled one of the conference chairs away from the table and sat down heavily. So Strain had gotten cleanly away, after all. He took a deep breath.

Calhoun stepped in close and bent down to look at his white face. "My God, man. You should be in hospital . . ."

Brogan shook his head irritably, then had to shut his one good eye tightly to wait for the pain to subside.

"No . . . no hospital. I spent a few hours there last night waiting for them to find a plane to fly me to Dublin. I'm all right except for some bruises." He took a deep breath, started to get to his feet and thought better of it.

"Okay. Let's start at the top again. You say he left about eleven, and that's the last he was seen. What time did you get to his flat?"

Calhoun consulted a small notebook. "Six forty-five. He lives in a new series of American-style apartments on North Strand Road. There is no one who saw him enter or leave his flat. We've combed every known place he might go in the city, but he's dropped out of sight."

"Wonderful," Brogan muttered. "What about the farm, then?"

"Clean sweep," Vandervoort answered. "The Army occupied the area at eight o'clock."

"Who the hell asked you?" Brogan muttered, got up and wandered out into the outer office, where two clerks were glancing apprehensively around at the armed policemen. Strain's secretary was still crying quietly at her desk.

Brogan moved some papers and an in/out box, sat down on the edge of the desk and sighed.

"What did Strain tell you when he left yesterday?"

The woman snuffled, dried her eyes, then shook her head. "Only what I have told you already."

Brogan shook his head. "Don't think I've anything to do with these heavy-handed idiots. Now, I want you to think back. What did he say and do? Did he just come out of the office and just leave? Or did he say anything to you? Was he wearing a coat? Did he have a briefcase with him, or what? Tell me everything you can remember."

The phone buzzed, and the inspector moved in as she picked it up and answered in a trembling voice.

"Hello . . . Commissioner Strain's office, may I help you? . . . no sir, he is not in today. Would you like to leave a message? . . . yes, sir. Yes, I will tell him. Thank you for calling."

She hung up the phone and looked up at the inspector. "That was the Assistant Secretary for the Home Ministry. He wanted a luncheon appointment with Mr. Strain." Her voice broke and she choked back a sob as Calhoun nodded to a policeman.

"Go out and make certain that they got that call on tape.

Have them trace it back and find out if it really came from the Home Ministry and who placed it. Then check him out." The policeman hurried out and Calhoun turned back to the secretary, but Brogan held up his hand.

"You've had all morning. Now it's my turn." Brogan shifted to a more comfortable position on the desk. "By the way, do something useful." Brogan handed him a crumpled slip of paper. "See that these people get taken care of. Their property got damaged a little. Charge it to that idiot over there," he waved at Vandervoort, then turned back to Strain's secretary.

"All right, from the time he came out the door," he prompted.

"Well, he was wearing his overcoat . . . it had been raining earlier, and he was carrying his briefcase, the one he usually takes to meetings. That's all."

"No, it's not," Brogan said sharply. "What did he say when he came out? Everything now."

"Well . . . he paused at my desk and said he forgot to mention a meeting that he had arranged earlier in the week. That was like him, he sometimes forgot to tell me about the appointments he set up himself. Then he said he would be back at five, but if not, he would be in first thing this morning. Then he left. That's all."

Brogan shook his head. "No, it isn't. It can't be. Think, now. There must have been something else."

The woman took a deep breath and rubbed her brow nervously.

"What did he do when he first came in until he left? Did he go straight into his office? Was there any dictation? Did you go into his office at all before he went to the meeting? Were there any phone calls . . . ?"

At that she looked up. "Yes, yes there was. I remember now that about ten minutes before he left he received a phone call. Long distance, I believe. From London . . . yes, it was from London."

Calhoun snapped his fingers at the officer standing by the door. "Get onto the phone exchange as quickly as you can. Have them find out where that phone call came from." The officer nodded and moved over to one of the other desks and lifted the phone.

Brogan shook his head. "It's a long shot . . . but it might just pan out. It could have been word that they had spotted me or that the truck was missing. Look," he said in an urgent voice to the secretary, "what time exactly did he get that call? It's very important. You said about eleven. A few minutes before or after the hour? Five, ten, fifteen, how many?"

The woman shook her head. "I really do not remember. He gets so many calls sometimes . . ."

Brogan got up from the desk and worked his shoulders around to loosen the muscles, which were beginning to cramp.

"What are you digging for, Cole?" Vandervoort asked.

Brogan started a sharp retort, then thought better of it. "I'm not sure yet. I hijacked that truck just after ten yesterday morning. And Strain got a call around eleven. Who warned him? It's possible that the trucks were to pass checkpoints on the way to Cork, and when mine didn't, they hit the panic button. They must have, because by three o'clock they had me."

Vandervoort nodded. "It might be significant. We should be able to get the exact time of the call, and where it was placed, from the post office."

Brogan nodded and sat down again. "You're right. The important question now is, Where has he gone? You say that . . . oh, my God, that's it." Brogan slapped the desk and jumped up again.

"His boat! His goddamned boat! Have you sent anyone down to see if it's still there?"

"What boat are you talking about . . . ?" Calhoun asked.

Brogan stared at him in amazement. "For God's sake, what the hell kind of investigations do you people conduct? Strain owns a boat, a forty-foot cabin cruiser which he keeps at Greystones."

"Forty feet!" Calhoun exclaimed. "He could go anywhere in that size boat."

"Exactly," Brogan said in disgust. "And he's had nearly fourteen hours to get there too."

"Jesus H. Christ," Calhoun breathed, half in prayer.

"Yeah, him too. Also, there are two girls to be picked up. I don't know if they are involved, but they might be able to add some information. Their first names are Kathleen and

Glynda, and I don't know their last names. But they are supposed to be actresses and shouldn't be hard to find."

"How in the name . . ." Vandervoort began, but Brogan was already out the door with Calhoun in hot pursuit. Vandervoort shook his head and lumbered after them.

The space at the marina was empty. The mooring fenders had been thrown down onto the dock, and the caretaker clucked in dismay as he carefully sorted and stowed them away in their locker. In spite of two carloads of policemen hovering around, throwing questions at him right and left, he still went methodically about his housekeeping duties. When everything was to his satisfaction, he straightened up and, holding his back, he nodded to the east and said in his heavy brogue, "All I can tell you is that he motored down yesterday afternoon. Around two o'clock it was, and went right aboard. Didn't even stop to talk, like he usually does, just started the engines and left. I saw him stop across the way for petrol, and that was the last of him. I expected him back about dark. Doesn't do much night sailing, Mr. Strain doesn't."

Calhoun put his hands to his face and shook his head, then turned and walked slowly back to one of the police cars and slid into the driver's seat. He sat for a moment, then picked up the microphone. Brogan sat down on the dock and shook his head also. Vandervoort lowered himself down alongside with a grunt and took out his pipe.

Brogan glanced at him. "You know something? I have the damnedest urge to kick you in."

Vandervoort smiled. "Always the cowboy!"

He packed the pipe, lit it, then dropped the match into the quiet water. "Where would you be going in that boat if you were Strain?"

"Where?" Brogan muttered and made the effort to get his thoughts in order. "Somewhere that I could make before dawn. Let's say that he figured he had eight or nine hours to dark and then about eight more to dawn, seventeen or so in all."

He dug into his jacket pocket for the battered and worn map he had taken the previous morning from the lorry and spread it open on his knees. The map showed the coast north to the Dublin/Galway line. A ferry route was marked from Dun Laoghaire east across the Irish Sea to Holyhead. A time of seven hours was marked above the curving line.

"Look here. If he started out at about two yesterday afternoon, he could have made it to Holyhead by around midnight, assuming his boat to be a few knots slower than the ferry."

Vandervoort took the pipe out of his mouth and considered for a moment. "Why would he want to go to Wales?"

"Not Wales, for God's sake. London! If he can make it to London, he can get so lost we'll never find him. In a few days or weeks, when the racket dies down, he can leave the country."

"Why would he take his boat? Why not fly? It would be faster, and there are any number of flights . . ."

"Because he did not know what the situation was . . . only that I had taken the lorry, apparently. He could not be sure that his people would catch me, and besides, if he flew, he could be traced too easily."

"Why go all the way to London? Why not Liverpool or Manchester?"

Brogan shook his head. "I don't know why, but I'd bet money on it. Liverpool or Manchester just wouldn't appeal to a man like him, nor would he be likely to know anyone there with the facilities to help a man on the run. London is two to three times as large as either of them, and Strain fancies himself a sophisticate."

Vandervoort glanced over at the map. "I don't think he would have gone across to Holyhead. Look here. There is only a bridge off the island, here at Menai. Strain impresses me as a person who never leaves himself only one exit."

Brogan studied the map again. "Yeah, you might be right. But what if he went further east, along the North Coast to Llandudno? That's a fair-sized town with a river harbor. With no customs to worry about, he could bring the boat in there without exciting much attention, leave it, pick up a car and head for London."

Vandervoort considered for a moment. "Assuming you are right and that he wants to go to London, then I agree, it is very possible that he might have done so. How much longer would it take him to get to . . . how do you pronounce that?"

"Llandudno . . . Clan-dud-no. The double *l* in Welsh is pronounced like a *cl*," he sighed. "It looks to be about thirty or forty miles more, say another three or four hours if he's making ten knots cruising."

Vandervoort glanced at his watch. "Then, that would put him into the port there about three or four A.M. . . . and it's nine-fifteen now. At most, then, he has a six-hour lead on us . . . if you are right." When Brogan started to bristle, he went on hastily. "Let's see what we can do about it." He got up and walked down to the police car, where Calhoun had been reduced to shouting into the microphone.

Brogan slept through most of the flight across the sea to wake as the chartered Piper Comanche landed at the small airport near Llandudno. He woke feeling even worse. The cramped seat had stiffened his aching joints, and to top it off, he was dirty and his mouth full of gummy muck. The sponge bath the nurse had given him at Shannon the night before had only removed the surface dirt and was in no way a substitute for a good hot shower. He stumbled out of the aircraft after Vandervoort into the bright morning sunshine of Wales. A police car waited for them beside the runway and Brogan climbed in, slumped gratefully into the seat and listened while Vandervoort questioned the driver, a local constable.

The man shook his head and replied in his thick Welsh accent: "No, sir, we haven't been able to trace his whereabouts since he arrived. Holyhead has been checked as well, but we found the boat here, as you suspected. It was very early morning apparently and no one saw him land or leave. No passports or customs to check through," he said half-apologetically, "and so there was no fuss."

"What about car-rental agencies?" Brogan asked. "Any of them rent a car earlier this morning?"

"No, sir." The policeman shook his head. "We've checked them all hereabouts. We are checking all the petrol stations 'round about as well, but so far, none of them remembers anyone of that description."

The policeman drove them into town to the police station.

Brogan dredged up enough strength to follow as they left the car and, as he walked inside, spotted a telephone.

"I want to call Sandra," he muttered and started for the phone. But Vandervoort grabbed him quickly by the arm and steered him away.

"Cole, I did not want to speak to you about this now, but I don't think it would be a very good idea to phone. Wait until you get back to London."

For a moment the meaning of what Vandervoort had said refused to register.

"Why?"

"Because," Vandervoort replied bluntly, "Sandra's convinced that you have had a nervous breakdown."

"I don't believe it . . . For God's sake, I've been proven right, haven't I?"

Vandervoort jerked his head away and stared out the window for a moment.

"Well . . . haven't I, damn it?"

"Cole, come over here and sit down. I want you to tell me everything you did from the time you left London four days ago."

He urged Brogan over to a seat near the wall and asked the constable for some coffee. Two other policemen had entered, and now they both stopped what they were doing to listen. The constable brought him a cup of black coffee and Brogan nodded gratefully. After a few sips, he was able to think coherently again and he related the entire story in detail, ending with the crash of the syndicate helicopter. When he finished, the three policemen were staring at him openmouthed, while Vandervoort's face was even grimmer than when he had begun.

"So," he took up when Brogan lapsed into silence, "you asked Sandra to come to me two days ago with that story?"

"That's right," Brogan nodded. "For God's sake, she did, didn't she?"

Vandervoort shook his head. "Cole . . . I'm sorry, no. She spoke to me yesterday, just before lunch, and she did not tell it just that way." He paused and gripped Brogan's arm.

"Cole, she told me that you had gone to Ireland, which I

knew you would do. Sandra told me that you had called her from some little town in Ireland, only she could not remember the name and had been afraid to ask you to repeat it. She was terribly upset. She said that you had babbled something . . . those were the words she used . . . about finding poppies, but that you were almost incoherent and she could understand very little of what you said.

"Cole," Vandervoort said softly, "she was very worried about you. She seemed to think that you had suffered a nervous breakdown. It was all I could do to keep her from going to Ireland after you." Vandervoort let go of Brogan's arm and leaned back against the wall.

"Damn it," Brogan said wearily after the shock had worn off. "Answer a couple of questions for me, will you? Did you take her to the director to hear her story?"

"The director came down to hear it."

The phone rang and, reluctantly, the constable moved to answer it.

Brogan nodded. "And she told you this yesterday?"

"Yes."

"Did she tell you that I was sending a package containing film and two sample poppies?"

"No. Look, Cole, she said it was almost impossible for her to understand you over the phone. Possibly you were excited, and also, the connection might have been bad."

"Mr. Vandervoort," the constable called across the room. "We've just had a call in from the Esso garage on A-496 south of Llandudno Junction. They report that a man answering the correct description stopped for petrol about five o'clock this morning. He was driving a blue Austin and there was a woman with him."

Vandervoort nodded grimly and walked over to the wall chart displaying the northern part of Wales, and England east to Crewe. Brogan stared quietly at the floor for a moment, stunned by what Vandervoort had told him. After a moment, he got up and walked slowly over to the map.

"A-496. That means he could be heading for the south or the west," Vandervoort muttered. "Look here, he can make connections with several other roads, all heading east. If you are right about London, then we can rule out any of the connecting roads west." He contemplated the map for a moment, then put his finger on a junction. "A-496 joins A-5 at Betws-y-Coed." The constable winced at his pronunciation.

Brogan stared at the map, forcing his personal problems into a subordinate position for the moment. "Damn, it's just too easy. That ties him to one main road until he reaches Tyn-y-cefn." The constable smiled wanly.

"Hell, we could put a roadblock there and have him easily, unless he wants to waste time jogging all over the countryside."

He turned away from the map and walked over to the windows to watch the traffic. Finally, he turned around. "Something's wrong. It's just too easy. Strain's left a clear trail. It's as if he wants us to follow it."

Vandervoort watched him, not quite understanding what Brogan was getting at.

"Look," Brogan tried again. "Apparently this woman picked him up. She could be anybody, because I know for a fact that he is quite a swinger. Now, wasn't it obliging of him to stop for gasoline. Anybody with half a brain would have filled the tank before . . . Hey, we can check that easily enough. Find out how much gas—petrol, I mean—they bought."

The policeman nodded in understanding and picked up the phone. While he dialed the number, Brogan went on.

"What if he wanted us to waste time looking for a blue Austin on the main roads south of here? There is a lot of empty space out there, and we could spend hours waiting for him to show at a roadblock."

"Well, what else could he do?" Vandervoort demanded.

"About three years ago I was driving through central Wales. I was using an ordnance map to follow the back roads. I remember turning off on what I thought was a 'B' road to drive up through the Brecon Beacons. About twenty miles in, I discovered that I wasn't on a road, after all, but a sheep track. Wales is honeycombed with sheep tracks, and some of them make usable unpaved roads. I remember talking to the owner of a hotel in MacLlenyth where I stayed that night, and he told me that you could drive all over Wales on sheep tracks.

They are marked on the ordnance maps, and that's what I was following."

Vandervoort snorted. "What kind of driving can you do on a sheep track?"

One of the two policemen who had been listening answered for him.

"I've driven them several times to take my boys camping. Some of the better ones are like a country road."

Vandervoort shook his head. "It seems a very long shot to me."

"Hell, this whole thing has been a 'very' long shot. Look, you've overruled me on every point so far. This time we'll do it my way," Brogan said with finality.

Vandervoort started to bristle, but before he could reply, the constable hung up the phone and came around the counter. "You were right," he nodded to Brogan. "They bought two gallons and one for an extra tin. That's why he remembers the man."

Brogan turned to look at Vandervoort. Vandervoort fiddled with his pipe for a moment, then stuck it in his pocket and shrugged. "All right. What do you want to do next?"

In ten minutes they had procured a quarter-inch ordnance map of the area and laid out a search pattern for a police helicopter the constable was arranging for with the Liverpool police. Brogan convinced them that it would do little good to set up roadblocks inside Wales, as Strain would be unlikely to go near any of the main or secondary roads.

"By now he's had a four-hour headstart, and that means he's long past the roadblocks you set up south and east of town. Hell, he's probably out of Wales by this time."

Vandervoort agreed, and a series of roadblocks in a line from Manchester to Gloucester covering all "A" and "B" roads for the next four hours was arranged.

"Not that they are likely to catch anything, but . . ." Brogan muttered. He placed more reliance in the helicopter patrolling the back country.

17

Rather than mark time in Llandudno waiting for word from the patrols and roadblocks, Vandervoort suggested they start driving toward London. Brogan readily agreed and Birmingham was selected as an intermediate destination. The constable arranged a rental car for them from the local Godfrey Davis office. Brogan fell into an uneasy sleep within ten minutes of starting and Vandervoort resigned himself to a long stretch of driving. He stopped twice to phone the Llandudno police for progress reports as they left Wales and pushed on into Shropshire. Within the first two hours the helicopter had completed a sweep across the area between Betws-y-Coed and Wrexham, but with negative results.

At 10:30 A.M. they drove into the suburbs of Birmingham. The sky had begun to cloud over during the morning, and the car radio was forecasting rain for the late afternoon as a cyclonic low pushed inland from the North Atlantic. Brogan, awakened by the noise of the traffic, was already regretting the nap, much as he had needed it. His mouth was dry and sour, and the bruises that covered his body had stiffened until even the slightest move was painful.

"Where are we?" he groaned and pushed up into a sitting position.

"Birmingham. I last checked with London while we were in Wolverhampton, thirty minutes ago. There is still no sign of Strain anywhere along the road network to London."

Brogan rubbed his face and blinked at the overcast.

The day had started out as a clear and warm midsummer day. But, as so often happens in Britain, it changed to a gray overcast under the influence of the low-pressure area and was threatening rain by the time they stopped in the Birmingham police car park. Brogan followed Vandervoort inside and, while he established their bona fides and telephoned London, Brogan found a lavatory and washed his face and hands, then stuck his head under the faucet to let cold water run over his head until some of the fuzziness evaporated. Fortunately, the Navy had supplied him with slacks and a shirt, and some enterprising sailor had patched his jacket neatly. Even so, he certainly looked disreputable, he thought. As he contemplated his battered, unshaven face in the mirror, a policeman entered and Brogan was nearly hauled off to the drunk tank before Vandervoort rescued him. Still muttering to himself, he allowed Vandervoort to lead him into the chief inspector's office.

A late breakfast was sent in while they talked, and afterwards the chief inspector offered the services of the locker room to Brogan, who accepted happily. He was taken down to the basement, where he soaked himself in a long hot shower after first stripping away the bandages applied by the Irish Navy doctor.

Vandervoort came into the locker room with a police surgeon as he was toweling himself dry. The doctor glanced at the burns and bruises on his body and flushed angrily.

"Damn it, man, you should be in hospital! Those burns are going to . . ."

Brogan shook his head wearily. "Tomorrow, doctor. Tomorrow, I promise. But not until this thing is over."

The doctor shook his head and, without another word, treated the burns and bruises with an antibiotic ointment and rebandaged his ribs. Brogan sat in a half-stupor until the doctor finished and then dressed slowly. As he pulled on his boots, he decided that maybe he would live, after all.

When he was dressed again, Vandervoort looked him over critically.

"Do you feel up to more riding?" he asked.

"Where to?"

"Strain's car, by its registration, has been located at Cirencester, about sixty miles south of here."

"Cirencester?" Brogan asked in puzzlement. "Why there . . . ?" He sat down on the bench and stared at Vandervoort. "The time is about right," he said after a moment. "If he got onto M-5 south, he could be in Cirencester in about an hour. Has he been seen in the town?"

Vandervoort shook his head. "We don't know. The report is rather incomplete. I know only that the car is in Cirencester now. It was found parked in front of the cathedral in the center of town."

Brogan stood up, letting his aching joints adjust slowly. "All right," he said. "Let's go. We haven't anything to lose at this point, and it's at least in the right direction."

* * *

Now that they had something definite to go on, Vandervoort drove like a madman, hunched over the wheel as much as his bulk would allow, weaving in and out of traffic. Once onto the M-5, he moved over to the inside lane and held the speedometer to a steady eighty. Brogan hunched into the seat and tried to stay awake but was losing the unequal fight until a close call with two heavy lorries trying to occupy the same space in their lane shocked him awake.

Vandervoort's revelation that Sandra was convinced that he had had a nervous breakdown had come as more of a shock than he had thought. Fortunately, he had been so exhausted that he had slept all during the ride from Llandudno, allowing his subconscious mind some time to filter and sort through his conflicting reactions. Now that he was able to think coherently again, he realized that he probably had sounded paranoid over the phone—just as Strain had accused him of being, although for different reasons. From her point of view, it could very well have seemed as though he had gone over the edge. For a week previously, he had moped and brooded around the office trying to fit all the pieces together. Then when he thought he had the puzzle completed, he had encountered strenuous opposition, first from Vandervoort, and then from Strain. Added to that had been Sandra's kidnaping and his sudden resignation. Seen in that light, it was no wonder she thought he was ready for the funny farm . . . particularly following his last phone call to report that he had hijacked a truck.

Brogan watched the green countryside flowing past. Traffic

was light at this time of day on the M-5 and Vandervoort kept to the inside lane, jockeying for room with an occasional lorry that insisted on using the fast lane for passing. As soon as this business with Strain was settled one way or the other, he had no doubt that he could persuade her that he was perfectly sane. After all, there was the wedding to be planned.

In something less than an hour, Vandervoort was swerving recklessly through traffic on A-417 into Cirencester, horn blaring to warn other drivers out of the way. Brogan spotted a small blue sign indicating the route to the police station, and a few minutes later they swung into the circular drive in front of the beige-colored, two-story building and hurried inside.

An elderly sergeant showed them out back to the blue Austin in the car park. A fingerprint team was busy as they approached, and their guide leaned in and spoke with one of the men for a moment, then backed out.

He shook his head. "Nothing, I'm afraid. The car appears to have been cleaned properly. We have notified London and they are rechecking the registration now, but we are certain it is the vehicle rented in Llandudno."

"Was the car stolen?" Brogan demanded.

"No, not that we have been able to determine. If you ask me, the car was rented, but there is nothing to indicate . . ."

"Then, that's the car, for sure. Otherwise, why go to the trouble of wiping it clean?"

The sergeant nodded, surprised at the vehemence in Brogan's voice. Brogan took a deep breath and forced himself to sit down on the railing around the car park, where he fumbled for his cigarettes. He lit one and inhaled slowly. After a moment he had regained a semblance of calm, enough anyway to ask, "All right, where do we go from here? The railway station?"

The sergeant shook his head. "I'm afraid not, sir. There was only the one train through here this morning, two hours before your man could possibly have arrived . . ." And seeing that Brogan was about to ask, he answered the unspoken question: "The only passengers were two elderly men and a young woman with two children. All of them known to be local citizens by the ticket agent."

"An airport, then?"

"The nearest is at Oxford, but for a small field west of town. No one has been there this morning."

"Then, the bus station?"

"It's in the railway depot."

Brogan thought for a moment. "Then, how about one of the local buses? Strain might have caught one along the road," he said, turning to Vandervoort.

"That is a possibility," the sergeant admitted, "and if so, then I am afraid that it would be difficult to say. Roadblocks have only just been set up in the area . . . and only on the main roads. Apparently, your people were expecting to stop them further north."

Brogan nodded in irritation and flicked the cigarette away. He glanced again at Vandervoort. "Any ideas?"

Vandervoort shook his head.

"Then, how in hell could he have gotten out of town, Sergeant?"

The man shrugged. "I don't know, sir. Unless, of course, he did not leave. We are checking the hotels now, but it is not likely that we will find anything."

The bells of Cirencester Cathedral began to toll. "Hell," Brogan muttered, "it's noon already. Where the devil could he have gone and how? You know this area. What would you do?"

The sergeant shrugged. "Very difficult to say, sir. If he has gone by road, then he may be stopped at one of the roadblocks before much longer."

"Then, it's for damned sure he's not going by road," Brogan snarled. "How else can you get to London from here?"

"Why are you so sure that he is making for London?" Vandervoort insisted.

Brogan shook his head. "I don't really know . . . it's just a hunch. But so far, it looks to me like he is. He crossed the Irish Sea, was met by this woman in Llandudno, then drove east as far as Cirencester. I just have a feeling that he has connections in London . . ."

"He could be going to Oxford or to any one of the northern ports," Vandervoort interrupted.

Brogan pushed his long hair back out of his eyes before answering. "Yeah, he could. But then, why come to Cirencester?"

Vandervoort snorted. "Why come to Cirencester if he is going to London? There are certainly more direct routes for a man in a hurry."

"Yeah, I know. And if he's trying to confuse us, he's done a damned good job of it on me." Brogan shook his head. "Right now the problem is to figure out where he went from here. I think it's obvious that he is not still in town; otherwise, he wouldn't have left the car to be found so easily."

Brogan wearily unfolded the by now almost unreadable map. Vandervoort and the sergeant continued talking nearby in low voices. A raindrop spattered the map and Brogan glanced up. The sky was now positively lowering. Mumbling to himself, he went back to studying the map.

He was not certain that he knew, in fact he had not the faintest idea, what to look for as he traced out the alternate routes to London. Bristol was a thirty-minute drive south and west and might have been a logical place to run, but somehow Brogan did not think so. London might be the most obvious, but it also offered the best haven. Putting himself in Strain's place, he would have made for London as fast as he could go.

The map showed two possibilities, both "A" roads, to Oxford and London. These he discarded as too dangerous. After a few minutes' thought, he discarded all the "B" roads as well. To the east of the town lay the rolling hills of Lambourne Downs. No matter whether Strain went south or east, he would have to cross the Downs, and the few roads could easily be blocked.

"Is there an airport around here?" Brogan asked for the second time.

The sergeant looked over. "No, sir," he said patiently. "The nearest one is at Oxford and we have already checked it."

"How about those local bus routes?" Brogan asked finally. "Where do they lead from town?"

The sergeant scratched his head and walked over to peer at Brogan's map. "Let's see now. One goes to Bristol, southwest. The other north to Cheltenham by A-435. There is one that goes as far as Whitney where you change for Oxford, and the other one goes to Wantage and on to Abingdon."

Brogan nodded and absently traced them out. "The one to Wantage, that's where Alfred the Great was born . . . wasn't it?"

The policeman nodded and Vandervoort began to look anxious, as if he were beginning to doubt the firmness of Brogan's sanity.

"It goes through Fairford, Lechlade, Faringdon, and finally Wantage, sir."

"Lechlade," Brogan mused. "That seems to ring a bell."

"Yes, sir," the sergeant answered politely. "It is a little market town . . ."

Brogan snapped his fingers. "*Here I could hope . . . that death did hide* . . . Shelley! By God, Shelley lived there and wrote 'A Summer Evening Churchyard,' Lechlade. Damn it all. I remember now!"

"Cole!" Vandervoort started but Brogan had jumped to his feet and was running for the front of the building and the car. Vandervoort hesitated, then followed, leaving the surprised policeman staring after him.

Brogan reached the car first and yanked open the door on the driver's side. Vandervoort puffed up as Brogan yelled to him, "Give me the keys and get in!"

"Cole, wait just a mom . . ."

"Damn it, we don't have time to argue. Give me the keys and get in. The Thames becomes navigable at Lechlade."

He reached across and snatched the keys from Vandervoort's hand and slid in. Vandervoort struggled in as the engine roared to life, and Brogan shot out of the car park before Vandervoort had the door closed. Brogan cursed in a dull monotone and held the horn down as he broke through the traffic and slipped past signals by a hair's breadth. As soon as they reached the open highway, Brogan turned the headlights onto high beam and, with the horn still going, pushed the car to seventy miles an hour on the narrow two-lane road.

"Cole, pull up immediately. You've lost . . ."

Brogan cut him off. "Listen to me carefully, for just once in your life. The name of that town struck a chord. Shelley lived there for several years. He used to walk through the churchyard every evening and down to the river. If you take that same walk today, you'll see a boathouse near the end where you can rent cabin cruisers to sail on the Thames. If you want, you can go all the way to London."

"Ach, my God!" Vandervoort gazed at him in astonishment.

"Yeah, my God is right. While we are searching all up and down every road in England, Strain is leisurely cruising down the Thames to London. Who the hell would ever think of looking for him on the river? He drives to Cirencester, dumps the car, rides a local bus to Lechlade . . . that takes maybe another half to one hour. Then he rents a boat—or hell, has one there, for all I know—and takes a couple of days getting to London after all the hue and cry have died down."

Several drivers and one or two lorries gave Brogan a bad time, but the insistent horn and his reckless driving soon scared them off. Fifteen minutes later they thundered into Lechlade and swung around the traffic circle, cutting off a Moped rider. Brogan spotted a traffic warden a block ahead and screeched to a stop beside him. Vandervoort was ready with his identification card, which he flashed at the man.

"Where do you go to rent a boat to cruise on the Thames?" Brogan demanded.

The warden, caught by the sudden flurry about him, only gaped in surprise and Brogan had to repeat the question.

"R . . . right through the roundabout. Foll . . . follow the road south two miles to the river . . . there's a sign . . ."

Brogan yelled his thanks and was already pulling away before the warden had finished. He cornered through the traffic circle, horn blaring, and shoved the accelerator to the floor.

"My God, you'll kill us both . . ."

But Brogan wasn't listening. He shot through the small town and barely made the turn onto the secondary road. Two minutes later he skidded into the graveled car park and stopped beside a small building as the astonished owner stepped outside. Brogan threw the door open and pelted up the steps.

"What is going on here . . . ?"

"You rented a boat to a man and woman this morning! They weren't driving a car when they arrived. How long ago?"

The owner, a large, burly man with a cigar, removed it from his mouth. "Who wants to know?" he asked in a heavy Devon accent.

Brogan stiff-armed him against the wall. "Listen, mister, you talk, and fast, or I'll break your arm off."

Vandervoort came puffing up the steps and grabbed Brogan by the arm.

"Let him go . . . now!"

Brogan released the man's arm and stepped back, his face pale with anger. Vandervoort interposed his bulk between the two and held his I.D. card under the man's nose.

"We want answers to our questions and we want them quickly. Either give them or talk to the police." Vandervoort's tone brooked no nonsense, and the man, looking from the card to the huge Dutchman and back again, nodded.

"All right," Brogan said in a calmer voice. "What time did you rent the boat?"

"There wasn't no man and woman . . ." the owner began, but this time Vandervoort grabbed his arm in one heavy hand and squeezed.

"We want no lies now. The truth, or you will be charged with being an accessory . . ."

The threat deflated him. Possible involvement in an unknown crime or crimes erased his belligerent attitude instantly.

"At ten o'clock or so . . ."

"Try again, you . . ." Brogan broke in. "It couldn't have been at ten . . ."

"But I tell you it was, I have it on my sheet. They came at ten o'clock this morning by cab. Said they wanted to rent a boat to cruise to Oxford and back. Said they was going to be gone for four days. They paid the rent and the safe deposit in cash. If I gets that, I don't care who I rent to. The boats is all insured."

Brogan glanced at his watch. "Ten o'clock . . . damn, they have nearly a three-hour start. What did they look like?"

The boat owner shrugged. "He was tall, about your size.

Gray hair and mustache. Was wearing a business suit. The woman was dressed in slacks and a mac. She was a looker. That's all I remember."

Vandervoort shook his head and glanced at Brogan. "Well, what do you think?"

Brogan shrugged. "I don't know. It could have been Strain . . . Are you sure they walked here?" he asked the boat owner.

The man shifted the cigar around in his mouth and mumbled past it. "Look at the car park. There's three cars there. Mine, yours, and one other customer who's due back today."

"Hell, then, it couldn't have been anybody else. The time is right if they rode the bus from Cirencester." He walked to the railing and stared out at the river, flowing as limpid as quicksilver between the narrow banks.

"How long," he asked, turning, "would it take me to get to Oxford from here by boat?"

The man shook his head. "Depends on how fast you went. If you was to keep the throttles open all the way and stick to the center of the channel, you could manage in three or four hours."

"And he's got at least a three-hour lead on us," Brogan muttered. "So there is a chance, then"—he turned to Vandervoort—"that we might be able to get him at Oxford if we move fast."

"And if he stops somewhere along the way . . ."

Brogan shrugged. "There is that possibility. But if he does, it won't be to leave the boat. He may tie up somewhere between here and Oxford to make sure that he isn't being followed or to give the excitement a chance to die down, or both. But either way, if it really is him on this damned river, I know for sure he won't leave it . . . today anyway. It's just too good a chance to break loose."

"Here now, one of you two's got to tell me . . ."

"Shut up!" Brogan snapped. "Look, I'm going to take another boat and follow him downriver just to make sure. You phone the Oxford police, then go on up there and make sure they conduct a proper search this time. If we lose him now, it may be for good."

"Cole," Vandervoort protested. "You are in no condition to

go off like that . . . Look at yourself. You should really be in hospital."

"Damn it, Van, there isn't any other way, and besides, I'm all right. The aches and bruises aren't going to kill me. You've got to get to Oxford and make sure the Yard gets involved. For God's sake, Van, do it my way for a change," Brogan pleaded.

Vandervoort nodded reluctantly. "All right. It is against my better judgment. Be careful." He thought for a moment. "You had better take this, then," and pulled a pistol from his jacket and handed it to Brogan.

"Okay. Is it loaded?"

Vandervoort nodded and handed him a spare clip of ammunition. "Are you familiar with this one?"

Brogan nodded. "Yeah. A Walther P-38. I know it. Look, Van, do me a favor, will you? Call Sandra and let her know that I'm all right and that I haven't gone completely crazy yet. Tell her what's happened so far . . ."

Vandervoort nodded and studied Brogan's battered face, knowing that he should not let him go. Then he sighed. There was really no way to stop him. "All right. Good luck. I'll meet you at Oxford."

"Here now, you two. Who's going to pay for another boat . . . ?"

18

Rain was falling lightly to spatter the quiet surface of the Thames as Brogan turned the twenty-foot cabin cruiser they had convinced the boat owner to *lend* him into midstream and pulled the throttles wide open. The boat surged ahead, and for a few minutes Brogan was fully occupied with trying to make it go in a straight line. As the boat disappeared into the mist downstream, stern swinging in drunken arcs, Vandervoort stared after him and slowly shook his head.

Brogan had wanted a ship-to-shore radio to maintain communications with Vandervoort and the Oxford police, but the only radio to be had was a citizens-band walkie-talkie with a range less than half a mile. Reluctantly, at Vandervoort's insistence, he had agreed to stop at boat landings on the way downstream to telephone.

In the first two hours, Brogan had checked four villages, five boat landings and several minor streams emptying into the Thames. Only one of these had been large enough to take a good-sized boat into and within two hundred yards, a weir stretching from bank to bank blocked further ingress. All of the villages he passed were typical riverside towns catering mostly to river tourists . . . and were now full of those tourists seeking shelter from the rain. Brogan quickly discovered that the owners of concessions, food, petrol and other small shops lining the quays knew most of the boats on the river by sight. This simplified his task immensely. Each one he questioned along the way stated categorically that neither Strain nor his boat had stopped. One young man in Radcot, where Highway A-4095 crossed the Thames, remembered seeing a cruiser pass that matched the description of the one rented by Strain. But he could not recall with any accuracy how long before it had been or whether or not there had been one, two or three people aboard.

"Sorry," he shrugged. "But after you've been here awhile, watching them come and go, they all seem to run together, if you know what I mean."

Brogan said that he did, thanked him and left. The rain was still thin, but steadier now, tending to obscure the remoter corners of the river, necessitating a more time-consuming exploration of every little bay and bend, and the smaller rivers and creeks that debouched into the Thames grew in number as the river widened.

The hours passed swiftly and Brogan's progress was not keeping pace. Although he was pushing the boat wide open whenever he could, in defiance of the speed laws and pursued from time to time by profanity hurled at him by other, more law-abiding boat owners, he was still several miles from Oxford by late afternoon. The rain had been falling in earnest for some time and Brogan had given up on the thorough exploration of every nook and cranny of the river. At Chimmeny, he had gone ashore to telephone Vandervoort in Oxford. At the suggestion of the police there, Brogan was to push on ahead as fast as he could while local police would mount a more thorough search behind him. Brogan readily agreed and went on.

At the boat landing below Farmoor Reservoir, he ran into his first bit of luck. The attendant at a small tea stand remembered seeing a blue-and-white boat tie up briefly a few hours earlier. A man had come ashore to buy sandwiches. What had attracted her attention was the woman who had remained aboard. She had stood beneath the bridge canopy watching the shore and the wharf with binoculars. They appeared to be in a great hurry and had left as soon as the sandwiches were ready. It had seemed strange at the time, but then it had started to rain heavily, and in the scramble to get her wares under cover, she had forgotten the incident. Brogan managed to pinpoint the time at one-thirty and left her on a dead run for the telephone box on the end of the pier. A moment later he was through to Vandervoort, who could again only report that no boat of that description had as yet passed through Oxford.

"Damn it, Van, then I think he's beat us through. Either that, or he's holed up somewhere. It's possible that he could have gone through Oxford before the barriers were set . . . or else he saw the activity and turned back upstream."

"You might be right," Vandervoort admitted. "What do we do now?"

"I'd say keep the barriers at Oxford but shift downstream farther, maybe as far as Reading. Set up again there. It's about ten miles by river to Oxford from here, and he could have done that in less than an hour, if he wanted to. But I don't see how the devil he could have gotten as far as Reading yet. I'm going to keep on the river through Oxford and follow up behind. Maybe it would be a good idea to start a police launch down-river from Oxford just in case. And for God's sake, make sure that nothing suspicious is visible from the river. Now that I've been on it for a few hours, even one or two boats stopped together in midchannel looks damned funny."

Vandervoort agreed, cautioned him again about going easy on himself, and Brogan hung up the phone impatiently and hurried back to the boat, shouting his thanks to a thoroughly puzzled concessionaire. This was a damned funny time for Vandervoort to be so concerned for his health.

Brogan swung aboard and started up the engines, furious with the weather that prevented the Oxford police helicopter from patrolling the river, furious with the police, who always seemed to be just one move behind Strain, and furious with Vandervoort for his earlier idiotic handling of the entire situation.

The river ran between high banks for the next few miles, with only a few inlets big enough to hide a cruiser, to be explored. In spite of the need for haste, Brogan did a thorough job wrenching the boat through high-speed turns, risking submerged snags and sand bars.

He reached Oxford an hour later, passed through the first barrier and was waved ashore at the A-4141 overpass south of town, where the second barrier had been set up. Vandervoort was there with two police officers to report that there was still no sign of Strain. A police launch had gone downriver a few minutes after Brogan had called and was reported to have reached Clifton Hampden. The police were, however, out in force on the roads along the river, as several roadblocks had been set up between here and London.

"It is only a matter of time," Vandervoort finished gloomily. "But the police are stretched very thin, and I don't know how much longer we will be able to maintain this level of effort. Already, I must beg and plead just to keep what we have now in the field. There is a growing conviction at the Yard that we are on a very expensive and fruitless wild-goose chase."

Brogan shook his head in exasperation. "If as much effort had been expended in trying to break this operation as has been spent in griping and obstructing everything I've tried to do, we wouldn't be in this fix to begin with. God damn it, he can't be that far ahead of us! He's either holed up above Oxford or he got through just ahead of the blockade, and if so, we can catch him at Reading. And unless somebody has done something very stupid, Strain should have no idea that we are this close to him. The safest course for him at this point would be to stay on the river all the way to London."

Vandervoort sighed. "I agree with everything you have said. But don't forget, the idea of growing opium poppies in Ireland, especially without petals, is very difficult to accept seriously, or was until yesterday. You cannot blame anyone for not believing you, especially when you had no hard evidence. As it is now, we have almost the entire police forces in the south of England hunting for Strain. No pun intended, but it does place a terrible strain on their manpower resources."

Brogan shrugged. "Too damned bad for them, then. If they need more help, they can call out the Army." He was silent a moment, staring down at the gray bar of river, forlorn and empty in the rain.

"How is Sandra taking all this? . . . Is she ready to accept the fact that I haven't gone crazy, after all?" he asked quietly.

Vandervoort shrugged, and a worried look that he could not quite hide flashed across his face. "I do not know. She did not come in to work. One of the clerks said that she was talking about going to Ireland yesterday to find you. She may have left last night."

"Aw, hell," Brogan muttered. "Damn it all, I thought she was supposed to be under the Yard's protection. How the devil could they let her dodge them like that . . . ?"

"All right," he said finally, not knowing what else to say. The two policemen exchanged puzzled glances.

"We are driving south to Reading," Vandervoort said. "Do you want to come with us?"

"Just a minute." Brogan slithered back down the bank and climbed onto the boat to check the fuel gauge. There was still sufficient left to make Reading.

He stepped out onto the deck and yelled up to Vandervoort. "No, thanks. I'll stay on the river and meet you there."

Vandervoort waved and he and the two policemen climbed back up to the road, where their car waited, its lights flashing in the waning afternoon light. Brogan watched them for a moment, then climbed back up to the bridge and started the engines. At least Sandra, if she was running around someplace in Ireland, was safe enough for the moment.

The rain was falling steadily now and visibility was bad. In another two hours it would be dark, and if they hadn't found Strain by then, their chances of ever doing so would be very remote. With miles of riverbank to patrol and their force of police already stretched thin, there would be no way to stop Strain if he realized the danger to himself and decided to abandon the boat.

The river curved west for a few brief miles south of Radley to pass around the ancient Saxon town of Abingdon. The town's buildings lent a medieval aspect to the flat river plain, half obscured by the driving downpour. Below the town, the river separated into two channels, and half blinded by the rain, Brogan chose the righthand channel instead of the left. A bridge loomed suddenly. Stone walls on either side of the channel narrowed abruptly, closing him in. From his vantage point on the bridge of the cruiser, Brogan found himself staring over the walls into terraced gardens and lighted houses. Startled, he closed the throttles, then reversed the engines to slow the boat as he realized he was no longer on the Thames.

The boat lost way, but Brogan was forced to go ahead again to keep from drifting into, first, the walls, then the bridge itself. The boat, idled down for steerage only, drifted beneath the stone bridge. On either side were the flat, open grounds of a park. Looking back, he found the bridge too narrow to reverse back through and he was forced to continue on upstream until the channel widened enough to permit him to turn the boat.

A quick glance at the map showed that he had taken the channel leading into the mouth of the river Ock. Cursing at the time he was losing, he opened the throttles angrily and the boat surged ahead.

A few hundred yards past the bridge, the buildings of the town, many of them seeming to date from the Middle Ages, lined a stone quay on the north side of the river. A housewife, standing well back under the eaves of her porch, was shaking a dustmop. She watched him a moment, then shook her head at the peculiarities of people who prefer to sail boats in the pouring rain. Brogan agreed with her wholeheartedly. A man carrying an open umbrella and wrapped in a raincoat hurried along the quay, paying no attention to him. Several cruisers and houseboats lined the quay, a convenient mooring place from which to reach the Thames and London or even the Channel.

Just past the edge of the town, Brogan found that the river began to widen. A cut in the bank on the far side seemed large enough and he slowed preparatory to making a 180° turn. As he scanned the near bank to make sure that there was sufficient room for a turn, he almost missed the blue-and-white cabin cruiser moored directly behind a large houseboat. Urged on by a sudden premonition, he spun the wheel in the opposite direction and drifted past the houseboat. The registration of the cruiser was the same that Strain had rented in Lechlade. With a whoop of joy, he cut the engine and slid toward the quay, letting the boat's forward momentum carry him alongside. The cruiser banged the houseboat hard, crumpling a portion of the overhanging rear deck. Ignoring the damage, Brogan vaulted down from the bridge, raced back to the stern, grabbed a mooring line and dragged the boat against the quay. The houseboat was nudged twice more, each time scraping paint away in large gouts.

As he secured the bow and turned abruptly, he slammed into a very angry houseboat owner.

"What in the hell are you doing?" the man screamed as he scrambled to regain his balance. "Look at my boat."

Brogan pushed past the man and hurried around to the stern of the cruiser. The man ran after him, yelling incoherently. The cruiser appeared deserted and the mooring lines had been secured hastily. Brogan grabbed the man by the arm.

"Look, I'm sorry about your boat, but this is police business. The damage will be made good. How long ago did this cruiser tie up?"

"I don't care what you . . . police . . . what . . . Hey, that still does not give you the . . ."

Brogan shook his arm angrily. "Look, mister, I already said I'm sorry about your boat. I also said it would be paid for. Now answer my question. How long ago did that cruiser tie up?"

The man glared at him suspiciously. "You're damned right you'll pay . . . less than ten minutes ago. There was a man and a woman on board. They tied up and left."

"A man and woman? Are you sure about that?"

He shrugged. "Yes, I think so. I wasn't paying that much attention. I just happened to see them come out and drive away."

Brogan turned toward the boat, reaching for his pistol at the same time. "Look, you had better get back inside. If you've got a phone, call the local police and have them send someone over right away."

The man needed no more urging than the sight of Brogan's pistol. He scurried back to his houseboat. Brogan forgot about him for the moment and walked slowly toward the cruiser. He slipped around to the stern, pulled himself through the railing and down into the cockpit, wincing at the pain in his leg and ribs as he did so.

So far so good. The cruiser was similar to his. The cockpit was just forward of the stern and was roofed with a flying bridge. An awning sheltered the controls. The cruiser was about twenty-five feet long and could sleep four or six. Below, in the main cabin, would probably be the galley/living quarters. He wasn't sure about that, since he had not had time to go below on his own boat. Brogan edged up against the bulkhead and gingerly tried the hatch. It was not latched and swung outward at his touch. Brogan pulled it all the way open. After a moment, he stuck his head around the jamb, close to the deck. The dim interior was empty and he stood up, made sure that the pistol was cocked and the safety off, and stepped inside.

Except for a hatch leading into the narrow engine compartment, the main cabin took up all the space belowdecks. Brogan made a hurried search but found nothing that could be used to identify the boat's renters without a fingerprint team. He went back up onto the deck, climbed down onto the quay and walked toward the houseboat as the owner came to his door. The man hesitated for a moment, then pushed open the screen door and came out onto the deck.

Brogan stopped on the edge of the quay and thought for a moment. "You say that the man and woman left the boat and got into a car?" he called up. "Which way did they go?"

"They drove west onto A-415. This drive leads to the highway, right over there."

Brogan turned as he pointed. A lorry passed in the gathering darkness, its headlights flaring mistily in the rain.

"What kind of car?"

The man shrugged. "I don't know. A Capri, possibly. I wasn't paying that much attention. Why?"

Brogan ignored the question. "Did you phone the police?"

The man shrugged. "I don't have a phone."

In exasperation, Brogan swore. "Oh, hell, where is the nearest phone?"

The man pointed to a phone box across the road and Brogan hurried over to it.

"Hey, what is this all about . . . ?" the man shouted after him, but Brogan was already shutting the door. He fumbled in his pocket for some change and found that he had none. Swearing, he grabbed the receiver and dialed 999, the police emergency number. A moment later, a man's voice on the other end answered.

"Shut up and listen to me carefully," Brogan broke into the first question. "My name is Cole Brogan. I'm an investigator for the International Narcotics Control Commission. You should have received word by now from the Oxford police or Scotland Yard that we are chasing a suspect believed to be in this area."

"Yes, sir," the voice replied in surprise. "All of our officers are now out . . ."

"Good," Brogan broke in. "I want you to do three things . . ."

"Just a moment, sir, let me connect . . ."

"No, damn it. Take this down and do it yourself. I don't have the time to wait. Number one, notify all the roadblocks around Abingdon to stop a man and a woman driving a Capri. I don't know the registration number or the color of the car. They will have to depend on the description of the man they already have. Stop and hold them until I get there. Pay special attention to A-415 because they were seen heading west on that road, about ten or fifteen minutes ago.

"Secondly, notify Commissioner Vandervoort. You can reach him through the Reading police. Tell him to get up here damned fast.

"Third, send a car out here for me as quickly as you can. I'm at a phone box on the west end of town, by the river, just off A-415."

"Yes, sir, I'll take care of it right away. But it will be at least twenty minutes before I can send a car. Everyone is out on the roadblocks except for one car which is handling an emer . . ."

"All right," Brogan shouted. "Get it here as fast as you can and get those messages out at once." He slammed the phone down, swearing in frustration, and kicked open the door to the phone box. The man from the houseboat had pulled on a raincoat and was crossing the road to him.

"See here. Are you really a policeman? What is going on here?"

Brogan started to swear at him wildly, then realizing that he was fast working himself into a state of hysteria, he took a deep breath.

"Yeah, I am," he answered slowly, methodically, concentrating on each word. "I'm a narcotics agent."

"Narcotics?" the man said in surprise. "What the devil are you doing here?"

Brogan pointed to the cruiser. "I've been chasing one of the people on that boat downriver all the way from Lechlade. All of your police are out on a roadblock and I'm stuck here . . . unless . . . Look, there's a roadblock just west of town. I've got to get out there. Will you drive me?"

The man glanced nervously around at his houseboat. "Well, I don't know as if I want to get . . ."

"Look, there's a Crown reward for anyone aiding in the capture of these two. It would go to you if you drive me out there in time to catch up with them."

The man's eyes lit up at that. "A Crown reward, you say . . ."

Brogan nodded vigorously. He had not the faintest idea if there was even such a thing as a Crown reward, but he would have to worry about that later.

"All right. I'll do it," the man answered, visions of money and newspaper publicity dancing in front of his eyes. "My car's just over there. I'll just leave a note for my wife . . ."

But Brogan was already running across the road. "We haven't time for that," he yelled back. "You'll be back in less than an hour."

The man hesitated, then hurried after Brogan. As he came around the car, the keys already in his hand, Brogan shouldered him roughly aside and grabbed the keys. The man started to protest, but Brogan already had the door to the driver's side open and was sliding in behind the wheel. The car's owner danced for a moment in anguish, then raced around for the other door as Brogan started the engine. He jumped in just as the car jerked forward, almost hitting the railing along the quay. Brogan banged the gearshift into reverse and backed wildly, then into first gear and shot toward the highway. He took the turn onto the main road in front of a heavy lorry and accelerated away as it swerved and sounded its air horns.

"Here!" the owner screamed. "Easy now! You'll wreck my car!"

"With the reward, you can buy ten of these if you want," Brogan snapped. "Now shut up and let me drive."

With the car in third gear and the speedometer nudging seventy, they sped down the rain-slick road. Fortunately, traffic was light and, by passing wildly, Brogan was able to maintain a high rate of speed.

"How much will the reward be?" the man asked abruptly, breaking a long silence.

"Huunh . . . ? Reward? Oh yeah, the reward." Brogan peered through the rain-streaked windshield at the glistening pavement and tried to concentrate on keeping the car on the slippery asphalt. A lorry loomed ahead on the curve just past Marcham and, gritting his teeth, he yanked the wheel to the right, then slewed back to the left as headlights showed ahead in the other lane. The brakes refused to hold on the wet pavement and Brogan pulled left and passed the lorry on the shoulder. The car bumped and tried to swerve on the wet verge, but Brogan managed to hold it safely around the lorry and back onto the road as the astonished truck driver let loose with a long horn blast in protest. Brogan drew a deep breath, thankful he was driving an Austin. The suspension on any other car would never have allowed that maneuver.

In the glare of passing headlights the owner's face was pasty white. "It should be ten per cent of the haul, something like that," Brogan finished his answer.

"Ten per cent!" he breathed, his narrow brush with death quickly forgotten. "Ten per cent. How much is involved?"

"I don't know. It could be millions . . ."

The man settled back in silent contemplation of the riches about to descend, and Brogan concentrated on his driving.

Ten minutes later, a bright hue of red brake lights blossomed ahead and he slowed.

"What's ahead?" He had to ask the question twice before he broke through the man's reverie.

"Ahead? The junction with A-338, I believe. Where are we . . . ?"

Brogan slowed, then pulled over onto the verge and edged past the waiting line of cars. At the road junction, a police Jaguar with a flashing blue light blocked the intersection. Cars were lined up in four directions with people milling about in the rain. Brogan stopped and, alarmed, vaulted out of the car and shouldered his way through the knot of people. A policeman was lying on the grass, his face, illuminated by a red flare, was streaming with blood from a cut forehead. A second policeman was leaning on the Jaguar, speaking urgently into the radio microphone as people tried to get him into the car.

"What the hell's going on here?" Brogan demanded.

"Just a minute, sir, he may be here." The policeman looked up at Brogan and shook off two good Samaritans. "Are you Mr. Cole Brogan?"

Brogan nodded and stepped back to examine the police car. The right fender had been crumpled, torn half away from the car and wrapped back around the grill.

"Yes, sir, it's him. Just a moment."

"Officer Sithmore, sir. Your fugitives came through here less than five minutes ago. Driving a blue Capri they were, sir, ran right through us. Never even tried to stop. They struck my partner and kept right on going." He cast a worried look at the other policeman, who was trying to sit up while several people attempted to restrain him.

"I don't think he's hurt bad, sir, but I did call for an ambulance."

Brogan looked around. "Which way did they go?"

"Turned onto A-338, sir, south."

"What's down that way. Any towns?"

"Yes, sir. The town of Wantage, sir. There are a few small roads that they could turn off onto, but it won't do them no good in this rain, sir. They are both unpaved and they'll be all mud by now."

Brogan kicked at a rock in frustration. He had lost count of the times that Strain had managed to slip through their traps. What in hell had happened to convince them to abandon the boat?

"Didn't you have a gun?" Brogan demanded.

"A gun? Yes, sir. There is a service revolver in the car."

"Damn it, next time have it with you and use it . . ."

The young policeman, shocked at his suggestion, shook his head after a moment. "Oh, no, sir. Can't do that. Regulations specifically state that weapons are not to be employed except in emergency, and then only with proper auth . . ."

"Damn your regulations. Give me the keys and get someone to a telephone. Tell the Wantage police to get roadblocks set up all south of here."

"Yes, sir. I mean no, sir. I mean I will about the roadblocks, but I can't give you the keys." The young policeman was in an agony of indecision and confusion.

Brogan stepped in close until he towered over the policeman. "Give me the keys, mister," Brogan roared at him. "That's an order. Or when this is all over, you won't even have a beat to pound."

The policeman hesitated a moment, then dug into his pocket. Brogan snatched the keys from his hand before the policeman had time to recall that he had no authority to order him to do anything, and hurried around to the front, where he yanked and kicked the fender until it was clear of the wheel. As he climbed in and started the engine, the owner of the houseboat, who had been hovering about, rushed up.

"See here, my reward," he shouted, but Brogan was already steering the Jaguar out of the knot of people and cars at the intersection and bumping down the verge until he could swerve back onto the road. In spite of the damaged fender, the Jaguar would have the turn of speed to catch the Capri that the Austin with its 1300cc engine did not.

He glanced at his watch. It was quarter to eight and almost dark. Unless police managed to cordon off the area effectively, there was not even the remotest chance that they would catch him tonight . . . and if that happened, he could very well be gone for good.

A-338 ran fairly straight for the ten miles to Wantage, and Brogan pushed the Jaguar to its utmost, blue light flashing and the damaged fender banging and screaming in the wind.

He did not dare use the siren for fear that Strain would hear it, but the warning light seemed to be enough to clear the light traffic. South of East Hanney, he caught sight of a long goods train on the open valley floor to the west. Cursing steadily, he kept the accelerator pressed to the floor and sped toward the crossing gate. As the front tires hit the raised grade, there was a solid bang on the roof as the crossing gate came down, but he was through and, a few minutes later, a long curve showed him the lights of the village. Red flares glowing along the pavement in the slanting rain marked the roadblock on the north end of town. Two policemen were trying frantically to reverse their car out of the mud along the side of the road. Brogan slowed as one of them jumped out and ran to the road.

He waved his arms and shouted: "He turned onto B-4507 . . ."

Brogan did not wait to hear more but hit the siren and shot away. He tore through the center of the village, narrowly missing the statue of King Alfred in the center parking area, sending the few pedestrians scurrying for safety. A minute later he cut sharply to the right, just in time to make the turn onto B-4507. The road narrowed abruptly and he whipped through an intersection, the siren barely warning a car, waiting to turn into a side road, in time. B-4507 was a winding, hilly road in contrast to A-338. It led away from the village and out into the Lambourne Downs. He saw a straightaway ahead, just past the turnoff to Childrey, and pressed the accelerator down hard and shot through the stop sign. He prayed that there would be no roundabouts along the way. On the wet asphalt he would never be able to slow enough to make the circle. A car appeared ahead in the distance as he topped a rise, and he bore down on it, but a moment later it pulled off the road and, as he shot by, saw that it was not a Capri.

A few miles later on, a set of red taillights appeared in the distance, and as Brogan closed the gap he knew that the car was not going to stop. The Jaguar crept up on the smaller car, but the twists and turns of the road gave the edge to the smaller Capri. For several minutes they sped through the countryside, the Jaguar riding the Capri's bumper. Brogan strove to edge past so that he could use the Jaguar's bulk to run the Capri off the road. A flat stretch gave him a chance. The road straightened and, ahead, the wire fences fell away from the narrow road to a dirt verge. He moved the Jaguar over into the oncoming lane and slowly began to gain. As he came abreast, the window opened. At almost the same instant, the thin crack of a pistol sounded and his windshield shattered into a star-burst pattern and he was driving blind. Brogan braked hard and with his right hand punched through the smashed windshield as the car swerved crazily. Bits of glass and plastic flew at him, but there was no time to shield his face as he fought the wheel until the Jaguar was back under control. Through the broken windshield he could see the taillights of the Capri rapidly receding. He downshifted to second gear and sent the Jaguar screaming ahead.

The gap closed again between the two cars and Brogan fumbled inside his jacket for the pistol that Vandervoort had given him. His bloody face, a momentary reflection in the rear-view mirror knocked askew, was an ugly sight in the dash lights. He concentrated on the red taillights of the car ahead as the Jaguar drew nearer. The Capri was veering back and forth across the width of the road, headlights flaring insanely as they cleared the tops of hills. A small car was run into a ditch by the Capri as its driver, ignoring the whoop of the police siren, tried to insist on his half of the road.

The Capri was less than four feet ahead when Brogan suddenly wrenched the wheel to the left and, before the pistol could appear again, had sped ahead to hit the smaller car a heavy blow with the Jaguar's already ruined right fender. Metal screamed and buckled, and the Capri wavered but held to the road. Brogan came on again from the right by cutting inside, but when he swerved the Jaguar this time, he met empty air. A long curve led left away from the highway to an adjoining road, and the Capri's driver had swerved onto it. Brogan yanked the wheel over hard and the heavy car screamed in distress and jolted over the intervening ground to the paved surface. The Capri had gained fifty yards. The Jaguar lurched sickeningly as it hit a bump and for a moment was airborne. It hit the road again, hard, swaying on its springs and something snapped. At the same instant the Capri's brake lights flashed and Brogan cut the wheel hard, hit something, pulled left, and went out of control into a spin, slashed through a small stand of trees and shuddered to a stop. Brogan tried to open the door but found it jammed. He rolled down the shattered window and wriggled half out into the rain, then lost his grip and landed heavily in the wet grass, stunned.

The Capri had fared little better. The road on which it had turned was barred by a metal stock fence. The Capri had smashed into the gate, slewed around and rolled against an embankment.

Brogan crawled to his knees and swiped ineffectually at the door handle for support. After a moment, he hooked his finger over the opened window and pulled himself up and hung onto the door while the earth spun beneath him. He lurched back and yanked at the door until it sprang half open. The interior was a mess of tangled seats and shattered windshield. He saw the pistol on the floor, managed to reach it, then staggered over to the Capri. Both doors were sprung open and a body lay crumpled beneath the dash, half hidden by the ruined seat. The rain was slanting down hard, long spears that snapped and shattered on the vegetation. He stumbled around to the front of the car and stared around, wondering where in hell he was. In the rain and nearly complete darkness, all he could see were the grass-covered Downs. To his left, a steep hill climbed up into the gloom. The white gleam of chalk sheep paths showing through the grass were barely visible as they edged up the slope. Brogan climbed the embankment and, moving cautiously, followed the nearest path onto the slope. There, the meager light reflected from the clouds was better, and several hundred yards ahead he could make out a figure struggling to climb the hill.

In the distance he heard the whoop of a following police car, and knowing that they would probably miss the turnoff and have to backtrack, he began to run.

For some reason, he found it impossible to force himself into more than a shambling trot. The long grass, beaten down by the rain, was treacherous, and several times he slipped. The insistent rain lashed his face and the wind clutched at his jacket. A narrow path worn into the chalk subsoil veered left and led upward. The hill was exceptionally steep and Brogan was struggling upward, trying to get above the fleeing figure less than thirty yards ahead, when he stopped and spun around. He heard a pistol go off and the bullet whistle past. Brogan threw himself down on the wet grass and saw Strain running toward him, firing. A bullet cut into the grass by his hand and a third went past his head. Brogan fumbled for the pistol he had dropped; he got to his knees, scrambling wildly before he found it. He spun around, still on his knees, sighted in on the looming figure and slowly squeezed the trigger. The Walther bucked in his hand and Strain stopped as if he had run into a brick wall, then clawed feebly at his stomach, collapsed and began to roll down the hill.

He heard the whoop of the police siren as the car came back along the highway, slowed and turned. Strain had stopped rolling some fifty feet below, and Brogan staggered down to him. His breath was coming in exhausted gasps and he fell to his knees beside Strain. Strain's eyes were open and he stared at Brogan. Brogan took the hand he raised, but Strain coughed once, took a deep breath and burst into a coughing fit that sent a gout of blood from his mouth. He tried to sit up, then fell back, his head lolling lifelessly. Brogan let go of his hand and stood up.

The police car braked to a halt below, and Brogan, pistol clutched in his hand, started down the slope to meet them.

19

"Cole . . . ?" Brogan forced his head up and looked through the open door of the police car to see Vandervoort, clad in a policeman's rain cape, standing beside him.

"Strain is dead," he mumbled.

"I know. The police have brought his body down."

"Sandra was the woman with him," Brogan said after a long minute. Except for that thought, his mind, fully as weary and exhausted as his body, was a blank.

He heard Vandervoort take a deep breath. "How did you find out? Did you see her?"

Brogan closed his eyes for a moment, then opened them again. "No."

He was silent and Vandervoort waited patiently, ignoring the heavy rain spattering on his cape and seeping down his neck. When Brogan spoke again, his voice was barely audible and Vandervoort leaned down to hear.

"There had to be someone in London feeding Strain information. Sandra was kidnaped the evening I got back from seeing him. They knew exactly where I lived, even though my phone is unlisted. And before that, I told you someone was waiting for me in the hotel parking garage in Copenhagen? She made the airline reservations for me, and I called her from the hotel to let her know where I was. I also called her from Abbeyfeale to tell her that I was mailing the package containing the film and poppies to myself, but I told Strain that I had mailed it to you. The package never arrived. I called Sandra from Scartaglin to tell her that I had stolen a truck. Two hours later they found me, and Strain had disappeared to be met in Wales by a woman, the morning after Sandra left London. It's all highly circumstantial, so far. But the clincher is this: Only Sandra knew exactly how the Space Watch II satellite had spotted the farm . . . by identifying the acetic anhydride source."

Brogan took a deep breath at this point and stared past Vandervoort at the rain. Vandervoort hunched his shoulders a moment, then dug beneath the cape for his cigarettes. He offered the pack to Brogan, who accepted one mechanically and Vandervoort lit it for him. A policeman came up, but Vandervoort waved him away impatiently.

"What about the acetic anhydride?" he prompted.

"Sandra knew about the satellite identification," Brogan went on. "She was in my office when I got the call from Washington. She was the only one in London who knew, and she told Strain and his people."

"How do you know . . . ?"

Brogan smiled slightly, but even in the dim dash lights Vandervoort could see that there was absolutely no humor on Brogan's tightly drawn face.

"In the helicopter, one of them, a man who called himself MacArthur, asked about the satellite. He said they had other sources of information. And he specifically mentioned the acetic anhydride."

"I see," Vandervoort said after a moment. He straightened up and, shielding his cigarette from the rain, inhaled deeply. He studied Brogan for a moment before speaking again.

"Cole, we have known for some time that there was a leak somewhere in the London offices. The Director and I were trying to solve two problems at the same time; find the leak and stop the Irish operation."

Brogan looked up at him but remained silent.

"Of course, we could not tell you about the leak since it could very well have been you. But, since you were low on the list, we thought that, if we discouraged you on the Irish investigation, something just might break in our favor. We tried to monitor you closely, but you just moved too damned fast." He paused a moment. "If it is any consolation to you, Sandra was lower on the list than you, and that is where we made our mistake. The question is why did she do it?"

Brogan shook his head. "I don't know. I hired her right after

I moved up to inspector. She came through Personnel with a clean sheet . . . who the hell knows?" he shrugged. "That was two years ago, about the time the syndicates would have started the Irish operation. What better place to put someone than in the central clearinghouse for worldwide narcotics activities. If they wanted her badly enough, they would have found a way."

Vandervoort nodded, then turned to the policeman who had been hovering about near the front of the car. He stepped forward and touched his cap.

"We've found the woman, sir. She's dead."

"Dead," Vandervoort echoed, and turned swiftly to stare at Brogan.

"Yes, sir. In the automobile, sir. She must have been killed instantly when they overturned."

Brogan closed his eyes.

"All right," Vandervoort answered quietly and waved the man away. "Cole," he said, turning, "I . . ."

"Shut up," Brogan said. "Just shut up."